Bertolt Brecht: Plays, Poetry and Prose
Edited by JOHN WILLETT *and* RALPH MANHEIM
Short Stories: 1921–1946

Brecht's Plays, Poetry and Prose
annotated and edited in hardback and paperback
by John Willett and Ralph Manheim
Methuen London publish all titles. Methuen New York only those
marked †

COLLECTED PLAYS

Vol. 1   Baal; Drums in the Night; In the Jungle of Cities; The Life
(*hardback*   of Edward II of England; A Respectable Wedding; The
only)   Beggar; Driving Out a Devil; Lux in Tenebris; The Catch
Vol. 1*i*   Baal (*paperback only*)
Vol. 1*ii*   A Respectable Wedding and other one-act plays (*paperback only*)
Vol. 1*iii*   Drums in the Night (*paperback only*)
Vol. 1*iv*   In the Jungle of Cities (*paperback only*)
Vol. 2*i*   Man equals Man; The Elephant Calf
Vol. 2*ii*   The Threepenny Opera
Vol. 2*iii*   The Rise and Fall of the City of Mahagonny; The Seven
               Deadly Sins
Vol. 3*i*   Saint Joan of the Stockyards
Vol. 3*ii*   The Baden-Baden Cantata; The Flight over the Ocean; He Who
               Said Yes; He Who Said No; The Measures Taken
Vol. 4*i*   The Mother; The Exception and the Rule; The Horatii and the
               Curiatii
Vol. 4*ii*   Round Heads and Pointed Heads
Vol. 4*iii*   Señora Carrar's Rifles; Fear and Misery of the Third Reich
Vol. 5*i*   Life of Galileo
Vol. 5*ii*   Mother Courage and her Children
Vol. 5*iii*   The Trial of Lucullus; Dansen; What's the Price of Iron?
Vol. 6*i*   The Good Person of Szechwan
Vol. 6*ii*   The Resistible Rise of Arturo Ui
Vol. 6*iii*   Mr. Puntila and his Man Matti
Vol. 7   The Visions of Simone Machard; Schweyk in the Second World
               War; The Caucasian Chalk Circle; The Duchess of Malfi
Vol. 8*i*   The Days of the Commune
Vol. 8*ii*   Turandot; Report from Herrenburg
Vol. 8*iii*   Downfall of the Egoist Johann Fatzer; The Life of Confucius;
               The Breadshop; The Salzburg Dance of Death

POETRY
† Poems 1913–1956   † *Songs and Poems from the Plays

PROSE
  Brecht on Theatre   † *Dialogues
  Diaries 1920–1922   † *Letters
† Short Stories 1921–1946   *Selected Essays

ALSO
† Happy End (by Brecht, Weill and Lane)

*in preparation
The following plays are also available (in paperback only) in unannotated editions:
The Caucasian Chalk Circle; The Days of the Commune; The Good Person
of Szechwan; The Life of Galileo; The Measures Taken and other
Lehrstücke; The Messingkauf Dialogues; Mr. Puntila and his Man Matti;
The Mother; Saint Joan of the Stockyards

Bertolt Brecht Short Stories 1921–1946

Edited by
John Willett and Ralph Manheim

Translated by
Yvonne Kapp, Hugh Rorrison
and Antony Tatlow

Methuen · London and New York

First published in Great Britain in 1983 by Methuen London
Ltd, 11 New Fetter Lane, London EC4P 4EE.
First published in the United States of America, in 1983
by Methuen Inc, 733 Third Avenue, New York NY 10017.
Published by arrangement with Suhrkamp Verlag, Frankfurt am
Main.

Original work entitled Geschichten *being Volume 11 of*
Gesammelte Werke *of Bertolt Brecht*
© *Copyright Suhrkamp Verlag, Frankfurt am Main 1967.*
Copyright in the individual stories:
Kalendergeschichten *Copyright 1949 by Gebrüder Weiss Verlag,*
Berlin.
Geschichten aus Prosa I © *Copyright by Stefan S. Brecht 1965.*

Translation copyright © *1983 by Stefan S. Brecht.*
Introduction and editorial notes copyright © *1983 by Methuen*
London Ltd.

ISBN 0 413 37050 X (Hardback)
ISBN 0 413 52890 1 (Paperback)

Library of Congress Cataloging in Publication Data
Brecht, Bertolt, 1898–1956.
   Bertolt Brecht, short stories, 1921–1946.
   "German texts taken from volume 11 of Brecht's
Gesammelte Werke (Prosa I)"—T.p. verso.
   Includes index.
   I. Willett, John.   II. Manheim, Ralph, 1907–
III. Title.
PT2603.R397A2   1982   833'.912   82–14095
ISBN 0–413–37050–X

Printed in Great Britain by
Richard Clay (The Chaucer Press) Ltd,
Bungay, Suffolk

Contents

THE TRANSLATORS
Yvonne Kapp *pages* 129–131, 139–170, 178–182, 188–203.
Hugh Rorrison *pages* 57–129, 131–138.
Antony Tatlow *pages* 3–53, 183–187.
John Willett *pages* 170–178, 207–224.

Introduction

Brecht is so often thought of nowadays as one of the great twentieth-century innovators – a literary-theatrical equivalent to Picasso, say, or Stravinsky – that we tend to overlook the more conservative or traditionalist aspects of his work. Admittedly his traditionalism was of a special kind, in that it tended to go behind the accepted traditions of his time and his country in order to re-establish a simpler, often more popular approach. It was neither the reverentially academic traditionalism of a conventional German upbringing – or, for that matter, of the dominant line in Soviet cultural thinking in the 1930s and 1950s – nor was its quite conscious naivety that of the primitive or the amateur. Its essence was directness and lack of affectation, and nowhere did it matter more to him than in his preference for straightforward narrative forms such as he found in ballads, folk tales, newspaper reports and what he termed 'the narrative pictures of the elder Brueghel'. This highly unfashionable insistence on the story-telling aspect of all art was the basis of Brecht's approach not only to the silent cinema, with its linear progressions and its externalising of complex human relationships, but above all to the theatre. Look, for instance, at the well-known table in his 'Notes to the Opera *Rise and Fall of the City of Mahagonny*' and you will find that the very first requirement of his Epic Theatre, as opposed to the conventional Dramatic Theatre of those days, was 'narrative' as against 'plot'. This was the foundation that he always set out to establish both in planning his own plays and in criticising others. Called on to analyse a work of art, in whatever medium, he would look for the story even before he commented on its social attitudes or 'gests'.

Stories can be seen to form the basis of the greater part of Brecht's work. Thus for several of his plays there is not only a more or less elaborate narrative scheme, showing the main events of each scene, but also a coherently written summary of the story, sometimes in imitation of a newspaper report. A number of these can be found in our notes to such plays as *Baal*, *Man equals Man*, *The Good Person of Szechwan* (in the American edition), *Simone Machard* and *Mother Courage*, while the scene headings too generally attempt to resume the episodes to come. Similarly his film treatments were written in story form, so that it is sometimes hard to distinguish them from the stories proper (this was the case with 'Caesar and his Legionary' in *Tales from the Calendar*, which is in fact a film project for William Dieterle in Hollywood) or, in the case of the *Simone Machard* story, from a working résumé of the play. In *Puntila*, again, stories not unlike some of those in the collected *Geschichten* make up one entire scene of the play. As a result the categories become blurred, between treatment and short story, between story and report, report and anecdote, anecdote and aphorism. There are unrealised schemes for a 'Factual Series' – apparently crime fiction somewhat in the style of Chesterton – and a set of 'Proletarian anecdotes for those who live in cities', as well as the published Keuner and Eulenspiegel stories. But what is clear is that Brecht's imagination got to work in the first place neither on visual images nor on conceptions of character but on a consecutive thread of narration. Language, music, roles for actors, the theatrical devices of director and designer only came into the picture once the story was firmly there.

Given this lifelong narrative bias on Brecht's part it is typically paradoxical, if not positively perverse, that he should have been only sporadically drawn to the recognised short-story form. However much his plays and, to a surprising extent, his poems set out to tell a tale, by far the greater part of his prose writing is not narrative but expository, argumentative or theoretical. Six volumes of his collected works (in the 1967 German edition) contain theoretical notes and essays on the arts (primarily the theatre) and political matters, as against four nominally devoted to 'prose', of which only one contains short stories strictly speaking. This 370-page book includes the seven stories from the *Tales from the Calendar* of 1949, which was the only book of stories to be published in Brecht's lifetime even though diluted with Keuner anecdotes (Mr Keuner being Brecht's reflective *alter ego*) and interspersed poems. The other three 'prose' volumes contain the *Threepenny Novel* and the unfinished Caesar and 'Tui' novels which followed it, along with the anecdotes, the (essentially political) *Me-Ti* aphorisms and the *Dialogues between Exiles* which more properly belong with other works in dialogue form.

In the selection which we have made from the 1967 volume there are thirty-seven stories and one long appended fragment, representing all Brecht's finished work in the short story medium; and between them they cover the most important part of Brecht's literary life, from his twenty-third to his fiftieth year. Close as they are to the core of his creative method they remain an interesting sideline rather than a perpetual semi-private outlet like the poetry or an all-absorbing concern like the plays. They gear into his other work; they reflect many of its features at different periods. They contribute to it and are sometimes outstanding in their own right. But the virtual absence of any concern with them in Brecht's diaries, letters and literary notes, along with the lack of evidence of any radical working or reworking of the surviving scripts suggests that he gave them a relatively low priority. Like the Singer in *The Caucasian Chalk Circle* he prided himself on being a highly professional story-teller. But if he was a short-story writer it was by the way.

*

The short stories proper group themselves around three main periods of activity, generally preceding rather than coinciding with their author's most productive spells as a playwright. First there are the early stories written in Bavaria before he had become at all firmly established in the theatre. At that point he was still a drop-out student whose writing might have become canalised into any of a number of directions: poetry, plays or stories and scripts for the new film industry which was then becoming active not only in Berlin but in Munich too. Every possibility at first needed to be exploited; thus 'Bargan gives up', the opening story in our collection, was the first work to make Brecht's name known outside Southern Germany, and it was no doubt because of this that his negotiations with Berlin publishers in the winter of 1921/22 centred on his ballads and stories rather than on his hitherto unperformed plays. Within a few months however the

issue had been decided by the success of *Drums in the Night*, and
from then on the name Brecht stood above all for a new force in
the theatre. Since one result of the new demands on him was the
delaying of his first collection of poems till after his final departure
from Munich it is hardly surprising that all plans for writing
further stories should have been likewise shelved.

His definitive move to Berlin in the autumn of 1924 gave him
more time for non-theatrical work: 'In these years,' he told his
main critical supporter Herbert Ihering, 'my affairs are in something of a vacuum'. It also introduced him to Elisabeth Hauptmann, who was sent by his publishers to help bring the book of
poems out. With her aid he began submitting short stories to a
number of newspapers and magazines, partly perhaps as a means
of keeping his name before the reading public, but also as a
source of income till his new plays should reach the Berlin stage.
It was not till 1928 – the year of his prize-winning story 'The
Monster' – that he scored his enormous and largely unexpected
hit with *The Threepenny Opera*, but if this gave him added reason
to circulate his secondary writings in the wake of that work's
triumphal progress it once again distracted him from producing
more. Only a few sporadic stories followed during the period of
Hitler's rise to power and the early part of Brecht's exile, and
none of these, it seems, was published before 1937. That year,
however, marked the start of his most creative spell of all –
covering the greater part of the *Svendborg Poems* and the big
Scandinavian plays from *Galileo* to *Arturo Ui* – and between then
and his departure for America in mid-1941 a number of his best-
known stories were written for the Moscow German-language
reviews. From that point on he once again neglected the form,
partly no doubt because of the lack of outlets in the United States,
but also because his main concern in California was with the
devising of film stories rather than the writing of short stories
for publication. These were at once less relaxed and less polished
than the more literary variety, and tended also to be more
collaboratively written. The hope was no longer that they would
be published in German but that they would get translated into
acceptable studio English.

To this changing role of the short story in Brecht's life and
work correspond some of its more notable thematic and stylistic

changes. Looking through the present book any reader familiar
with his other writings will find some evident connections with
them. The early stories thus carry overtones of the Bible and of
the brothers Grimm. 'Bargan gives up' and the very notion of
writing a group of such 'tales of filibusters' is all of a piece with
the romanticised toughness of the 'Ballad of the Pirates' of 1918.
'Java Meier', despite the Brechtian geography of its name, not
only anticipates his lifelong interest in crime stories but bears
directly on his efforts to devise such plots for the silent cinema:
efforts which never reached the screen. 'A helping hand' and 'The
death of Cesare Malatesta' both have the very strong but restrained
stoicism which emerges from some of the story ideas in the early
Diaries and comes to inform so much of his later work. 'Four
men and a poker game,' whose opening phrase always struck
Elisabeth Hauptmann as classic Brecht – to be compared with the
first sentences of *Man equals Man* – relates, along with 'Hook to
the chin' and the unfinished Samson-Körner biography included
in the appendix, to Brecht's sporting phase of the mid-1920s, when
The Little Mahagonny was set in a boxing ring and the revised *In
the Jungle of Cities* presented as 'an inexplicable wrestling match
between two men'. 'The Good Lord's package' reflects his mental
picture of 'cold Chicago' as epitomising the cruelties of urban
life.

There are stories which had other functions, or acquired them.
'A mean bastard' is thought, for instance, to embody an abandoned one-act play, while the first part of 'Before the Flood'
became a soliloquy in the 1926 version of Brecht's youthful play
Baal: Baal viewed as a lumbering prehistoric monster (and
thereby very indirectly as an ancestor of Puntila in the play of
that name). Then there are the major exiled stories with their
mainly remote historical settings and their evident role in the
development of such plays as *Galileo*, *Lucullus* and *The Caucasian
Chalk Circle*. Surprisingly enough there seem to be only two
stories which express Brecht's most direct and didactic phase of
political involvement between 1929 and 1937 – the period of the
Lehrstücke and the militantly anti-Nazi poems and sketches. One
of them, the 'Soldier of La Ciotat', is scarcely a story in the
conventional sense, and it seems to have been prompted by the
news of Mussolini's invasion of Ethiopia. The other, 'The job',

springs like Brecht's film *Kuhle Wampe* from the German economic crisis of the last years of the Weimar Republic and is closely and uniquely akin to contemporary stories by Elisabeth Hauptmann (see in particular her 'Gastfeindschaft' in Wieland Herzfelde's *30 Neue deutsche Erzähler*, 1932) and Anna Seghers. With these two exceptions Brecht's stories are his least overtly political works.

There are also two categories which correspond to nothing much else in his writing. The more prominent, and also more conventional of these is the button-holing yarn told by a semi-detached 'I' narrator in the tradition of Kipling and Maugham, not to mention the *Strand* magazine. A good number of the stories submitted by Brecht (or on his behalf by Hauptmann) to German magazines in the 1920s follow this pattern, and one or two of them seem (like 'Barbara' for instance) intended simply as light entertainment. At the same time, however, there is a sprinkling of highly imaginative stories from different periods which may well surprise even those familiar with the plays and poems. This applies not so much to 'The revelation' perhaps, since the Rimbaudesque echoes there are also found in *In the Jungle of Cities* and the early Psalms; but the studies of sheer nastiness in 'A helping hand', 'Letter about a mastiff' and the later 'Gaumer and Irk' seem like nothing else that Brecht wrote. If there is a precursor here it is Kafka, whom Brecht recognised as an 'epic' novelist and a 'really serious phenomenon' already in the 1920s. Though Brecht was for the most part highly critical, if not positively insulting in his view of his German language fellow-writers, he put Kafka among a very small nucleus of avant-garde authors from whom realistically-inclined socialists could learn about technique; and in conversation with Walter Benjamin he praised Kafka's precision and visionary powers, even if these were restricted to seeing 'what was coming, without seeing what *is*.' It is only in Brecht's prose, and that at rare intervals, that he seemed to be trying to take Kafka a step further, by applying all his capacity for imagination and precise description to the grim unpleasantnesses of the everyday world.

*

In deciding what to include in the present book we have eliminated the unfinished or fragmentary stories apart from the long and unique 'Life story of the boxer Samson-Körner' which Brecht, a somewhat exceptional ghost, wrote under the direction of the German middleweight champion. We have left out all anecdotes and very short stories, along with the play summaries already referred to and any film stories detectable as such. This leaves a hard core of genuine short stories which have been put as far as possible in chronological order, in three main sections corresponding to the major divisions in Brecht's life (i.e., respectively, to sections II, III/IV and V–VIII of *Poems 1913–1956*). It has meant splitting the *Tales from the Calendar*, though these are given individually in the same versions as in the 1961 Methuen edition of that book. The poems originally included there are now all but one of them in *Poems 1913–1956*.

The notes have been arranged similarly to those to the *Poems*. There is a brief account of the collections planned or made by Brecht, and of the main publishing events since his death, followed by detailed notes on the separate stories, their dates and places of original publication. Though there seems little likelihood of a substantial number of further stories coming to light – as against the scores of long-unpublished poems – there may well be discoveries to be made about those included. Grateful as we are for the help given by Herta Ramthun, their original editor, and the Brecht-Archive in East Berlin, we are very much aware that this is one of the least researched areas of Brecht's work, and one where there is relatively little material to go on. Of course this relates to the point already made: that the short stories were never among his primary concerns. But it also means that there are some unsolved problems waiting to attract the attention of scholars. As it is, that damned elusive author still cannot be pinned down.

THE EDITORS

The Bavarian stories (1920–1924)

BARGAN GIVES UP

At midnight we made the ship fast in a bay which was sleeping under thick, fat-leaved trees, put biscuits and dried dates in our pockets and, treading carefully as if on eggs, pushed on westwards through the bush. Bargan who led us like a swarm of kids – not that we buccaneers were exactly babes-in-arms – Bargan had a flair for the stars and when it came to getting his bearings he was as good as God Almighty. We found our way through the monstrous forest, which was more tangled than a ball of twine, to the clearing, and ahead of us in the mild light lay the town, which we had been looking for like our own home before daybreak. Silently we began our terrible business; at first none of them bothered us but then, awakened from their sleep by destroying angels, they turned nasty and a dirty battle was fought in the houses. All of us together would run into a house, scuffle with men in shirtsleeves who struck at us with tables and doors, and defend ourselves against the women who behaved like hyenas. Their screaming filled the air like an icy mist as step by step we pressed towards the citadel, which consisted of wooden buildings leaning against a bare mountain. A group of us, myself among them, pressed on through an open gate, on the heels of people fleeing; the gate closed and the women standing in their shifts on the walls and scaffolding threw stones and wooden objects at our heads, so we didn't feel too comfortable. Our heads were already bleeding and we were whistling like mad to make Bargan hear us when he came up from the rear with some men. Ahead of all the rest, he had swum down the small swift river under the trussing into the citadel, where a fish would have slit its stomach on the jagged stones, but Bargan couldn't stand even one of us dying. From then on things went faster, and all the more so since Bargan had one of his incredible ideas. The most tenacious of the enemy had barricaded themselves in the topmost wooden house which couldn't be reached except with wings. Those who hadn't yet been killed ran towards it from all sides. This soon made the house very strong and if it swallowed any more of the enemy that way (and they were able to arm themselves inside) this could easily turn it into a damn rat-trap, because we buccaneers were scattered all over the settlement and many of us had already started satisfying the women; you can leave children to slaughter turtles. That's why Bargan had a number of women strung together, and some of us, in full view of the blockhouse, began to rape them, which looked terrific and made such an impression on the woodworms that, against all the rules of cut and thrust, they broke like young bulls out of their wooden security and were slaughtered like young lambs, trembling and helpless, one after the other or in groups of ten. And so the town was taken thanks to Bargan's wisdom and knowledge of human nature, and when the fine houses woke up we were stomping around inside them admiring our new possessions. It was a good caper but if we had seen the snag – sharp, crooked and murderous – as we do today five weeks later, we would all rather have conquered flaming hell than that beautiful town filled to bursting with useful things. The prisoners – there were around seventy, the others slept on in their houses till the day of judgment, it won't rain on them – we herded together into a courtyard of the town hall, where they could sit on the stones and rest. For a few hours we were drunk with victory and nobody had time to bother about them, it wasn't until midday that Bargan arrived to call the roll and then he too went in to have a look at the women. They got up and stood around in the yard, trembling with the cold for they were mostly wearing only their shifts, it all happened so damned quickly, with God turning his face away from them to have a look at the harvest in Brazil instead. By the way there were a few pretty women among them, that is to say they were in their shifts and shivering and we hadn't seen any young flesh for seven weeks. A shark would have thought we were dying for it like God for a repentant sinner and Bargan made a start straightaway by picking a young woman to come to his tent. We didn't look at them carefully at first, Bargan hadn't much taste, he slept with all kinds of scum, and it wasn't for nothing people said he had the American sickness that rots a good Christian bit by bit. But then a quarrel arose between Bargan and his friend Croze, the 'Clubfoot of St. Marie', and it was about this young woman both of them wanted. Bargan would have knocked down anybody else immediately – for we friends never fought among ourselves over brandy or money, nor over honour either, only over women – but for some ungodly reason Bargan had taken a fancy to the fat fellow who had lain on the road like an unwanted dog till Bargan drew him to his bosom. Now he was swollen like a poisoned dog, drank all over the place, played with Bargan's gold pieces to which everybody's good sweat stuck except his own, and now before our very eyes he was arguing with Bargan himself over a woman who belonged to Bargan just as surely as did his own foot. Soon we all began to shout, so Bargan, being by no means certain if his own foot belonged to him or not, finally had to take the woman, whereupon he held roll-call as usual while the Clubfoot of St. Marie stumped along the line behind him. All the time we looked into his eyes and I can tell you and could have done so then, treachery lay in their depths – slime and rotten fishes.

We spent the whole day over drink and women, we were like the beggar who threw an old louse-ridden shirt over the hedge saying: Live and let live! Only Bargan worked in the tent – he never moved into a house, always said the ceiling would fall down – pretty well the whole day, distributing the booty among other things, in so far as it consisted of pure gold. He didn't see the young woman even *once* and in the evening we all shook our sodden heads over the fact that Croze had the wench; Bargan himself had her brought over to the house where the Clubfoot of St. Marie had lain the whole afternoon with another slut. Later on we said his hatred of Bargan, who loved him like a child, came about because when Croze got the woman in the evening he couldn't do it any more, and that irritated him. Anyhow, that same night some of us discovered the young wench in Croze's room with her throat cut, but he had made off, after slaughtering her like a hen, at the dead of night. Together with seven or eight more young fellows who weren't too keen on Bargan because they were born with rotten souls. When we told Bargan early the next morning he didn't give anything away but afterwards he drank and stared into a hole all the time, right in the middle of our victory celebrations which lasted three more days. On the evening of the third day, when the women had all been used up and the brandy was getting bitter, fat Croze came back, but on his own, and behaved as if he had been relieving himself in the bushes and looked questioningly into all our faces. And though we would have liked to pull his thick skin over his gristly ears, we pretended we hadn't missed him and hadn't found the hen, just because Bargan did nothing at all to hide his joy over his return, which did him no credit. And during the following days, while we prepared to move off, the two of them lived together as before like brothers who together had committed murder.

We loaded the best of the stuff – the merely good we had to leave behind – on the ox-carts, chose the draughthorses and made everything ready, for we had planned an expedition of two or three days and now it had turned into a week. But as we were about to leave, we noticed the ammunition was missing. There had been heaps of gunpowder, we had taken even more as booty, now the whole lot had disappeared, blown up without a sound. The guards had heard nothing, perhaps they'd been sleeping it off; it was just a curious fact that the chests up on top were the old ones, only there was sand in them, while instead of the barrels under them lay chests and herring casks, all kinds of old junk. We searched like bloodhounds and put off our departure The next day we came across the good powder-kegs in a pond, you could have slept on them. It was a neat bit of work to bring them that far without strangers getting alarmed, nobody had a scrap of proof but nobody in the camp doubted that Croze was as closely connected with this nasty business as a mother with her baby's belly button. The umbilical cord had been bitten off, but from then on we kept an eye on the Clubfoot of St. Marie, who was hopping about among the herring barrels like a furrier whose furs had floated off after he had already sold them, and we didn't forget the fellows who had been swallowed up by the forest either.

Our column had a swollen stomach – the crowd of carts and draught oxen – and a lame fist in the shape of those empty powder-kegs; we waddled at an easy pace through the wood, which we had to demolish with axes, and we had to stuff up the crevices in the ground to get across. It was dull work. Then we got some entertainment, more than we bargained for.

On the second day of our march, as we were forcing our way through a picturesque region with attractive cliffs to right and left, it began to rain stones the size of ostrich eggs, or even bigger. We were wedged between the carts and the oxen which wanted to scatter in all directions, because the stones seemed to be harder than we were and we could only hide under the wheels and wait till Heaven showed us some sympathy or ran out of stones. Under different circumstances we would have fired up at them and then, in addition to the stones, a couple of skinny angels would have fallen down, but not even Bargan could use herrings for bullets. We'd have been buried slowly or quickly, and the fellows up above who arranged for the rain would have looked down on a field where useful stuff once grew but where after the hail there lay nothing but stones with no names written on them – but then one of us had a bright idea and, risking his life, seized the Clubfoot of St. Marie by the collar and pulled him out of his cart where he was squatting in safety like the yolk in an egg. And the ones up above must have had good eyes and remembered his cart with gratitude, for the rain stopped straightaway and we were able to continue.

That was a clear signal from Heaven, and if Bargan had only been blind, he would have seen it. But he loved fat Croze and told us there was no proof and we should be ashamed of ourselves. Then Croze, who was standing beside him looking at the sun, shook hands with him before our very eyes. So we arranged that one of us should watch Croze all the time, day and night, because Bargan didn't, he closed his eyes, he lived with Croze like two friends in a gloomy wood who don't have anybody else. So we had to keep our eyes skinned, because Bargan was the sort of person we would all rather have gone to the Devil with than hurt.

But then came the business about the right direction.

Somehow or other we must have lost our way. God was wrong about the stars. In earlier times Bargan used to cast one glance at the night sky and afterwards we could march straight to a peg in the forest. Now he stood outside the tent for hours on end and made calculations, so our guards said, and sometimes in the middle of it all he had an argument with Croze who grew more insolent all the time. And then he'd make mistakes and we did all we could not to let him notice it. Later on something went wrong with his orders now and again, but it began with the business of the stars.

We thought he was worrying about Croze whom he had taken up with after all, he probably felt like a man who would rather mend

an anchor chain five times than buy a new one, even though there
are storms. In short, we forgave him, the bad business with
Jammes as well, whom Croze accused of stealing his knife and
whom Bargan ordered whipped, though we all knew that the
knife belonged to Jammes and Bargan must have known that the
knife didn't belong to Croze. Croze stood there and didn't even
bother to fabricate any evidence. He just stared at his friend as if
he had wanted to test him. Afterwards there was even a rumour
that the Clubfoot of St. Marie had told Bargan he recognised the
knife as his own, because it was the one with which he had cut the
throat of the woman Bargan had given him. That was the limit.
It was Croze all over.

The mistake about the direction became very embarrassing. We
arrived far beyond the place in the bay where the ship lay. Then
Bargan decided, despite all that had happened, to send Croze on
ahead to inform the ship's crew of our approach. We all objected
but it was no use. The Clubfoot of St. Marie had his way and rode
on ahead of us. We watched him, fat and bilious, bounding off
through the bush on his horse. We all had crabs in our
throats.

We had been marching for a bare two hours when the man who
had ridden with Croze came back with a message that the latter
and the whole ship's crew would come and meet us in a dried-up
creek which led to the bay, so we should march in that direction.
We smelt a rat, yet Bargan actually directed us to the river-bed,
and even though we had figured out that the Devil would take
over, we still didn't know what he had in mind; so because of
Bargan we obeyed. With a cool breeze blowing, we marched over
the close-set stones of the river-bed until well into the evening.
The river-bed widened very considerably till in the end we lost
sight of the banks and swore that the bed had dried up completely or that we had already left it. Bargan on his black stallion
had the route firmly fixed in his head. In the mild light of the
first stars which surged out of the darkening sky and which for
certain reasons I remember more clearly than those of any other
night, we pressed forward in good order and suddenly felt water
in our shoes as the darkness gathered, observing without pleasure
that it was rising steadily and none too slowly. The waves of
shallow water also followed a certain course opposed to ours,

and then it dawned on us that we had no more lost the river-bed under our feet than we had our shoes, that it wasn't a river-bed at all but a bay and that the tide was doing its level best to drown us all, men and horses and carts, before cock-crow. At first the darkness was kind enough to let us stare at one another but then a soft and disgustingly whitish mist veiled the few stars and the water round our ankles rose with the determination of a phenomenon that knew how to do its job. The acquisition of our booty had cost us and its former owners much sweat and blood but now we had to leave it for the cold water which, preoccupied with its own meaningless ascent, was no more troubled by us than by dry stones. The river looked like an eye which for some reason or other was growing darker and darker as happens in love at the onset of ecstasy. When the waters had risen high enough to disconcert us even if they had been still, they began to take on the agitated life of a whirlpool. The carts were getting stuck and we swung ourselves on to the bulls. But then the bulls too began to find it tricky, and it must have been a little after midnight when the first bull sank soundlessly into the waves and drifted away. And then we had to resort to swimming, we did it like brothers with the help of wooden planks. We managed to stick together, not all of us of course, some swam away for a long time, I've never seen them again. But Bargan stuck with us.

Around two hours after midnight we felt firm ground under the clods that hung from our knees and climbed in Bargan's wake on to a small stony island where, hungry and without fire or blankets, and wet to the skin, entertained by concern that the water might follow us, we waited till morning like a sinner on Judgment Day waiting for God's voice to give him permission to go through the right-hand door into that famous state of bliss.

During all these hours Bargan didn't say a single word, though we were all thinking about the seventy men and women whom Bargan had had slaughtered at Croze's request before we marched off.

Towards morning the water subsided, and once the icy morning wind had dried out our clothes we were able to go on and look for our ship, without booty and bereft of the things we had taken into the wood and of many comrades as well. And we didn't find the bay until around midday. We hadn't had too good a time, we had stood in cold water and under a shower of stones and frozen like dogs waiting at night for a bitch in heat, but we still had our eyes in our heads and evidently this was the bay, we recognised it like our mother by the fat leaves on the trees. It was just that with our weakened eyes we could see nothing of our ship, though it had two sails hoisted and was made fast to those fat-leaved trees. There wasn't even a hawser any-where. But the Clubfoot of St. Marie hopped out from among the trees, pale and somewhat dishevelled and swung his backside as if everything was in good hands. Then he asked Bargan where he had been, said he had been waiting in pain for hours, there was nobody there, had they wanted to leave him alone among the wild animals? Bargan just looked at him and didn't even ask about the ship but walked away from us, past Croze, in among the tree trunks as if he were looking for something which you couldn't see so well from far away. But to us Croze said abruptly over his shoulder, the ship was gone when he arrived, it was full of rogues or the wind and the tide had torn away the cables. Then he limped off after his friend, probably because he had judged the look on our faces correctly.

Weak-kneed we stood around between the trees and stared the eyes out of our heads; but if someone has lost his glasses, he can't see anything, and he can't find his glasses for the same reason. He'll stay blind for all eternity if nobody helps him. So we too couldn't catch up with our ship without growing wings and for that we would at least have to kick the bucket first. All the same we didn't want to throw away the gun we had no more powder for, if only Bargan had been healthy again. So we sent some men to him and they found him sitting on a root, his arm round Croze's shoulder. They told him plainly that he was to blame for the slaughter of the seventy, for the seven deaths in the quarry and for the fact that many of us had floated off to an unknown destination and that the ship had gone to Heaven; he, Bargan, was responsible for this and not the Clubfoot of St. Marie, whom they'd have drowned right away like a fat dog. However, they wanted to ask him, Bargan, to lead them again, because he was worth all the trouble he'd made. But they wanted to bump Croze off quickly and bury him no less than seven feet deep. Better to bite off a disgusting wart than throw away the whole man. Bargan listened to this very calmly. And when they had finished he asked them what they intended doing if he refused to abandon his friend just on account of their suspicions that didn't hold water. Then they began to enumerate everything for him, piling one piece of evidence on top of another, last of all how Croze had sent away the man who he knew would be keeping an eye on him, with a message that was intended to send him and all the rest into the water, while he himself took care of the ship. And while it all became clearer and clearer to them as they spoke, the Clubfoot of St. Marie sat grinning on a tree-stump and running his splayed fingers through his black hair which he wore long and combed back and which the dirt had matted into greasy strands. But Bargan asked just what did they intend to do if he simply refused. Then it suddenly dawned on our men how matters stood with Bargan, that he knew it all even better than they did and still didn't want to abandon that fat dog, God knows why. So they turned back without a word and came and told us the whole story.

We now grew very sad for we all saw that something had happened to Bargan that had never been told him in his cradle or at the coffins of his enemies, something that can befall any of us: a disaster under full sail and in brilliant sunshine. Just this happened to Bargan as he sat alone in the bush with the Clubfoot of St. Marie and showed his obstinacy. We didn't blather for long because the best man among us had got cancer, but made the sign of the cross in the air and a clean break between him and us. Some wanted to leave a bag of dates for the man who had nothing but the friend who had betrayed him, but we were all against stuffing a corpse with food if the living had empty stomachs. So on a warm day in summer, in the bush near Mary's Bay in Chile, we went away without again seeing Bargan, a man who had been a dear friend.

We tried for two whole days to find the ship, with a feeling inside us that crabs can't catch greyhounds, then we found a tub swaying in the bay with two sails which looked about as strong as St. Patrick's Christmas crib, our ship's twin brother. That twin brother was drifting under the full midday sun. If we could have waited till the mild light of evening it would have been a pleasant trip, with eggs and bottles of wine, to honour St. Patrick's Christmas crib with our visit; a fine raft was built in less time than it once took us to come by our dear cockleshell. However the dear cockleshell seemed to have her cargo on board already for she abused the wind with all her canvas even though, sensing the state of play, it scarcely danced attendance, and they sailed as badly as if they had been let loose on a modern two-master straight out of navigation school. Anyhow we had to hurry up, so we jumped on to the raft and rowed with powerful ease towards our fat fish. It frittered away its precious time with droll dancing practice till we got within shot, while we went flat out like with another man's wife and as if we had stolen the raft. Then the first bullets whistled their welcome over our heads. One of us who had secured his powder-bag round his neck also fired a shot for honour's sake, but then something happened that really gave us the shivers. After our first shot there appeared at the rail, upright, a good target which we knew well and which bore the name Bargan. We were far from pleased that Bargan should be the man who wanted to get our cockleshell out on the high seas as quickly as possible without us. And here he was, trusting so firmly in our kind hearts that he was acting as cover against our shots for the whole of his new crew! We didn't yet realise that we were doing him wrong when we stopped shooting because it was him.

When we clambered on to the ship – Bargan himself lowered a rope – it was as quiet as a church and there was nothing to be seen. Bargan himself was no longer exactly a tourist attraction, he was wearing a disgusting garment, probably a present from his friend Croze, and he would have done better to put on a mask for he was hardly able to parade his new face. But he probably looked like that because of the disgusting garment. Good morning, we said, on board St. Patrick's Christmas crib, no doubt you've been waiting for us? No, he said. Then we saw that he could only manage to get out *one* word and since that's not much for the kind of man Bargan used to be, we were ashamed of our unjust anger and asked very gently: so you found the ship again? They must have sailed to meet us and then came back? We wanted to help him out in this way, because he was standing there like a child and we couldn't bear it. But he got his mouth open and said:

no, it wasn't like that. So we saw that he couldn't lie, he hadn't learnt how. And we left him standing there and went down into the ship and he remained standing in the same place, motionless, as if he were a prisoner.

Down below we came, of course, upon the dear fellows who had emigrated from the town earlier on and arranged for the rain and rolled the gunpowder with great difficulty into the wells and finally didn't think it would be too much to recuperate with a little trip on St. Patrick's Christmas crib. They squatted around the walls and busied themselves trembling. In the middle their God Almighty sat on a coil of rope, the Clubfoot of St. Marie, fat and shameless, looking at us as if we were his wedding guests; only his skull twitched a little and his front view was a little pale when he grinned. We ventured with the greatest respect to ask what he believed in just now, about his religion, his business prospects, the future of his unborn children and what he thought about life after death. Then one of us asked why had they steered so atrociously when after all they had Bargan on board? Then it emerged that Bargan's job was to scrub the awning, that's what the clubfoot wanted, and they had dragged him to the washing trough with their knives; for he was really going to have to earn his meals on Croze's ship. We were just about to knock the sweet monster in the teeth when Bargan came down the steps and asked us to leave Croze alone and deal with *him*. He wasn't all that long-winded about it. Then we looked at each other and just for the sake of saying something one of us tossed a little question into the black bilge, namely: do you happen to know where the good lads are who were supposed to defend the ship against enemies whilst we conquered the town and took all this booty? But not a sound came out of the brute's maw which was black and showed stumps of decayed teeth; it was suffocating in there. Then we understood that the poor lads had swum off to tell us that St. Patrick's Christmas crib was going to set sail and we should hurry up if we wanted to come along. And without a word two of our men took Bargan between them and went back up the steps with him, while in the half-darkness the rest of us dedicated our hands to the memory of our dear brothers. We only left Croze's neck intact because he went up after his friend and we wanted to keep him for later.

When we got up on deck we locked the Clubfoot of St. Marie in a wooden cage where a monkey had once been imprisoned. We let Bargan walk about, for what's the use of talking with a man who has a disease and thinks about the stars? We hoisted the sails and put out of the bay.

In the evening we celebrated our return with a few good gulps of brandy and also commemorated our dear corpses which now, as one of us put it rather nicely, were swimming up from the depths under the mild light of the stars, face upwards, towards some goal or other which had been forgotten and like someone who has no home and is homesick none the less. Bargan didn't show himself, it wasn't until right at the end when most were asleep that he came up to me as I sat on guard in front of the wooden crate, and he said: would you let me into the crate, or have you some objection? He was standing in the starlight, I can still see him and hear him too, and he's surely been decapitated a long time now or perhaps not, who knows. And the question cost him a lot of effort. We didn't look into the cage but the Clubfoot was sitting inside, listening to every word. So with no lessening of the respect I had always had for him, because he was far the best buccaneer captain from here to Ecuador, I said: wouldn't you rather go to your cabin? He thought about it and said: I suppose you don't think much of this ship? I said: I'd give a great deal for it. He thought again and said: I love that man in there. Then I understood him, but I still couldn't contain myself properly and said: so you wouldn't give much for the ship? Now he didn't understand, so after a while he said: but I beg you, let us go! I have to admit I had some brandy under my belt but I really was deeply affected by the fact that he wanted to leave the ship and couldn't speak about it and only said 'but', which covered everything he could suggest; and he certainly read all this on my face, for he continued: if I leave all of you the ship and you give me that man there, then we're quits, I mean as far as I'm concerned, because I haven't got much else that I could give for him. I considered the matter and he added: of course it would be an act of mercy too; and that word was a thrust with a good knife into my crocodile hide. I considered it for a long time, and all the while, as under a light wind we rocked over the water which you could hear, he stood there quietly and I couldn't see his face which was in the dark. And although every breath of wind took us farther out to sea and away from the land where he wanted to go, he said nothing to hasten my decision.

But that night I thought of his whole fate and everything lay before me like a meadow in the full light of morning which is slowly being devoured by a forest and is only there temporarily. This man had put all his money on one card and now he was defending it. But the card was a loser and the more he put on, the more he lost; he knew all about it, but he probably just wanted to get rid of his money, he couldn't help it any more. That's what happened to him, this great man, a special effort on God's part, and it's what could happen to any of us: you get assaulted in broad daylight, that's how secure we all are on this planet.

And then I opened up the cage and carried fat Croze into the little boat with my own hands and Bargan followed behind me. He didn't look to left or right when he got into the boat, and yet it was his ship where for ten years he hadn't always done good, though good had been done too, but at least he had lived and worked a lot and had been just and had stood in good repute, he didn't look at it as he joined his friend in the small boat, and he didn't say anything either.

And that night as he slowly rowed away and I watched him go (I never saw him again or heard any news of him or the clubfoot) many things occurred to me concerning life on this planet, and I came closer to God than in a lot of dangers I myself had been through.

For all of a sudden I understood God, who, for a scabby fat dog not worth wasting your knife on, that you wouldn't have butchered but should have left to die of hunger, sacrificed a man like Bargan who was incomparable, who was just made for conquering Heaven. And who now, merely because he needed something he could be useful to, had attached himself to this lump of mange and given up everything for him, and was probably even glad that it wasn't a good man he loved but an evil, gluttonous child that sucked him dry like a raw egg in a single draught. For I'll be hanged, drawn and quartered if he didn't actually enjoy destroying himself and everything that was his for the sake of that little dog he'd set his eyes on, and that's why he gave up everything else.

STORY ON A SHIP

For four days we had been rolling around under a grey-green soapy sky; it wanted to gobble us up straightaway hair and hide, and our hide was thick and we were down to our last hairs, we had already lost so many. But on the evening of the fourth day which I'll never forget, with the indifference of its waters and the failing light above the hatches, we prepared for the night like widowers wanting to marry for the last time without being too happy about it, particularly about the accompanying fuss. We finished off the last of the whisky and lit the last candles and put on the best faces we could, and persuaded ourselves not to pump water in our last hour because it was undignified and anyway not worth the trouble.

So light spread over everything, a particularly good and expensive light; there wasn't a dark corner in any of us, nor in the old floating coffin which was a blank we had drawn, and we too had probably been blanks, and the light too likewise was dwindling. But once we were sitting together in the dining saloon with our candles and our whisky and our very special light, everything changed again and it was no longer necessary to have such a special light, such exceptionally expensive light for a few corpses, and we created a little darkness and didn't look into the corners, for it was no longer worth the trouble to trouble ourselves. And we stopped speaking crudely and awkwardly like greenhorns who think that you have to have the last word on everything and that speaking the truth is always permissible, which is nothing more than a way of excusing brutes and schoolteachers. That's why we spoke in a refined kind of way, as best we could manage, for we cursed like demons, believe you me, but with enormous care and delicacy. 'Dicky' we said and 'good old fellow' and nothing about the wind which ended after us or about the floating coffin which was coming to an end with us, or the water which was without end. Yes, with some whisky which there was no point in saving we even managed to spread a specially dense darkness over these particular things and though we didn't waste a syllable on tomorrow or the like, a sort of tacit supposition arose, that we'd be able to talk about it the day after tomorrow, and everyone tried his best to encourage the others in the belief that there was nothing so permanent as himself and that a dining saloon was not a nice place to be. Manky, for example, said we absolutely shouldn't save up the whisky, since we couldn't father any children and heirs on board, in view of the total absence of those long-haired creatures which the process calls for. And all in all, and taking the special circumstances into account, that was a good remark of Manky's.

But now I'm coming to the matter I wanted to talk about and the reason why I'm gassing so much; you'll see in a minute that it was necessary. For one of us – his name no longer carries any weight on this planet, it refers to nothing, though once it intro-duced a man who wasn't all that fat, with red hair and two teeth missing and a faint talent for cooking – one of us, I say, now said something which we noted carefully and still recall many years afterwards, and I don't intend to forget it today. On the contrary, I can still remember him standing up with his glass and walking up to the bulkhead and carrying the glass along and putting it on a small table as he said it, and doing so in such a way that it wasn't quite certain whether he was putting much thought into it. He said: *Well, I'm fed up. I'm fed up with this rolling around. I'm going home.* Yes, that was all.

It may not seem all that much to you people now, and none of you grew any paler as I said it, although I had my special way of laying such stress on it: but here you're not in a dining saloon and that wind isn't blowing and so on, and I doubt if you can really understand how after that remark silence spread, as if one or ten men saw a light in the darkness and then it fizzled out and was a cigar-end. Of course Ferry – and now I've mentioned his name after all – understood pretty well, just looking took his breath away, you could see how he immediately turned pale, paler than the bulkhead he was standing by. And then he immediately left the comfortable saloon, which was bloody crazy with those waves, and he never came back again and up till now none of us has ever asked where he went. He had a home, a little house in the state of Arkansas with a wife in it, but he didn't go there, as we knew very well when he said it, just as we knew that we our-selves would never go anywhere else on this planet, we who had no 'home'. And although we knew that neither he nor we would ever go anywhere at all, and that water is just as wet for everybody, our hatred was still so great that he immediately felt it and walked out into the water; for we didn't know that the wind was going to stop towards morning, and the water was calm in a few hours, and we finished the voyage with no cook and no whisky.

THE REVELATION

A middle-aged man was taking a walk one evening in the avenue of poplars when, on seeing a large dog chasing pigeons beside a black stream, he observed that he was not welcome. He went home at once.

Nothing special had occurred that day. His business was doing well, his mistress was the only girl among his acquaintances who was not stupid. At the barber's that morning somebody had told the story of the thirteen year old Apfelböck who had shot his parents. Now the man's knees were shaking as he climbed the stairs.

As he went back to thinking about the Apfelböck case – the boy had kept his parents' corpses in a chest for seven days – it struck him that he could easily kill the dentist tomorrow, with a knife, say. The dentist had a stout white neck. But he could equally well not kill him.

He wanted to sit down at the piano and play Haydn; but Apfelböck had waited seven days, during which time (because of the weird smell) he had moved first of all to the living-room and then to the balcony. Haydn couldn't disguise that.

The man prowled around the dark room, from one window to another, stared into the void and down at the blue roofs far below, and he wrung his hands. It was unendurable. By now seven days had passed.

Then he got into bed. We're not responsible, he thought. This planet is a temporary affair. It's whizzing with all kinds of other ones, a whole range of planetary stuff, towards a star in the Milky Way. On that kind of a planet we're not responsible, he thought. But then it grew too dark in bed.

He had to get up and light candles. He found five; these he took and lit and placed at the corners of the bed, two at the head, two at the foot, and one on the bedroom table. Five candles in all. It must mean something, he thought.

After going to all that trouble, he smelt the corpse smell of his parents. Shouldn't he move on to the balcony? He definitely would not. These were figments of the imagination. Anyway there was no balcony.

If I were to die, the man said to himself; but it's a vicious circle. I am helpless. The carpet is red even if I don't like it. After my death it will still be red. The carpet is stronger than I am. It clearly has no wishes. It can't behave foolishly.

The flies buzzed. He caught one. He knelt up in bed to do it and his hand skimmed the wall with shirtsleeves flying. Lit by five candles. Having caught it, he thought what a useful thing to do in your dying moments.

Suppose I did die, he thought. I'd like to have a child. Perhaps I have got a child. If I die nobody will give a damn. If I stay alive nobody will give a damn either. I can do what I like, nobody gives a damn.

Troubled, the man got up and put on an army greatcoat over his shirt. Thus clad, he went out into the street. It was not all that dark; clouds passed, visible, damp, compact. Stiffly the black chimney-pots pierced the sky.

The man walked on, his hands in his pockets. He hummed: 'How gently falls the bridal tear, When the bridegroom slugs her on the ear.' Then he walked faster, past the other people, in the end singing loudly in his shirtsleeves; for he threw off his coat; on a planet like this nobody needed a coat.

Loudly intoning, he strode through the streets, and no longer understood anything.

THE FOOLISH WIFE

A man had a wife who was like the sea. The sea changes in response to every breath of wind, but it does not grow larger or smaller, nor does it change colour, nor taste, neither does it grow harder, nor softer; but when the wind has passed then the sea lies still again and has grown no different. And the man had to go on a journey.

When he went away, he gave his wife everything that he had, his house and his workshop and the garden round his house and the money he had earned. 'All of this is my property and it also belongs to you. Take good care of it.' Then she threw her arms around his neck and wept and said to him: 'How shall I do that? For I am a foolish woman.' But he looked at her and said: 'If you love me, you can do it.' Then he took leave of her.

Now that the wife was left alone, she began to fear for everything that had been entrusted to her poor hands, and she was very much afraid. And she turned to her brother, who was a dishonest man, and he deceived her. Thus her possessions dwindled, and when she noticed it she was in despair and resolved to stop eating lest they decrease still more, and she did not sleep at night and as a result fell ill.

Then she lay in her chamber and could no longer take care of the house and it fell into ruin, and her brother sold the gardens and the workshop and did not tell the wife. The wife lay on her cushions, said nothing and thought: if I say nothing, I shall not say anything foolish, and if I eat nothing, then our possessions will not decrease.

And so it came about that one day the house had to be auctioned. Many people came from all around for it was a beautiful house. And the wife lay in her chamber and heard the people and how the hammer fell and how they laughed and said: 'The roof leaks and the walls are falling in.' And then she felt weak and fell asleep.

When she awoke she was lying in a wooden chamber on a hard bed. There was only a very small window high up, and a cold wind was blowing through everything. An old woman came in and snapped at her viciously, telling her that her house had been sold but her debts were not yet met, that she was feeding on pity, although it was her husband who deserved it. For he had nothing left at all now. When she heard this the wife became confused and her mind was slightly touched and she got up and began to work in the house and the fields from that day on. She went around in poor clothes and ate almost nothing, yet earned nothing either, for she demanded nothing. And then one day she heard her husband had come back.

Then she was seized by a great fear. She went indoors quickly and tousled her hair and looked for a clean shift but there wasn't one there. To cover up she ran her hand over her chest and found her breasts had shrivelled. And went out through a small back door and set off, blindly.

After she had been walking for a while it occurred to her that he was her husband and they had been joined together and now she was running away from him. She turned round at once and walked back, not thinking any longer of the house and the workshop and the shift, and saw him from afar and ran towards him and clung to him.

But the man was standing in the middle of the road and from their doorsteps the people laughed at him. And he was very angry. His wife was clinging to him and would not lift her head from his chest nor take her arms from around his neck. And he felt her trembling and thought it was from fear because she had lost everything. But then she finally raised her face and looked at him, and he saw it was not fear but joy, she was trembling because she was so glad. Then he realised something and he too faltered and put his arm around her, felt unmistakably that her shoulders had grown thin, and kissed her on the middle of her mouth.

THE BLIND MAN

A simple man lived decently for thirty years, without excesses, then he lost his sight. He could no longer dress himself properly, and washing too proved difficult. Things came to such a pass that death would have been a release – and not only for him.

And yet he bore the beginning with a certain composure. This lasted about as long as he remained able to see at night in his dreams. Then things got worse.

He had two brothers who let him live with them and who kept an eye on him. During the daytime they went to work; then the blind man was all alone in the house. For eight hours a day or more. For eight long hours the man who for thirty years had had his sight without being aware of it, sat on his bed in the dark or walked around the room. Early on men with whom he had formerly played cards for low stakes came to see him. They talked about politics, women, the future. The man they were looking at had none of these three things, and no work either. The men told him what they knew and never came again. Some people die sooner than others.

The blind man walked up and down his room for at least eight hours a day if he was lucky. After three days he stopped bumping into things. Just to keep himself amused he thought of everything that had ever happened to him. He even recalled with pleasure the blows he had been given by his parents as a child to make him grow up into a good person. All this went on for a certain time. But then the eight hours became too long for him. The person in question was thirty years of age and a few months. With luck a man can live for three score years and ten. So he could hope for another forty years. His brothers let him know that he was growing visibly fatter. That came from his easy life. If things went on like this he might eventually get too fat to squeeze through a door. Then, when the time came, they would have to cut up his corpse if they didn't want to damage the door. For far too long he entertained himself with thoughts of this kind. In the evening he told his brothers he had been to the music-hall. They laughed.

They were very goodnatured and loved him as men love one another, because he was a decent person. Keeping him wasn't easy for them but they never gave the matter any thought. At first they took him along to the theatre every now and again; he enjoyed that. But when he discovered the ramshackle nature of words, it only made him sad. It was God's will that he had no understanding of music.

After a while his brothers remembered that it was many weeks since he had last been out. They took him along once: he felt faint. When a child took him out for a walk it ran off to play and he was seized by a great fear and was not brought home till late at night. Then the brothers who had been worried about him laughed and said: 'You must have been with a woman,' and 'We can't get rid of you, you see'. They meant it as a joke, being glad to have him back again.

That night he could not get to sleep for a long time. Those two sentences settled down like squatters and made themselves at home in his brain which had become as inhospitable to the brighter side of life as a house without windows is to cheerful lodgers. He had not seen their faces; their remarks were nasty. When he had thought about this for a long time without coming to any conclusion, he put such thoughts aside like chewed-up grapeskins which lie on the dirty floor and make your feet slip.

One of the brothers once said to him at mealtime: 'Don't push your food with your hand. Use two spoons instead.' Deeply shocked, he put down his fork and in the air he saw children eating. They straightaway calmed him down but after a while that brother started having his food brought to him in the factory. This was because of the long journey. The blind man, who went walking by himself for at least eight hours a day, had not yet composed his thoughts about it when the other brother idly asked if he was having a lot of difficulty washing himself. From that day on the blind man had an aversion to water, like a dog with rabies. For now it appeared to him that he had been patient long enough and that there was no reason why his brothers should live in pleasure if he was perishing in misery and loneliness.

He grew a beard and could no longer recognise himself. His clothes were cleaned by his brothers but from then on the stains from the food which he spilt on his shirt grew worse and worse. Around the same time he acquired the inexplicable habit of wanting to lie on the ground like an animal.

He grew so dirty that his brothers could not take him anywhere. Now he had to spend all Sunday alone, going for walks. On such Sundays various mishaps occurred. Once he fell with the washbasin and spilt it on his brother's bed, which took a long time to dry. Another time he put on his brother's trousers and soiled them. When the brothers realised that he was doing this deliberately they felt very sorry for him at first, then they asked him not to do such things; their misfortune was great enough. He listened quietly, his head bowed, and guarded the sentence in his heart.

They also tried to get him to work. They had absolutely no success. He was so purposely clumsy that he ruined the material. They came to see that he was growing more ill-natured every day, but could not do anything about it.

So the blind man walked in darkness and pondered how he could increase his sufferings in order to endure them better. For it seemed to him that a great torment was easier to bear than a small one.

He who had always been so clean that his mother in her life-time had held him up as an example to his brothers, now began to foul himself by urinating into his clothes.

This made his brothers deliberate how to get him into an institution. He listened to their deliberations from an adjoining room. And when he thought of the institution, all his past suf-fering seemed bright and beautiful, so much did he hate the prospect. There are more people like me there, he thought, ones who have come to terms with their misery, ones who endure it better; in that place we shall be tempted to forgive God; I'm not going there.

When the brothers had left he sat for a long time in deep con-templation, and five minutes before he expected them back he turned on the gas tap. He turned it off again when they were delayed. However, when he heard them on the stairs he turned it on once more and lay down on his bed. They found him there and were seized with a great fear. They took pains with him for one whole evening and tried to revive his interest in life. Obs-tinately he resisted their efforts. That was one of the best days of his life.

But then the procedure to admit him to an Institution for the Blind was speeded up.

On the evening before the appointed day the blind man was in their home alone and set fire to it. His brothers returned un-expectedly early and put out the blaze. While doing so one of them could not contain his anger and began to yell at the blind man. He enumerated all the misfortunes they had endured on his account, omitting no cause of ignominy or occasion for anxiety but on the contrary exaggerating every single point. The blind man listened patiently and his face showed his distress. Then the other brother, who still took pity on him, tried to comfort him as much as possible. He sat up with him for half the night and held him in his arms. But the blind brother did not say a word.

The next day the brothers had to go to work, and did so with a heavy heart. And when they came home that evening to take him to the Institution, the blind man had disappeared.

When evening came, on hearing the town clocks strike, the

blind man had descended the steps. Towards what? Towards
death. He had groped his way laboriously through the streets, had
fallen, been laughed at, pushed and berated. Then he reached the
edge of the town.

It was a very cold winter's day. The blind man was actually
glad to be freezing cold. He had been driven out of his house.
Everyone had turned against him. He didn't care. He made use
of the cold sky for his own destruction. God was not forgiven.

He could not accept it. An injustice had been done to him. He
had gone blind, blind through no fault of his own, and had then
been driven out in the ice and the snowy wind. This was the work
of his own brothers, who were privileged to see.

The blind man crossed a meadow till he came to a stream. He
stepped in. He thought: Now I shall die. Now I shall be forced
into the river. Job was not blind. Never has anyone borne greater
suffering.

Then he swam down the stream.

A HELPING HAND

In a harsh land there once lived an evil man by the name of
Lorge; he had a heavy hand and where he struck the grass did not
grow again. He choked the life out of the peasants and slept with
their wives by force; he devoured the property of orphans; he
swigged brandy from a cask as a bull swigs water and when he
was drunk he spoke with the trees at night. Nobody could touch
a hair of his head, even though he was a sore trial, for he was very
strong.

In a fight one day this man was struck across the eyes and as a
result grew blind. He stood in the centre of a meadow in the
midday light, and now his sun set rapidly and the wind grew very
loud around him. His servants chased his enemies away but
Lorge sat on a tree-stump the whole day and reflected.

When the news reached the villages there was great rejoicing
everywhere. People believed that God had intervened; for they
did not yet know that Lorge's adversary was even worse than
Lorge.

This man extended his protection to the defeated Lorge and let it be known that he would be as hard as Lorge himself on anyone who tried to hurt him and this would shorten their life. When Lorge heard that he laughed again for the first time.

He stayed in his farm and nobody did anything to harm him. The servants lived riotously off his property, and left the blind man sitting in his room. However, they set his cask of brandy in front of him.

Lorge did not touch the brandy cask and when the servants saw that he had grown pious and that this alone was bringing him low, they took it away again. Lorge said nothing. He was waiting for something.

Lorge waited for three weeks and nothing came. Then he began to understand that nothing would ever come to him again. In the wall there was a hole; through it there came a weak cold sun or a weak warm sun. In the table in front of him there were a number of streaks and hollows which never changed. Sometimes the servants sang outside. If you walked around, you fell down easily. It was hard to sleep. These were Lorge's experiences now and for evermore. Perhaps the Amen would be added sometime later.

Once he went out of his room and leaned against a linden tree which he loved very much, particularly its crown. When he pressed his cheek against the trunk, he felt the tree trembling and he could imagine its top again swaying in the wind. The tree could not see either, and lived for centuries. It had a *different* way of living. Lorge went to it many times although people often laughed at him because he had a new lover.

But after three weeks he had the horses harnessed and was driven by his neighbour. This neighbour was a friend of his. He had been away at the time when Lorge had lost his eyesight. When he now saw the pale fat clod in the rack-waggon, he became very confused and afraid of fate. He stepped up to the waggon and greeted Lorge and Lorge stood up, reeling, and his thin fair hair blew about his great head and he opened his eyes wide and said: 'You must help me, brother. I cannot see any more.'

Then the other invited him into his house and promised to help him and they shook hands on it. They sat together at night and the neighbour drank. And Lorge didn't drink a drop for whenever he drank he was seized with an irresistible desire to go out and do evil. The neighbour was greatly shaken by the fact that Lorge could not do evil any more.

In the morning he gave Lorge into the care of his best servant and went out with the rest of his servants to avenge Lorge. And by the evening he was already a corpse and no longer in need of help.

Lorge never learnt of this. For when he heard that his friend wanted to avenge him, he was bitterly disappointed and said to the servant, 'Trusty servant, I have business to do. You must help me.' The servant agreed.

Then they retraced their steps to Lorge's farm, this time on foot and they walked all day. But a short hour's walk from Lorge's farmhouse he turned off the road and he had himself brought to the farm of his greatest enemy among the peasants. He knew that this man must be at a Midsummer festival that night. So he groped his way into the house with the servant helping him, and the two of them tried to rape the farmer's wife. However, they did not succeed. Instead, the wife ran away in her nightdress to her husband and the husband returned before morning. There sat blind Lorge in his room waiting for him. And as the farmer entered wanting to kill him he said: 'As long as I could see what your wife looked like, I didn't want to have her. But now she doesn't want me any more.'

So the farmer noticed just how much trouble Lorge was taking to provoke him, and simply got two servants to eject him from the house. And Lorge groped his way home. All was not going well on his farm; even in his blindness he noticed that, but it did not matter. In any case it was better than if everything had taken its normal course. No one bothered about Lorge, they often forgot to serve him his meals and sometimes they bolted the room so that he had to relieve himself beside the bed. In addition it rained through the roof and the wind whistled through the cracks. The fields were untilled, the animals were slaughtered or died in their filthy stalls. The servants quarrelled and spent the whole of February drinking, and the people from the neighbourhood went out of their way to avoid the house. From a distance they looked into this hell where the blind man sat and was sure to perish, and they were glad.

But in March just as the great storms began Lorge set out one day, walking off alone in the early morning. He walked along swampy roads, corroded by the black rain and lashed by the stormy winds, and he had to grope his way along the roads with his feet, but often strayed into swampy meadows. In places where he was unknown people sometimes took him in for the night, and those were his last good days.

Finally he walked day and night and in April came to his brother's farm. One evening when his brother came home from hunting there he was, standing among the servants. But his brother recognized him straightaway and reined in his horse. And Lorge, while the servants jostled him, spoke into the air: 'I've lost my sight. You must help me.' Then his brother dismounted, and saw that he was very dirty and had grown thin and blind as well, and he fell upon his neck and wept over him.

But that evening they sat together drinking and Lorge drank too; for now he no longer turned vicious. He told his brother everything that had happened to him, and when he came to the point where the farmer gave him two servants for his farm, his brother got up and closed the windows. Afterwards they went out into the farmyard arm in arm.

And Lorge began telling, and he told of how they had all forborne to hurt him and had avoided him and been unwilling to help him. Then his brother brought him to a place on the wall where there was a drop of around twenty feet into the castle moat and he said to him: 'Watch out; if you make one false step here you'll drive the bones through your body.' Then Lorge let go his arm.

But his brother saw how Lorge's legs were searching carefully for the path along the wall and Lorge made no false step. He said nothing more, but his face was grim and there was sweat on his forehead and he stepped carefully.

When they were both sitting again in the room and felt each other's breath – for both of them were big and strong, and the room was too small – and began to drink again, the brother complained about the world and called it a treacherous vale of tears. Then Lorge got up and bent forward and tried to locate his brother, and they stood opposite each other as in their youth and Lorge had been the younger one, but now he said: 'I tell you it's more beautiful than anything else, don't contradict me.'

Then his brother sat down and said nothing more, but he drank a lot. After a while Lorge, too, sat down again.

As it was growing light they went out of the chamber, and the brother put a sword in Lorge's hand. They had not exchanged another word since Lorge's remark about the world. As Lorge examined the thing and noticed that it was a sword, he hesitated and drew a deep breath and looked out of his blind eyes into the air and did not blink.

Then they both walked off beside each other, and his brother supported Lorge because he was blind.

They came to a place in the wood where there was a linden tree and they stood there with bare shoulders, powerful both of them, with swords in their hands. But Lorge himself struck the first blow.

Then his brother struck and now they fought fiercely for a long time and Lorge defended himself well and fought mightily and pressed his brother hard till he was standing by the linden tree and could not step to left or to right. Then his brother, who was in danger of his life, gripped his sword with both hands and closed his eyes and struck the blow.

JAVA MEIER

Come to think about it, Samuel Kascher was one of the oddest men I ever set eyes on. He was a fishmonger, but convinced you it didn't mean much since his father had married into the business. For many years it never occurred to him – and even before then it would have been too late to think of it – that he could have chosen his own profession. What's more, bankruptcy hovered continuously over his small white bungalow. And yet as far as one could see he only had one single passion, and it was this which brought us together. For he subscribed – a luxury way beyond his circumstances – to almost all the important German newspapers and read them carefully. The outlay was high and he justified it simply: he needed paper to wrap his fish in. He also had interesting attacks of conscience every now and again, during which he proved to anyone, rather ingeniously, that the sole purpose of all these forms of entertainment was to benefit his fish business (which his father had married into). It was purely for the sake of the fish business that he occupied himself with certain forensic exercises; for just as he considered a good newspaper to be a good advertisement for the fish wrapped inside it, he also believed he could attract connoisseurs of fish with interesting conversations. At least he believed this during his bouts of guilty conscience. One of his strangest cases was the episode of Java Meier.

One evening I was sitting with him in the brown wooden extension behind the shop, whose white curtained window opened to the yard, among old newspapers and the stink of blubber and fish. Kascher was drawing initials in his ledger and on the blotter as he recounted slowly, as was his wont, an event of the previous night in Well Lane (where his shop was) which he had heard from one of the cooks in the neighbourhood; for although he himself probably heard the shot, he had not thought it worth getting up for.

This is what happened. The inhabitants of Well Lane had been woken between twelve and one o'clock at night and drawn to their windows by a revolver shot in the street. In the middle of the lane, outside Number Seven where Meier the engineer lived, stood a man with a bicycle, holding a revolver. The neighbours opposite saw Meier come to the window in his shirt and the man shouted something up at him.

As he told this story, the fishmonger opened the door to his shop and stepped out into the dark room where the fish corpses were floating in their tubs. He opened a window which gave on to the street and said in an undertone: 'He must have been standing over there and shouted very loudly in the night.' But I didn't feel like walking past those fish, and was well able to imagine the man on the corner, likewise the engineer who was now lying stiff in the house opposite, probably under a linen sheet drawn up to his chin if not further.

The man had shouted: 'Don't forget Java, Hut 17 and poor Lizzie, and don't you leave town!' Then the man had mounted his bicycle and ridden off.

They had found Meier the engineer that morning, hanged, a short way from the path through a coppice where he used to go for a walk every day. The rope had parted, snapped in the middle, one end was swinging from the branch, the engineer was lying on the ground. The newspapers said the reason for his suicide was obscure, 'to be found perhaps in the impenetrable forests of far-off Java where Meier had once worked on the construction of a bridge.'

The fishmonger continued deftly drawing initials as he reported the story without embellishing it in any way. Then his tortoise-shell eyes looked at me and he said: 'Actually it's as clear as day-light even if a few details are missing. Perhaps I should add that it didn't rain this morning, that the branch which Java Meier was hanging from was a thick one and that Java Meier had originally intended – at least yesterday evening he did – to make a short trip to Frankfurt. Doubtless you can see straightaway from all this that it is certainly a case of murder.'

Whereupon Kascher stood up in his brown suit and walked again through his shop to the window to look out. He had a crafty way of dramatising his horror stories, carefully making use of the stinking fish, the darkness of the unlit room and the white curtain, nor was he above using the brutal trick of leaving me sitting on my own.

'I don't see it. You can skin me alive! It's straightforward suicide. The man wants to travel, and doesn't, so he has a bad conscience sparked off by a cry of alarm from that man the night before. That's all.'

In the room next door the fishmonger half turned and said somewhat tonelessly, 'Some people think the man wanted to warn him'. I noticed clearly how my idea was gaining ground:

'I see; so Java Meier respected this so-called warning enough to refrain from leaving town but didn't think enough of it to forgo his usual walk?'

'It seems to me,' said the fishmonger impatiently, 'you're forgetting that he was only warned not to leave town; so he could perfectly well have taken that warning seriously and still gone for a walk around here.'

'You admit that, do you? Right. A fine warning, wasn't it? A really excellent sort of warning to stay put, after which the fellow who stays put gets strung up . . . How about it? That's not really what you meant, is it?'

'Well, the murderers could have been here and not yet in

Frankfurt, could have heard about it or waited at the station this morning in vain. Besides, the man himself could have been involved in the plot, couldn't he?'

'Really, Kascher? Can you imagine anyone thinking you can do away with a man more easily on a journey than in his own home town, which follows his doings, and in the middle of his daily routine, which can be observed? Suppose he had really wanted to warn him, what a public, theatrical way of doing it; how ineffectual, about as good as shouting into the murderer's ears! And how imprecise! "Don't forget." No, my dear fellow, he wanted to scare the daylights out of him, that's all.'

'I think so too,' said the fishmonger in a monotone. 'It was probably something like that.'

'If you frighten somebody it is usually harder to kill him, wouldn't you say? He keeps a lookout, hears every leaf rustle, stops going into the wood where the thick branches are. Incidentally, how do you know this particular branch happened to be thick?'

'The milkman was there, and I asked him.'

'So you weren't there?'

'Did you think I was? I'm not a dog. The milkman gave me a full account.'

'Yet this business has been on your mind all day long. Anyhow, why did you ask about it at this particular moment?'

'Because it wasn't raining.'

'I don't understand you. I think you're too keen to create an effect. Who do you think is the murderer, then?'

'The murderer is the man with the bicycle.'

'The man whose warning led to what you call the murder? And who showed himself to the whole street in order to keep his man here (where he was undoubtedly more difficult to kill than anywhere else), and yet could hardly have meant his appearance to prevent his victim from stomping into the woods, presuming the latter had a bad conscience and was therefore bound to recognise him.'

'Yes, that leaves some points to be cleared up, or just one really. It wasn't among those you mentioned. But let's forget about it. This business isn't over yet. It's a splendid case, believe you me.'

After Samuel Kascher had seen me out and I had walked down the dark narrow lane, I passed by Java Meier's house. There it stood looking sombre.

When I went to the fish shop again three days later, it was full of people, as fresh cod had just arrived. The fishmonger quickly fetched me the paper I wanted and asked, without showing much interest:

'By the way, did you know that Meier the engineer – you remember, Java Meier – that Java Meier was Italian by birth? Yes, his mother was an Italian and married a German engineer. What does that signify? Like to know? Come round again. I've got some new cuttings.'

Kascher cut out interesting cases from the newspapers, and I went round to his place that same evening. He was still cleaning up in the shop.

'Did I ever tell you that I originally wanted to be a soldier?' he began. 'It came to nothing because I couldn't get a room of my own to sleep in. I couldn't bear it. Here at least there's only the smell of fish.'

'I'm not all that surprised,' I said with interest. 'You must have a cruel streak, I suppose. And your face is so gentle.'

'You see, I had been reading too much Stendhal. And the world is not aristocratic enough. It's turning more and more to the fish business.' He dragged a barrel of cod into the corner.

I laughed and enquired about Java Meier.

'They've buried him,' he said. 'What's more, it was the wrong one.'

'You said this morning he was an Italian. What difference does it make?'

'That was what needed clearing up, in my view. But the house-keeper herself told me.'

'Don't you think it was his bad conscience that made him give himself away?' I asked a little impatiently.

The fishmonger grew a little uneasy. He looked up from his barrel, sizing me up.

'Oh yes, I'd say so. Have you worked it out?' He sounded disappointed. He loved to create an effect.

'I mean, it was after that that he hanged himself. He must have been thoroughly frightened, surely?'

'Certainly.' The fishmonger sighed in relief. 'He was just as badly shaken as everybody else in the street. I'm glad *I* didn't look out of my window. I'd have been frightened too.'

'What do you mean? He didn't go on his journey?'

'Right. And he went for a walk before dinner. By the way, he would have had fish for dinner; he'd bought some of my dried cod, the idiot.'

'What's up with you?'

'Oh, nothing. It's a little annoying something like that should have happened to him. Like a printer's error.'

'To whom? Java Meier?'

'No, to the murderer.'

'Whose error?'

'Yours, saying Java Meier must have been stung by his conscience, if he didn't go away. That's idiotic. Oh yes, I wanted to ask you a favour, it's for someone else, I mean it's really for me. I wanted to ask you to put a small ad. in the Engineer's Journal. Something on the lines of: "Engineer named Meier, formerly active bridge-building Java. Contact undersigned." Would you do that?'

'Yes, but for God's sake why?'

'He'll write to you, give his address or something. At any rate the town where he is living.'

'And what do you want to do there?'

'Subscribe to the newspaper.'

'Are you . . . is this supposed to be a trick? Enquiring about Meier when he's dead? I don't get it.'

'It's for the living one. The living Java Meier. Not a case of mistaken identity. The still living tangible flesh-and-blood Java Meier.'

'Oh, to hell with your mysterious secrets! What are you really up to? Are you or are you not going to put your cards on the table?'

'No. Sooner not. You're too energetic. Too strong-minded. You're a little too enterprising, let's say too western. A little, a trifle too western.'

'What are you on about now? Do you want to sleep alone again? Does your fish stink better than me?'

'You've got me wrong. It's nothing so complicated. Do you or do you not want to hear a story?'

'Yes of course; you know I do. Go ahead!

'No. Just because you want a story you'll have to wait for it. Meanwhile put the ad. in.'

'I don't understand you, Kascher.'

'People who understand everything get no stories.'

Damn me if I didn't put an ad. in the Engineer's Journal. That was Tuesday; it was due to appear the following Monday. On Saturday the fishmonger beckoned to me.

'Your story is finished, everything's all right, here, the whole thing in print. It was a little sooner than I had anticipated. He was an idiot, but this will get him out of it. With luck he'll be all right.'

'What's it all about?'

The fishmonger led me into the shop. It was getting dark. He didn't light the gas, but he did light a candle.

'If you stand up in a hurry,' he said, placing a tub of carp in front of my stool, 'mind the tub.'

'Is this about Java Meier?' I asked. 'I haven't had any response yet.'

'You won't get one my friend, Hamburg is the town, and I've ordered the newspaper from there. But shall we go over the story again from the beginning? Although the point is quite a simple one, namely, that the rope had snapped. Get that firmly in your head, would you? Why did it snap, what was the reason, eh, given that it hadn't rained? Either a rope doesn't hold, in which case you can't hang yourself with it, or else it does, in which case you have to pull it apart if it is supposed to have snapped. It *had* snapped, so this affair wasn't a suicide. Don't say a word, not yet; I know the murderer's behaviour was most unusual, even apart from the way he pulled his victim down again – he was able to, the branch was thick, a thick branch – he showed himself in public, he shouted in the street for everyone to hear, in order to get a gentleman who had been in Java to come to the window by night with a candle in his hand. True enough, he shouted at him to be so good as to stay at home because of Lizzie, because of a certain Lizzie. Although it would have been better if the gentleman had gone away; not because he could have been done in more easily, but because he wouldn't have had to be done in at all. The question is simply: did the man feel inclined to stay here on Lizzie's account? And now we come to a big surprise, my friend; which is that the gentleman really did stay. Yes indeed, he didn't leave town, he went for a walk instead, although Lizzie had nothing to do with it, I'd swear he didn't even know her any more than you or I. But did his behaviour suggest that he knew her? Only to an idiot. The man stayed at home because he was shaken and surprised and had been woken up, denied his sleep. This is amply proved by his going unsuspectingly to the park and getting slaughtered without a murmur. Yes, he had shown himself in a particular way, as one never saw him on the street, holding a candle at the window and looking rather frightened. And then he didn't leave town; that was enough for the murderer. But don't ever hang anybody on the basis of such proof, let me tell you, such a shadow of a proof, you mightn't be able to cut him down again, not alive at least. Yes, nothing – neither the performance that night, nor the punishment for Java Meier's seemingly bad conscience – points as clearly to the murderer's terrible un-certainty – to his quite unbelievable and ridiculous uncertainty – as does the victim's descent from the tree after he had been hanged; and the uncertainty concerning Java Meier. It was the wrong man. That is the point, a rather bloody one if you like, but very special, selected with cunning. You may ask what it was in the short interval between the murder and the murderer's return that made it clear to him, after having first been quite sure that the Meier he had was the Meier he wanted, that it was the wrong Meier, this Meier who was seemingly stung by his conscience and had been revealed by the flickering light of the candle and had now been murdered. And that brings us to the nub.'

The fishmonger went into the dark shop and paced back and forth, peering into the dark. Then he continued rather wearily: 'It seems certain that it wasn't easy to reconstruct the right Meier in his pursuer's brain. The man's knowledge of him was probably quite inadequate; he only had a vague idea of him, no matter how strongly he hated him . . . Java is a long way off. And yet Meier must have done something in the brief period of his previous existence that sank into his pursuer's mind, some-thing indelible, more distinct than a face, more recognisable than the movement of a hand in fright, something that could be done in a very short time, that was done in great agitation and that –

pay attention, would you – that you do again in the moment of your death, with the result that it didn't strike the murderer straightaway, not at the moment of the murder, of all that hard work – just try stringing up a heavy man on a tree – but soon afterwards, on his way through the bushes, almost immediately afterwards all but in the nick of time. As I told you, this was an obscure point until I heard that Java Meier was an Italian by birth so that his mother tongue was Italian. You understand? He cried out before he died. He said something relevant, he spoke about the project, he probably got excited. And he spoke Italian. It was his natural instinct to speak his other tongue when he felt about to be strangled; at least I imagine that is what happened. And the other Meier, the real Java Meier, who knew Lizzie and Hut 17, shouted in a different language when he in turn appeared at the window in such a state of agitation.'

The fishmonger was silent again, but was breathing rather heavily; his breath trembled a little. He probably saw it all fairly clearly. He had not left his shop, yet he had seen everything in the dark while he was working.

I wanted to say something, if only to break the silence.

'What do you suppose happened in Java?'

He brushed his hand across his forehead:

'They were building a bridge. They were bridge builders down there, there were quite a lot of them, there were more than 17 huts and I assume that Meier had a wife, or the murderer, maybe the murderer also had a wife. It seems certain to me that in the process something happened to Lizzie: whether she was Meier's wife living in Hut 17 and the murderer was with her when Meier came home, or the other way round, it's pretty much the same. Anyway the murderer was standing down below and saw Meier up at the window either storming in or running away, probably running away, definitely for the first time in his life, and anyway something then happened to Lizzie, most likely she hanged herself or she was strung up, it doesn't matter which. Anyway Meier was to hang as well, that seemed the logical conclusion.'

'Tell me,' I said after a while, 'why didn't you go and look at the corpse and study the scene of the murder if the affair interested you so much?'

'What was the point? Perhaps I am too eastern, perhaps I still

felt I was too western. Corpses sour you. They are bad for ob-
jectivity. I didn't see Lizzie hanging. If I had seen her murderer
hanging, I could easily have misjudged his. And that was when
Java Meier was still among the living; the sun still shone on him.'

'So he's dead now?'

The fishmonger passed me the paper. On an inside page I
learned that an engineer called Meier had been found hanged in a
hotel under strange circumstances. And I heard the fishmonger
saying in his gentle way:

'In case you stand up in a hurry, please mind the tub. This is my
business. It's my business to sell fish.'

THE LANCE-SERGEANT

Karl Borg was a lance-sergeant in the artillery and all the scum of
the regiment were concentrated in his battery. They were always
drinking, and even when schnaps wasn't to be had anywhere else
you would find drunks there who should have been in the cells.
They'd have found schnaps to requisition in a shot-up graveyard.

There was pastyfaced Mayer, who had captured a French lady's
shift near St. Quentin and used to stand by the guns in laces and
silk, with some sort of a bosom, a ridiculous ghost except that he
handled a gun well. He also had a small pince-nez which he
perched on his nose like a professor of chemistry inspecting his
test-tube. But Mayer put it on when he was adjusting the gun.

Bernauer, with his griping idealism, also belonged to the
battery; when drunk he would sing 'Off to battle for Kaiser and
Country' and 'I'm a Prussian, do you know my colours', preferably
at night so that nobody could sleep until he had finished.

There were a few more of that sort, and with any other captain
but Captain Memming there would have been hell to pay. As it
was, things were tolerable, the battery endured its misery with
dignity.

Lance-sergeant Borg himself was the worst, the Lord have
mercy on him. He came to a bad end. He said he was a coward
and that that was why he drank. 'What else can I do?' he asked.

'God will forgive me, I have to fight for the Kaiser and I can't do it. He created swine, so he can't complain about them.'

When he had been drinking, the sky was all blue, there wasn't a cloud, everything was beautiful, so fine and mild, you stepped ahead like a white horse, you were satisfied with everything, even with death.

Whether God forgave him or not is pretty uncertain, for a lot used to happen in our billets; but the captain did, and he was a conscientious man. He was short and thickset, an impeccable horseman whom carried himself excellently and dressed with astonishing elegance. Under the heaviest fire he would walk around with a little stick, making a show of his equanimity among the guns. It was said that he was bullet-proof, that the Tommies were likelier to hit a fly than him. But he had murdered many men who he took with him on his excursions and didn't bring back; returning to the dugout with equanimity and no companions. He showed no trace of consideration or forbearance, but he didn't interfere with the drunks around Borg.

Sometimes it wasn't all that easy for him. For instance, when he got hauled out at first light because Borg and Mayer were 'murdering' each other, at first light and under the bleary eyes of the whole battery. When the captain arrived they were standing in an open space fifty metres apart, each with a carbine raised to his shoulder, and were sniping at each other in the half-light. Neither was in any danger, for they were dreadfully drunk. But everyone else was in mortal danger since the two of them, fervently and with trembling hands, were shooting holes into the morning.

If the captain had been incompetent he would have yelled and punished them but he only said: 'You're not hitting anything, why not beat each other up, that would make better sense.' After which they had a drunken brawl which was a pleasure to watch. Incidentally, this story has an appendage. For pastyfaced Mayer was weaker than Borg, but Borg was drunker than Mayer and so Borg got more blows, more than he could stand. So he got up and shouted that he was going to transfer to the infantry, he wouldn't stand for it any longer. Everyone laughed and he went up the line to the infantry, over the terrain which was under fire, up to the infantry. He woke up in a ditch and since he was sober he started trembling all over, he got a horrible fright and had to be brought back like a wounded man. For he was as scared as a child to go back alone and they didn't have schnaps available for a cowardly lance-sergeant from the artillery.

He and pastyfaced Mayer were always seen in each other's company, they drank and didn't have to talk when they were together, and besides they had developed the fine art of whistling duets, they did it with tunes which neither of them had ever heard and they did it without practising. That's how they passed the gloomy hours in their dugout; it entertained the others too.

For a long time the two of them had amazing luck, they were together the whole winter and drank their way through everything. But in the spring of '17 pastyfaced Mayer was killed in a barrage. He was hit in the chest – he wasn't wearing his lady's shift that day – he died as a man and behaved accordingly. Mayer slumped forwards silently, his pince-nez fell off and he lay fully conscious for an hour without saying anything before he died. He had nothing more to say. He had only sort of turned a little pale, but with him you didn't notice that.

Borg wasn't with the battery that day because he had sprained his ankle. He didn't come until the next evening, by which time pastyfaced Mayer already had the earth scratched over him. Borg didn't notice anything until Bernauer failed to look him in the eye, but slunk away instead. Then when they told him, he took it calmly. But that evening he drank more than usual even for him and around two in the morning the others were woken up by the sergeant singing at the top of his voice. He sang: 'Never have I felt so good!' and it sounded bad.

The days following the barrage were very quiet, a warm dark wind was blowing, the sky was full of damp clouds, everything was bare and it looked as if the war was never going to end. What's more, there was nothing to drink, only Borg had something because he had connections which he kept strictly secret. Things were going worse then ever for Borg, he staggered and cursed all day and had a new quirk: he insisted everyone should salute him like in barracks, and out here you didn't even salute officers. That's when the men got to hate him, for one thing because his appearance was going to the dogs. At night he lay quietly and studied the stars, he did whistle now and again but only for a short time, as if he'd forgotten himself. That's why the griping Bernauer said Borg was mourning for his mate.

And then the day came when things went wrong for Borg. One night he left the dugout and fell into a shell-hole, drunk. There he lay, probably unconscious, until morning. In the grey dawn he was found and brought in. His internal injuries were too severe for him to be evacuated.

He lay the whole day in the dugout without speaking; it was a day when not a shot was fired. He was conscious, his eyes wandered restlessly over the timbers. At night Bernauer sat and watched over him. But towards midnight he went to sleep because Borg didn't need anything and was lying still. Bernauer was woken by a thin, shrill whistling; Borg lay stretched out flat with a swollen red face and an untidy moustache and was whistling. 'Do you want something?' asked Bernauer in surprise. Only a miserable oil lamp was burning and in that light the lance-sergeant looked like a bundle of old clothes. He made a face and opened his mouth wide and just when you thought a roar was going to come out there came a murmur, you could hardly hear it and it said: 'let me have it, Mayer'. Then Bernauer understood that Mayer was with him and he was asking for a bottle that wasn't there. At least he realised it would be silly to interrupt a conversation between friends, one of whom had come a specially long way, but after all these were the last hours, and you never knew. So he said to Borg: 'If you want schnaps, there's none here but perhaps you have other things to settle. One never knows.' But Borg couldn't hear properly and didn't understand very well and anyway he was talking to Mayer, who was closer to him and had come specially in the dark warm spring wind and even so had forgotten the schnaps. It must have been like that, for he said in a frail voice: 'Stop that and let me have it!' This made it certain that Mayer was telling dirty jokes and Borg couldn't get involved, for he knew about his condition. When Bernauer had worked this out, he listened with a strange turn of his head, and for a moment heard the wind in the timbers and felt the misery in his heart, and he was a rough man. He looked across at the face of the drinker, on which lay a torment too great to be safely accommodated. The lance-sergeant lay there like a bundle and hadn't been consulted but had been left in the dark, and now he wasn't going to get a schnaps either which he really needed in order to remain in the dark, something that would have been an achievement.

That and no other way is how Bernauer saw it. Lance-sergeant Borg had to die without any schnaps and Corporal Mayer had to watch him doing it.

MESSAGE IN A BOTTLE

I am twenty-four years old. People say that is an age strongly inclined to melancholy. All the same I don't think my melancholy is a reflection of my age. My story is as follows.

At the age of twenty I got to know a young man in whose vicinity I felt lighter; and since he also seemed happy in my presence our union depended only upon the consent of our parents, who agreed without much hesitation. The evening after this had been decided, he told me that before we were joined in wedlock he meant to spend several years travelling in the tropics. Being ill placed to force myself on him, I made no attempt to hold him back; indeed with bitter pride I promised as calmly as I could to wait for him. Next day he informed me that his journey would keep him away longer than he anticipated, I would not have sufficient patience, his sense of honour forbade him to make such demands on me, and so he was releasing me from my promise. Deeply shocked but not without composure, I accepted a letter from his hands, and in a failing voice promised not to open it until three years had passed. We parted coolly. A few days later he left the town without saying goodbye, nor did we meet again. I know that the story of my love is commonplace, indeed banal, but that does not make it any less bitter. For three years I put the letter away as the writer had desired, for you cannot take what does not belong to you. After three years I opened it and found a blank page. It is white and thin and smells of nothing at all, not a single stain on it. It makes me very unhappy.

To start with, of course, I just felt like a blank piece of paper. But since then I have thought a lot about it and have gradually become more and more disturbed. I still blush at the thought that anyone might want to mock a woman in her bereavement. Nor can I believe it was chance since that would make me look ridiculous. For a while the following thought comforted me: sailors who go down off the coast of Chile bequeath to the sea a bottle containing notes on their last hours, then twenty years later perhaps Chilean fishermen will uncork the bottle and, though not able to understand the foreign characters, nevertheless feel what it is like to drown in alien seas. Water and spray may have dispersed the writers, but the characters, fresh as the day they were written, do not betray how long ago that was. Think how ridiculous the message would be if it were legible; for how impossible it is in one's lifetime to find words that won't shatter the silence following a death, nor say anything nasty.

But in the long run this thought did not satisfy me, being too deliberately comforting to be true. Soon I was convinced that during those three years the characters might have faded: time heals wounds. Perhaps I may be excused at this point if I mention a thought which might sound far fetched but which has been haunting me since I first had it. As you know, there is such a thing as magic ink which is legible for a specific period and then disappears, surely anything worth writing down ought to be written with such ink. I would also just like to add that about a year ago – that is, roughly two years after giving me the letter which is only a blank piece of paper – my beloved disappeared completely from my sight, presumably for ever. After waiting patiently for three years for a message which was less and less meant for me, I can only say that I always thought that love was outside any lover's control, and that it was the lover's business and nobody else's.

A MEAN BASTARD
Novella

When Martin Gair was taking the air one afternoon in a fashionable street under the good September sun he noticed the widow Marie Pfaff, clothed in bright muslin, striding past the shop windows on her sturdy legs. She was tall and vigorous, and blessed with a full bosom and evidently soft hips which the clinging material emphasised suggestively. She had a pale healthy face and her thick brown tresses were swept up into a bun at the back of her head. He liked that, so he followed her for a while. Then he accosted her, and asked if he might accompany her. Since he looked at her very boldly, and since he was a tall gaunt bastard with brown skin, she was frightened at first and didn't answer, but made him walk faster to keep up with her. He for his part said nothing more, and so, gradually regaining her composure, she got rid of him by turning sharply sideways on her heel into a lingerie shop which she left again presently through a back door. She failed to see Gair, who was standing behind a projecting wall. He then followed her nonchalantly at a distance until she reached her apartment. After that he went to a somewhat dubious restaurant for a meal and devoured a half-raw beefsteak with which he had ordered three eggs. After this meal he knocked back a small glass of schnaps, dug into his black stumpy teeth with a toothpick and cleaned his nails with the same instrument. He paid the bill, added a five per cent tip and left the restaurant. Pulling the bell of Frau Marie Pfaff's apartment, he walked past a pretty maidservant into the dark hallway and asked to speak to Frau Pfaff. Astonished, she came out, recognised him immediately, said to her maid at the door, 'I am not at home to the gentleman' and went back into her living-room where her half-eaten evening meal lay steaming on the table. 'What gentleman?' said Gair. The maidservant propped herself trembling against the door-post and quickly thought of the latest sex murder reported in the newspaper – one carried out with unparalleled cruelty. Finally she said 'The gentleman is not here. Frau Pfaff is a widow.' These last words were dragged out of her against her will by the black eyes of the intruder; she threw them in his teeth, hoping he might spare her because she was honest. He moved towards the door, opened it and stepped into the living-room. He didn't linger for one moment on the threshold but walked straight over to the window opposite, which was hung with white muslin, and said 'I love you. But please finish your meal. I have already eaten.' The widow had sat down again, after listening breathlessly and with heaving bosom to the scene in the corridor. Now a slight weakness came over her. She heard Gair saying 'You are a widow, so the cream has been skimmed off. But there is still something left for me to take over.' She lent against the chairback half conscious, then rose slowly as if hypnotised and tried to reach the door. But Gair forestalled her and pressed the bell above the table. When the maidservant appeared Gair said severely in a voice of iron, 'There's been a misunderstanding. Frau Pfaff wishes you to clear the table and wash up.' He looked at Marie Pfaff all the time, he was a tall black bastard with angular features but a soft solid body. Frau Pfaff drew herself up, pulled herself together and said with passable self-control 'Clear the table, Anna!' Then she turned towards her guest and pointed wordlessly to a chair. Sitting down at once, he manoeuvred his chair so that his face remained in the dark. The maid cleared the table in silence. Meanwhile Marie Pfaff went to the mirror and straightened her hair; she also took something out of a small box. She had brought her voice almost entirely under control by the time the girl had left. In almost singing tones she asked with a mixture of outraged severity and dignified irony, what the gentleman wanted. Gair took in every inch of her full figure with his penetrating gaze. 'You', he said. Her answer sounded less certain, although he was sitting in the leather chair, slightly bent and relaxed and obviously satisfied. 'I don't understand you at all.' At that he stood up. He stood there, dark against the muslin, broad, tall and strong. Then he sat down again: that was his answer. 'What do you really want?' she murmured. 'Is your memory all that bad? Put that revolver down!' She laid it silently on the table. 'Sit down.' She obeyed. 'My time is my own and I have good muscles. I am going to live here and you are going to keep house for me.' She sat there quite crushed, not daring to say more than 'But I don't even know you.' 'First of all I'm going to have a wash,' he replied, 'then we can get to know each other.' As he spoke he rose, walked up to her and seized her with his strong arms. 'That trembling doesn't matter; in fact it's a good sign. I am neither a murdering rapist nor a matrimonial swindler. I am a lover.' He didn't kiss her, but let her sink back into the chair from which she had half-risen. When she made no move to get up, however, he fell upon the semiconscious woman, carried her in silence to the couch, raised her arms and crossed them over her head. Then he left her there panting. She got up without a word, turned left into the bathroom and prepared the bathtub. He carried her to bath and bed, to which she steered him feverishly without knowing his name. In the half-dark of the alcove she learnt in torment and bliss to love his hard hands, and she surrendered herself to them body and soul.

When she opened her somewhat swollen eyelids the next morning, she felt akin to this strange bastard and she loved him, dirty underwear and all. She got up quietly, without waking him. She hummed as she washed herself; doing her hair she thought about the nocturnal paradise into which he had led her. But once he woke up the work began. He looked no worse in the daylight, he was so strong and had brown skin and much else besides. He wouldn't let her draw back the heavy yellow window curtains; that tall dark-skinned bastard felt good in the golden light. At night, as he tumbled with her, he had been like a pale fat fish in its pond and now he was lying high and dry in the golden warmth, sunning himself, strong and evil. He took his coffee in bed, and she saw his knees and thighs under the thin blanket and felt dizzy. But he was lazy and had had enough. Let her work for him. The improbable nature of their acquaintanceship no longer struck her, and she took no thought for the morrow. A new life was beginning. The bastard never budged from her rooms; he lay around, smoked or fooled about with the goldfish which shone only faintly in the dull light. She for her part went out to fetch cigars, she served him strong liquor, she smothered him in newspapers. Her life had acquired a meaning; she was a mother by day and a mistress by night. He knew his job. They were happy. The past didn't exist.

This lasted for half a week, three days and four nights, then he'd had enough. He simply needed a change. The lady of the house was well built; however, he could make do with the same liquor and the same cigar, but not with the same woman. So he took to reading the newspaper in bed, and impregnated paradise with the smell of tobacco. She found fear of his cold eyes replacing love of his brown chest; it was fright that made her work, he became increasingly relentless. In the course of the fourth night, towards morning, about five o'clock, it couldn't have been completely light, he embraced her for the last time. At midday he had yet another bath, then after the meal turned his back on her tor-

mented eyes and left the apartment. She waited for him at the
window, not daring to draw the curtains for fear he might step
in and find the light too bright; she held on to them with both
hands for half the afternoon. He strolled around the town, drank
in various bars (he had pocketed some money), tipped like a lord
and sometime after six that evening stopped a girl who was
leaving a shop. She was shy and pale. He took her by the arm,
they went to a third-rate restaurant and had a substantial dinner.
Her confidence grew; he said practically nothing, but for the
sake of the change he was after, adopted a flattering manner. Then
they walked through the parks for two hours during which he
kissed her pale arm, once among the dark bushes and once again
in the white light of the asphalt streets; then when nine o'clock
came he took her home with him. The widow Pfaff in person
opened the door, then recoiled – but quite lightly as if on springs.
His hand on her arm he led the girl through the hallway into their
room. Then he looked at the widow and she went out. He sat
down with the girl at the table, then with a rolling gait he brought
cognac and sweet wine and some pastries too. They ate, he kept
looking fixedly at her knee, she slowly got drunk, began singing
and laughing, finally she was shouting. He led her to a leather
sofa and told her to sleep it off. 'The bed is too classy for you,' he
said. Whereupon he got into bed himself with his boots on.
Meanwhile the widow spent the night in the bathroom out of
embarrassment at what the maidservant might say.

When morning shone grey and milky through the coloured
glass the conflict in her soul began to call for a decision. She
won. She got up and went into the hall. She took her coat and hat,
left the house. When she came back around ten the girl had gone,
the man was lying on the couch. The room was in a mess, as if
there had been an orgy. He was in a bad mood and greeted her
with bitter irony. Had she slept well? Hadn't she seen the ghost
on the leather sofa? There'd been one animal lying on the leather
sofa and another in the bed – hadn't there? Liquor was ripe for
drinking but his love was just in its early stages. Liquor, to be sure,
would have to be procured at once. He hoped she was in possession
of ready money and if not she should stick at nothing to procure
some. She stood by the table watching him. He sat up and observed that she was looking at him. A gaunt muscular bastard

with mean features. His power was gone. It had been a kind of intoxication. Hadn't she been drinking schnaps? Now she saw it all: the stained furniture, the bed, the ransacked sideboard. Her head was heavy but it sat on her shoulders. She said 'Get up and button your shirt!' Involuntarily he obeyed. 'What's the matter with you,' he said. 'Nothing. You can go, If you need anything ring for the maid!' He got up, large as life. All the same, the room was spacious enough for him. He said 'Stay here!' in a ringing voice – and away she went. He dropped into the chair and laughed, but that wasn't enough to suppress the revolution. She walked to the door and then she went out, on her sturdy legs. He stayed seated for a while and looked at the furnishings. There were several attractive pieces. Then he went out. For inside his skull he had seen a light. He seized a small box of cigars, took his bowler hat from the rack and left the apartment whistling, box under his arm, that was all. That was how he had come. (Apart from the box; but it was only half full.)

The widow Marie Pfaff took a bath. She washed vigorously, sat down to lunch in her dining room which had been tidied up, rang loudly for the maid and checked the household accounts before the meal. Then the bell rang and the man came back. He wanted to make a brutal entry straightaway but this time he didn't have the right momentum, he drew back, no doubt he smelt something fishy. He heard the woman say: 'Give him something to eat in the kitchen.' After that he whistled softly while the girl led him into the kitchen. He was hungry and something had struck him. As she drank her coffee the woman asked whether that 'bastard' had gone. She no longer felt any embarrassment. The maidservant said yes and the widow Pfaff went out. She went to a café where she found lady friends. There was a silence as she stepped up to their table. It was awkward; the group had been informed, they could smell it on her. She had gone to the dogs. She didn't stay long, she soon got up, she went for a walk. First she went round the shops without buying anything, then to the gardens and then even further afield. She had remembered the bastard, and she felt a weakness in her knees. She wandered around till evening. It was September, mild air, wide sky. At nine o'clock a man accosted her. He was a young person, rather slender with good-natured eyes. He was not insolent. She let him take her arm. They walked for another hour in the park. On every bench there were couples, making strange shapes, the leaves didn't always conceal them completely. They didn't speak much. He talked about his German studies. The stars shimmered damply. They went home. She thought 'I cannot spend the night alone. The first step is the hardest.' She thought of him. Her knees thought. So the young man was allowed to go upstairs with her. He didn't refuse.

They felt their way along the hallway, stepped into the room. The woman avoided switching on the light. In the dark they were closer. She took the young man by the arm and, pressing close to him, led him to the alcove. She pulled back the curtain and uttered a small weak scream. There lay the dark-skinned bastard with the maidservant. The young man recoiled to the middle of the room. The woman sank down on her knees, lowered her head on the bed, and her body shook with tears. The bastard was asleep.

THE DEATH OF CESARE MALATESTA

At fourteen Cesare Malatesta was already ruling the town of Caserta; and historians of the Campagna place in his seventeenth year his murder of a brother two years younger than himself. Over two decades he steadily increased his fame and his possessions through his boldness and ingenuity, and his name awakened fear even among those who loved him – though on account not so much of the blows he imparted as of those which he was able to endure. In his thirty-first year however he got involved in a small, embarrassing affair which not many years later was to cause his death. Today throughout the Campagna he is accounted the disgrace of Italy, the affliction and ordure of Rome.

It came about in the following way.

During a conversation with Francesco Gaja – a man famous for his elegant way of life and utter nastiness – Malatesta, among various jests which greatly entertained his guest, made a witty remark about a distant relative of the Pope, unaware that he was at the same time a distant relative of Gaja's. Nothing in his guest's behaviour indicated that this was the case. The two men parted on the friendliest terms after exchanging elegant courtesies and making plans to go hunting together in the autumn. Following this conversation Cesare Malatesta had another three years to live.

Gaja had meanwhile become a Cardinal, and whether it was that he was busy with financial affairs or whether he was disinclined to spend his time in the open air, for two years Cesare Malatesta heard nothing more from him apart from a few courteous but cool lines apologising that he could not keep their appointment to go hunting. Two and a half years after their talk, however, Francesco began to gather an army. Nobody in the Campagna suspected the purpose of these preparations, and he himself gave away nothing about his plans. Since the Pope was not restraining him, it had to be against the Turks or the Germans.

When he discovered that the march of the Cardinal's army would bring him close to the town of Caserta, Cesare Malatesta sent emissaries to him with courteous invitations. They did not return. Around this time Cesare was having trouble with a shameless monk who, in a little place not far from Caserta, spoke about him to any visiting Casertans in an unseemly and stylistically barbarous manner. He had had the monk seized and thrown into the dungeon; but after only a few days he fled, and his guards with him. From then on, thanks to the monk's provocations, there was no lack of talk in Caserta about Cesare's murder of his brother. The fact that four of his best people had run away with a prisoner who had insulted him seemed even more amazing when three more servants went missing one morning, including one who used to dress his father. In the evenings, as he walked down from the citadel to the wall, he often saw people standing around and talking about him. Only when Gaja's army was encamped a mere two hours from Caserta did Cesare learn from a local peasant that Gaja's campaign was aimed against himself. Nor did he believe this until some rabble one night nailed a paper to the gate of the citadel saying that Francesco Gaja summoned all Malatesta's mercenaries and servants to forsake him without delay. This same piece of paper told Cesare that the Pope had excommunicated him and condemned him to death. That morning the last people disappeared from the citadel.

And now began that strange siege of a single individual which the people of the time considered a successful jest and recounted with merriment.

Walking round Caserta at midday, the worried Cesare discovered there was not a soul to be found in any of the houses. Only a large number of ownerless dogs followed him when he returned to his deserted citadel, walking more hurriedly than usual and feeling like a complete stranger in his native city. From the tower that evening he could see the ring which Gaja's army was beginning to lay around the abandoned town.

With his own hands he locked and barred the heavy wooden gate of the citadel and went to bed without having eaten (from midday on there had no longer been anybody there to serve him a meal). He slept badly and rose restlessly soon after midnight to have a look at the largish force which was attacking him like an unexplained illness. Despite the lateness of the hour he could see camp fires still burning and hear drunken singing wafted across.

In the morning he cooked some corn, which he half burned and consumed hungrily. As yet he had no idea how to cook. He was to learn, however, before he died.

He spent the day barricading himself in. He heaved boulders on top of the wall, placing them in such a way that if he ran along it he could throw them down without much difficulty. With the help of his two remaining horses, he pulled up the wide drawbridge which he could not raise on his own; just one narrow plank remained which could be removed with a kick. He stopped going into the town in the evening because from then on he was afraid of being attacked. During the following days he lay up in his tower watching; he noticed nothing remarkable. The town remained lifeless, and the enemy before the gates was evidently settling down for a long siege. Once when Cesare went for a walk on the wall (for he was beginning to get bored) some sharpshooters shot at him. He laughed, believing they were unable to hit him – he had not yet realised they were deliberately practising *not* hitting him.

All this happened in the autumn. The harvest was being gathered in the fields of the Campagna and he could see clearly how they were bringing in the grapes on the heights opposite. The songs of the harvesters intermingled with those of the soldiers, and not one of the people who had been living in Caserta a week earlier ever returned there. In a single night a plague had arisen and consumed all but one of them.

The siege lasted three weeks. Gaja's intention, and the point of his jest, was to give the besieged man enough time to review his whole life and find where the rotten spot lay. Besides, he wanted to wait until all the men of the whole Campagna had arrived to witness the spectacle of Cesare Malatesta's execution. (They came from as far away as Florence and Naples, often with their wives and children.)

All through those three weeks crowds of country- and towns-folk stood outside Caserta's walls, pointing their fingers and waiting, and all through those three weeks, each morning and evening, the besieged man went walking on the wall. Gradually his clothing came to seem neglected; he appeared to have slept in his clothes and his gait became slower and heavier because of the poor food. His face could not be recognised on account of the great distance.

At the end of the third week those outside saw him lower the drawbridge, and for three and a half days he stood on the tower of his citadel and shouted in all directions words that were incomprehensible because the distance was too great. All this time he didn't put a foot beyond the walls and he did not come out.

During the last days of the siege – that is to say in the fourth week, when the whole of the Campagna and many people from every station in life had arrived in the camp around Caserta – Cesare rode his horses along the wall for hours at a time. In the camp they assumed, probably with good reason, that he was already too weak to walk.

Many recounted later, when it was all over and the people had gone home again that there were some who crept up to the wall at night in defiance of Francesco's strict orders and had seen him standing on the wall and heard him screaming to God and the Devil that they should rather kill him. It seems certain that up to and including his last hour he did not know why all this was happening, and certain that he did not ask.

On the twenty-sixth day of the siege with great difficulty he lowered the drawbridge. Two days later, before the eyes of the whole enemy camp, he relieved himself upon the wall.

He was despatched by three executioners on the twenty-ninth
day of the siege, at about eleven o'clock in the morning, with
no resistance on his part. By the way, Gaja, without waiting
for this last and rather cheap twist to his joke, had ridden off and
ordered a memorial column erected in the market place on which
was written: 'Here Francesco Gaja ordered the execution of
Cesare Malatesta, the disgrace of Italy, the affliction and ordure of
Rome.'

In this way he managed to honour a distant relative by forcing
Italy to remember the latter's calumniator – a man of some
achievements – merely as the originator of a single witticism,
the point of which Gaja claimed to have forgotten but could not
let go unpunished.

The Berlin Stories (1924–1933)

THE ANSWER

There was once a rich man, and he had a young wife who was
worth more to him than all his worldly goods, which were not
inconsiderable. She was no longer very young and neither was he.
But they lived together like two turtle-doves, and he had two good
hands, and they were her hands, and she had a good head, and it
was his head. She often said to him, 'I can't think well, husband
dear, I just blurt things out.' But he was sharp as a razor and so
his possessions grew and grew. It happened that one day
a man's debts fell due, and that man was not a good man and he
had property the rich man sorely needed. So he gave him short
shrift and seized his property. The man was to spend one more
night in the house where he had lived all his days in such a way
that he would now have to go among strangers; the next day
everything was to be confiscated.

That night the rich man's wife could not sleep. She lay thinking
beside her husband, and then she got up. She got up in the middle
of the night and went across to their neighbour whom her husband
was evicting. For she felt that she could not insult her husband
by helping their neighbour with his knowledge. Nor could she
bear to see the man suffering. The man was awake too, so she had
guessed right so far. He was sitting in his own four walls enjoying
these hours to the full. When he saw her he took fright, but she
only wanted to give him her jewellery.

Now because she took some time to do this, or because her
husband sensed in his sleep that she was not by his side, he awoke,
and he too got up, went all over the house and called her, and he
was afraid and went into the street. There he saw a light in his
neighbour's house and went across to see if the man was burying
something which no longer belonged to him, and in so doing, as
he looked through the window, he saw his wife in his neighbour's
house in the middle of the night. He could hear nothing, nor
could he see the casket in her hand, and so the blood rushed to
his head and he doubted his wife. At the same time he grasped
his knife in his pocket and wondered how he could kill the pair

of them. Then he heard his wife say, 'Just take it; I don't want my husband to burden himself with such a sin, nor do I want to wound him by helping you; for you are an evil man.' With that she moved towards the door, and the husband had to be quick to conceal himself, for she came out quickly and ran across to her house.

He followed her in silence, and once inside he told her he had not been able to sleep and had gone out into the field because his conscience was troubling him for wanting to take away his neighbour's house. His wife fell upon his breast and wept, such was her joy. But as they were sleeping together the man's conscience began to prick him and he was much ashamed, for he had now been petty twice, once in mistrusting her and a second time in lying to her. Such was his shame that he convinced himself he was no longer worthy of her, and got up and went down into the living room, and sat there a while, just like his neighbour in his house across the road. Then matters got worse, for he had no one to help him, and he had indeed been found wanting. With this on his mind he went out of the house towards morning while it was still dark and drifted off aimlessly like the shifting breeze.

He walked for a whole day without stopping to eat, along a road that led to a desolate region, and when he came to a village, he circled round it. In the evening he came to a black river beside which he found a deserted, dilapidated hut, and since lush herbs grew in the fields all around and the river was full of fish, he stayed for three years and spent the time collecting herbs and fishing. Then it became too lonely for him there, which is to say, the voices of the water became too loud for him and the thoughts, which are said to be like birds that cast their droppings on your food, grew too numerous. So he went into a town, then from town to town, following no direction, and begged and knelt in the churches.

But as time went by his thoughts tightened their hold on him and tortured him greatly. So he began to drink and run around like a dog that is not worth chaining up. He spent many years in this way. And once it came to pass, at a time when he had forgotten his own name, that he, by now half-blind, returned to the town where he had once lived those many years ago. He did not even recognize it and went no further than the outskirts, where he lay down in the yard of an inn.

Now one day about noon a woman came by and turned into the yard and spoke to the innkeeper. When the beggar heard her voice he started and his heart beat faster, like that of a man who has come by mistake into a room where there is beautiful music to which, however, he has no right. And the man saw that it was his wife who was speaking and he was unable to utter a single word. He just stretched out a hand as she passed. But the woman did not recognize him for he no longer looked like the man he had been, not in one single feature; so changed indeed was his face that one could not even see the torture he had undergone. So the woman was on the point of passing, for there were so many beggars about, and this one was quite without shame. Then the man managed to part his jaws and utter something that sounded like 'wife!'

Then the woman bent down and looked at him and her knees began to quiver and she went very pale. And when the sound of his own heart-beats subsided he heard her, and what she said was, 'My dear husband, how long you have kept me waiting, so long that I have now become ugly, and seven years have passed as pain passes and I *almost* lost faith in you.'

BEFORE THE FLOOD

Considerations in the rain

My grandmother used to say when it had rained for a long time, 'Today it's raining. Will it ever stop? I hardly think so. At the time of the flood it did not stop.' My grandmother would say, 'What has happened once can happen again – and so can what hasn't'. She was seventy-four years old and totally devoid of logic.

On that occasion all the animals went into the Ark quite peacefully. That is the only time when all the creatures on earth have been peaceful. And all of them really did go in. But the icthyosaurus stayed away. He was told in a vague sort of way that he should get in, but he had no time during the days in question. Noah himself drew his attention to the fact that the flood was coming. But he said placidly, 'I don't believe it.' He was generally unpopular by the time he drowned.

'Aha, aha,' they all said, as Noah, lighting the lamps on the Ark for the first time, observed 'It's still raining', 'aha, aha, he won't come, not the icthyosaurus.' That particular animal was the oldest of all the beasts, and given his long experience he was fully capable of telling whether anything like a flood was possible or not.

It is quite possible that I myself might not go in in similar circumstances. I think that on that evening, as the night fell in which he perished, the icthyosaurus saw through the corruption and chicanery of providence, as well as the unspeakable stupidity of all earthly creatures, the moment he realised how necessary these things were.

Fat Ham

It is said of the ass that he was not in the Flood, and that God didn't make him until much later, after all the other animals, on noticing a gap in Creation. That gap was to be filled by the ass. This view, it must be said, is contradicted by a Flood legend which circulates among the asses and has been handed down to the present day. It goes like this:

Among the sons of Noah, Ham the Fat was particularly important. He was called Ham the Fat although he was only fat in one place, and the reason was this: that, as we know from other sources, the Ark was constructed entirely of solid cedar. Each plank had in fact to be as thick as a man.

For several weeks during the building, Japheth, as we know, went around standing beside trees before they were felled. Trunks that were thinner than Japheth were just not used for the construction of the Ark. But then, at the last moment, when it was already raining terribly, Japheth decided he had had enough of standing around in cedar forests and asked his brother Ham to stand beside the cedars in his place.

But Ham was the thinnest of Noah's sons.

Then the Flood came and the Ark began to float, and Noah perceived forthwith that the Ark was floating excellently well except for one place where she was too thin. The Ark was terribly long and broad, and she also had a mighty draught, and the place that was too thin was no bigger than the orb of the sun at noon. But it was here and here alone that the Ark shipped water.

So Noah said to his sons, 'Which of you has done this?'

The sons said to Noah, 'Ham has done this.'

Thereupon Noah said to Ham, 'Arise, Ham, and go to the place that is too thin, and get thee down and sit upon it.'

Ham sat down, and the hole was plugged.

The Bible records exactly how long Ham sat on that spot, for he sat there until the Flood was over. And when the Flood was over Ham stood up, and that portion of Ham which had covered the leaky spot in the Ark had grown very fat. Apart from that, however, Ham was just as thin as before. This peculiarity in his physical constitution rendered Ham pretty useless for a good many things, but if there is ever another flood, and they build an Ark with a thin spot, then Ham will be indispensable.

It is this particular story of the Flood that has survived in the memory of the asses.

CONVERSATION ABOUT THE SOUTH SEAS

At my publisher's I met a man who had spent 15 years in Brazil.

He asked me what was on in Berlin.

When I told him, he advised me to head for the South Seas.

He said you can't beat it.

I had no objection. I asked what should I take with me.

He said, 'Take a short-haired dog. That is man's best friend.'

I naturally thought for a moment of asking him whether a long-haired one would do if the worst came to the worst, but common sense told me that long hair would get terribly matted with coconut needles.

I asked him what there is to do in the South Seas the whole day long.

He said, 'Nothing. You don't have to work at all.'

'Well yes,' I said, 'Work wouldn't satisfy me either, but there must be something one can do.'

He said, 'Well, there's always nature.'

'Fine,' I said, 'but what is there to do, say at 8 a.m.?'

'8 a.m.? You'd still be asleep.'

'And noon? One o'clock?'

'At one it's too hot to do anything.'

At this point I lost my temper. I gave him a nasty look and said, 'The afternoon?'

'Oh, you're bound to have some way of filling in an hour.'

At last he seemed to realise that I am not the sort of man who can busy himself on his own, and he made a suggestion. 'Take a double-barrelled shotgun and get in some shooting.'

I was now in a thoroughly bad mood and told him curtly, 'Shooting is no pleasure to me.'

'Well, how are you going to live?' he asked me with a smile.

I was getting steadily madder.

'That is for *you* to tell me,' I said. 'It's your job to make the suggestions. How am I to know anything about the South Seas?'

'Would you like to fish?' he proposed.

'I wouldn't mind,' I said huffily.

'Good. Take a steel fly-rod, you can get one in any shop, and in five minutes you will have two fish on your hook. Then you can eat fish if you don't want to go shooting.'

'Raw?' I asked.

'You surely have your lighter with you?'

'A fish cooked over a lighter is hardly a full meal,' I said, appalled by such lack of experience. 'Can I at least take photographs?'

'Now there's an idea,' he said, visibly relieved. 'You'll have the whole of nature at your disposal. Nowhere else is there so much to photograph.'

Now of course he's got the upper hand. He'll have me taking photographs all day long. It'll keep me busy and leave him in peace.

But you can take it from me that I have been put off the South Seas for years. And I never want to see another man like that again.

LETTER ABOUT A MASTIFF

One of the few events in my uneventful life that made an impression on me was the San Francisco earthquake – because of a dog.

I was twenty-three and alone in the world when I got to know a mastiff in San Francisco. I was living on the sixth floor in a dilapidated block and shared a stinking, badly whitewashed hallway with the other tenants. It was there that I used to run into the mastiff several times daily. He belonged to a family of five who were living in a single room no bigger than mine. They were unkempt people with dirty habits who left bins full of stinking refuse standing outside their door for days. To describe the dog is more than I can bear.

My first meeting with that mastiff I do not remember. But I think we can take it that the mastiff's first emotion on seeing me was fear, and that I too experienced an unpleasant sensation (probably as a consequence). At any rate it was the beast's obvious and totally unjustified antipathy that first drew my attention to him. On seeing me the dog, joyfully as he may have been romping around with the children (who were incidentally incredibly dirty), would slink sullenly round the corner, or better still would creep with his tail between his legs into an open doorway. Indeed once when I tried to stroke him to dispel his stupid fears, which were already, I seemed to observe, making the children stare at me in awe, he even trembled, and – it is with some reluctance that I record this – his hackles must have risen, for I was taken aback momentarily by the stiffness of his coat, and it only occurred to me later that this must be what people mean when they say 'His hackles have risen.'

If a man had adopted this attitude to me I would have been inclined to think he was confusing me with somebody else. But a dog! Right from the start, I remember, I was far from underrating the matter. In the days that followed I now and again brought something for the mastiff – food or bones. He would slink away without so much as a sniff at the bones, look up with an indescribably reproachful and at the same time perplexed air, then make off. Usually he was skulking in the midst of a band of scrofulous children, who were all too obviously the sad

offspring of the scum of the earth. The whole block smelt of children's piss. I only rarely managed to get the mastiff on his own,
and I was careful never to go near him in the presence of eye-
witnesses. Nevertheless the children had some damn way of detect-
ing my attempts to approach the dog, harmless though these
undoubtedly were; and from then on, far from recognising my
good nature, they began to point accusing fingers at me. All this
time I was convinced that the people who owned the mastiff were
not giving it enough to eat; it was probably not even getting the
bare essentials. I had, of course, no time in which to study this
dog. Since I was working by day in a car factory, I only had the
evenings for my own entertainment. Nonetheless I was able to
observe quite a few people in their dealings with the mastiff. There
was, for example, the tenant next door who got along, if not like
a house on fire, at least reasonably well with him. To attract him
he snapped his fingers, as many people do. As a result he quite
often got the dog rubbing himself without a qualm against his
dirty trouser leg. I even practised this little trick myself, which
incidentally anyone can master, but I had enough self-respect not
to try it out. There was an old woman in the house whom the
mastiff ran after whenever he saw her. This old woman, an unpleasant person with a piping voice which set your teeth on edge,
simply could not bear the mastiff and always tried to shoo him
away with her shopping bag, but never succeeded. To her annoyance she couldn't get rid of him. A heavily made-up girl from our
neighbourhood would often chat to the mastiff, fingering the folds
under his jaw as she did so. Once when I stood opposite this girl
on the bus – her trade, I would add, is her own affair – I noticed
that she had bad breath. Such personal attributes, harmless and
unimportant though they may be in themselves, are always indica-
tive, in my opinion, of more deep-seated aberrations. It surprised
me that a dog of thoroughly sound instincts, like the mastiff, took
no notice of this flaw in the girl. This observation soon led me
to doubt the dog's instincts; I began to think it might be some
quite superficial peculiarities of mine that were putting the mastiff
off. It seemed improbable, but I wanted to overlook nothing. I
changed both my suit and my headgear, and I even left my stick
at home. All this I did, as you might imagine, with the utmost
reluctance, aware, as I was, of the humiliation involved, but it

seemed to me that there was nothing else for it. One decisive occurrence showed me how closely all this concerned me. This was a time when I had unfortunately to make a tedious trip to Boston, since I had reason to suspect my younger brother of using some remarkably artful dodges to get the better of me in the matter of our mother's will. When I came back – without, I may say, settling anything, since there is no such thing as proof in this life, however blatant the injustice – the mastiff had gone.

In the initial excitement I was particularly hurt that he had just run off, indeed I thought I would have been less disappointed if he had been sliced in half by a truck. That a dog in whom I had an interest should simply run away from his master was merely further proof for me of the planet's unfair treatment of the life on it. Though his comments on my person seemed so ridiculously important to me, he himself of course was of an inferior breed. All the more distressing that I should be so upset when he failed to return. In the end my enquiries, coupled with the offer of a large reward, brought him back; but my mistrust accompanied him from that day on until his inglorious end.

After the trouble I had taken to recover him, I naturally considered the dog as my property. That the family to whom he officially belonged, acted as if they did not know how much their mastiff had cost me just discredited them further in my eyes. I had no wish to go on being treated as if I were not there.

Shortly after his return, I saw the mastiff going down the hall with the tenant next door. When the man stopped to fill his pipe by one of the windows that looked on to the yard, he again rubbed himself against his leg. The man took no notice. This struck me as most unpleasant. When I enquired, I discovered that he lived as a lodger with the family of five. In the next few days I casually asked the caretaker, whether to his knowledge it was permissible for tenants to take lodgers in their rooms. He told me in some embarrassment that he did not know, but would, if I thought fit, write a letter to the company. I left it up to him, since it was none of my business.

A week later as I came home from work I noticed a hand-cart with some ramshackle furniture in front of the house. On the stairs I passed a girl with bad lungs coughing as she carried a chest downstairs. I concluded that the caretaker's letter had done the trick; evidently it was indeed forbidden to take lodgers.

As I looked on and pondered the matter, I decided that it was hard for these people, on top of all their other difficulties – and there was seemingly no shortage of these; you only had to look at their clothes – to have to face the expense of a removal. Nor could it have been out of arrogance or for pleasure that they shared their none too spacious room with a stranger. So as I stood in my doorway smoking my evening pipe and heard them discussing what to do with their mastiff it was perhaps not only my interest in the dog that made me listen somewhat too sympathetically; and on having thus been drawn into the conversation and asked for my opinion, I declared that I was prepared to take the mastiff in. It seemed that in these new circumstances they could no longer afford such a costly luxury, for that is what a mastiff undoubtedly is; so they agreed to hand him over to me.

I admit that I was not dissatisfied with the way things had turned out, even if a certain ruthlessness had been involved. Especially as I have always been convinced that if one lets things take their course without interfering while at the same time snapping up any chances that may occur, things are bound to take care of themselves.

It was not altogether easy for me to move the mastiff into my room. He resisted with all his might, though without making a sound or taking his eye off me. A stout leather strap which I had bought a week earlier did yeoman service now.

The mastiff was not a pleasant sight. I kept him tied to the leg of my bed, and as long as I was in the room he always skulked under the bed, and whenever I went near him, or even when I went to bed, his whole body trembled. When I was out – or, more precisely, when I was watching him through the keyhole, he padded restlessly up and down in front of the bed, keeping as far away from it as the strap, which was not too long, permitted. For dog-lovers I would add that the tenacious fable about dogs mourning lost masters seems to be boloney. Though this rumour has been all too readily accepted, it is just another example of man's vanity. I could see no sign of mourning in my mastiff.

The fact that he would not eat anything was due to altogether different and, for me, unflattering reasons. He would take nothing from my hand. For three days he dumbly refused to look at the bones I bought for him, and on the third day he even scorned a piece of best beef. He ate none of the things I put down for him; nor did he eat anything I had touched.

I confess that this caused me embarrassment (he got visibly thinner and began to drag his feet as he padded round). In moments of anger I thought I might execute him simply by handing him food that he would not eat. But I realised in cooler moments that mere violence solves nothing.

So I brought home a young man I knew casually, a mechanic from the car factory, so that he could give him something to eat. Once I had got the man in my room it suddenly seemed uncommonly difficult to initiate him, and the conversation, in spite of my lemonade and cigarettes, moved haltingly. He was an unkempt fellow of poor breeding with rather too soft teeth and watery red hair. It was hard to stomach watching him sitting on my table, and listening to him talk almost made you sick. In addition to which he had a habit of laying hold of you constantly as he talked, which is something I cannot stand. After that he sensed that there was something wrong, and his malice knew no bounds. He poked slyly at the mastiff with his toe, talked hypocritically for a while as if he knew nothing, noticed my perplexity and finally blackmailed me, not without forcing me to go into a full explanation, into begging him to give the dog something to eat. (It is of course equally possible that he noticed nothing.)

He complied in the most tactless fashion, scolding the mastiff and reproaching him for his unloving attitude to me. The dog was fed in this fashion every evening for two weeks.

Oddly enough I could never abandon my vague hope, and it took an earthquake to convince me of the planet's firm and unalterable attitude towards me. On June 23rd, 1912 the San Francisco earthquake took place. On that day many people in the trembling city lost their lives. All I lost was a suit, a pair of boots and some household equipment, and I might have forgotten the disaster more easily than most; but it was not to be. Amid the tremors which were getting more and more violent, in a house which was on fire, I stood in my shirt-tails looking straight into the eye of the implacable mastiff whose backside was trapped in a wall that had collapsed; then, as I went to his assistance, I saw in his lack-lustre eyes an indescribable fear of me, his saviour, and as I reached out to free him, he snapped at me.

Since that day two years have gone by. I now live in Boston. My enquiry into the mastiff affair remained incomplete after his death. What was it that moved him to reject the hand I offered? Was it my eye whose gaze brought me success with a number of people (so I have been told), but put off the more sensitive creature? Was it a certain casual movement of my hands as I walk, which has recently been catching my eye in shop windows? Since that mastiff's attitude to me I have never ceased to wonder what kind of deformity (for that is what it must be) separates me from other people. Yes, for months I have even been coming to think that it may be due to deep-seated deformities within me, and the worst of it is that the wider I spread my enquiry, the greater the deviations from the norm that I find in myself; and then, as I add one thing to another, I begin to believe more and more firmly that I shall never discover the real reason; for it may perhaps in fact be my mind that is abnormal and thereby no longer capable of recognising revolting behaviour as such. Though I have no sympathy for such ludicrous phenomena as the Salvation Army with its cheap conversions, I am nevertheless bound to say that a profound change in my whole being, whether for better or for worse, can no longer be denied.

HOOK TO THE CHIN

After a big fight at the Berlin Sportpalast a group of men, four in all including me, were sitting, still in a relatively bloodthirsty frame of mind, over a few beers in a bar on the corner of Potsdamer Strasse and Bülowstrasse, and one of us, a professional boxer, told the instructive tale of the decline of Freddy Meinke, 'The Hook'.

'Freddy,' said the man, squinting for all he was worth and leaning one elbow in a puddle of beer, 'two years ago, Freddy had the chance of a lifetime. Freddy's real name was Friedrich of course, but he had spent six months in the States – whatever happened there, he kept it dark, nothing could get him to talk about it – and all he had brought back apart from a few unknown names on his fight record and two or three dollar bills, which he would now and then quite absent-mindedly take out of his trouser pocket, was the name Freddy.

'He boxed under this nickname of Freddy for a few months in second rate towns like Cologne and out in the sticks and then suddenly he acquired a new nickname, "Freddy the Hook", and an excellent reputation.

'When we got our first look at him here, we had quite a laugh at the preliminaries he went in for: having his picture taken in what can only be described as ladies' knickers, in lilac. He was the cutest thing you've ever seen in a ring. He strutted around as if he was on the stage. But then he k.o'd his man in the first round, and he did it with a right hook that was really something. You know, of course, that he was a bantamweight? They don't usually pack much punch at that weight, and on top of that Freddy was a rather puny figure just to look at. But then suddenly he would move as fast as a propeller and he would go in with the power of fifty horses, until finally the whole man was just one big hook to the jaw.

'When we were sitting together afterwards, patting him on the back fit to break his shoulder, he said it was only a matter of pulling yourself together. You could only get really tough if you knew for sure that you had yourself totally under control. He himself had to feel from the outset that he was not hitting a man, but hitting right through him, so his hand could not be stopped by a little thing like a chin. He said one or two more things along these lines, and anyway it was good for him to believe them, as indeed we had seen. He had had a thumping success that night and was heading straight for a crack at the championship.

'The date, when we heard it, seemed to us all to be a bit early; scarcely eight weeks later. Freddy floated gaily on in his lucky streak; he trained hard. Among other things he even took on me as a sparring partner. He seemed to have taken a lease on all the pace there was around, and my extra thirty pounds were just what he needed to test that unnaturally big punch. All the same he was a disappointment in training. This was probably because he didn't 'pull himself together', and of course you can't go around for eight weeks hitting right through people. So it did not really mean very much. What was more important was the razzmatazz he went in for. It was none of my business if he wanted to buy a motorbike on hire-purchase and choose that moment to learn to ride it. I thought to myself, he could just as well have let that wait. But when he also acquired a fiancée, with a firm engagement and full-scale domesticity on the horizon, even a walnut bedstead and bookshelves for all I knew, the whole works in other words, then there was no doubt he had gone too far. A man who gets involved in a big deal like an engagement at a time when his existence is hanging by a single thread has got himself in a spot where a hell of a lot, maybe even his entire happiness, depends on something that hasn't happened yet. A man in that position simply can't afford to lose. But I tell you men, it is a bad deal when too much depends on one thing. You should go into a championship fight like a salesman going into his shop. If he sells something, okay. If he doesn't sell anything then there is always the owner, let him have the sleepless nights. Well, the fight was on September 12th.

'Freddy completed his training on the 10th, and on the 12th at 7 o'clock we were sitting here in this bar, Freddy, me, and his manager, Fats Kampe. You know him, over there where the man with the toothpick is sitting. The balloon was to go up in an hour. It was a mistake, of course, to come in here. You can see how stale and smoky the joint is, but that was what Freddy wanted, and he had no time for people who have to be on the look-out for every little March breeze for fear of their lungs. To cut a long story short, we were sitting here in a fug you couldn't have cut with a power-saw, and Kampe and I ordered beers, and that was the start, in the fifteen minutes we had left, of a very rum business, though I was the only one to notice it. Freddy decided he fancied a glass of beer.

'In fact he called the waiter. But Kampe stepped in and said firmly that that was sheer madness just before the fight; he would do better to eat hobnails than drink beer.

'Freddy muttered "nonsense", but he let the waiter go away. As far as Kampe was concerned that was the end of the matter, but not for Freddy. Kampe went through everything he knew about Freddy's opponent, the good things as well as the bad. Freddy read an evening paper. I had the feeling that behind the small ads his mind was still on that beer, or more precisely on his wish for that beer.

'Right after that he stood up and sauntered over to the bar unnoticed by Kampe. He stood there for a while, not trying to push his way in, he even let one or two other people by, and once he let a waiter through. Then, with a rather stupid look on his face, he took a few cigarettes and stuck them in his waistcoat pocket.

'When he came back to the table, he seemed to have changed somehow, and he toyed with the cigarettes in his waistcoat pocket and looked somewhat irritable. He sat down again behind his *Achtuhr-Abendblatt*. Then I began to run down the beer without taking any notice of what Kampe was saying. I still remember telling him it was a tepid, sickly brew, that you could actually taste the horse-shit it must have been made of, and must be good for a nice little dose of typhus. Freddy grinned.

'I think he had pretty well finished struggling with himself. It was quite unbearable for him to sit here without a drink just because something depended on his not having an off night, and at the same time still to want some of that typhus-bilge inside him, and yet be too weak to go ahead and do what he so illogically wanted, and to be annoyed at his own unreasonableness. He was probably also seeing the girl with her engagement face, along with the walnut beds and bookcases, and he stood up and paid.

'We didn't say a word in the taxi to the Sportpalast.'

When the boxer reached this point in his story he noticed his elbow in the puddle of beer, and dried it with his handkerchief. Although we were all pretty clear in our minds about the outcome of the fight, I nevertheless asked for the sake of completeness, 'Yes, and –?'

'He was knocked out in the second round. What else did you expect?'

'Nothing, but why was it, do you think, that he was k.o'd?'

'Quite simple. When we went out of the bar I knew Freddy had a low opinion of himself.'

'That is pretty clear,' I said, 'but what, in your opinion, should a man in Freddy's position have done?'

The man emptied his glass and said, 'A man's got to do what a man's got to do. In my opinion. You know, caution is the mother of the knock-out.'

MÜLLER'S NATURAL ATTITUDE

We had finished eating and were sitting over our cigars, going through our stock of conversational topics. Current affairs had been exhausted, so, just to be on the safe side, we addressed ourselves first to the decline of the theatre for the umpteenth time, and then plucking up courage we gradually came round to Müller. Müller, Müller the engineer, the arch-enemy, Müller was a ticklish subject because he could always put the cat among the pigeons, even when he wasn't there.

He had repeatedly caused trouble of late, as we all knew to our cost, but Pucher was determined to raise an old, slightly be-whiskered story for discussion. He evidently needed to get it off his chest.

'I once had a deal with Müller,' he began. 'It involved me in flying with him. We flew from Berlin to Cologne. Müller wanted to introduce me to a company there which would give my self-starter the once-over with a view to distributing it on a large scale. We were going into the business together. Müller would concentrate on the marketing side, since, as I've told you, he was bringing in the other company. Müller said he thought we suited each other all right, and he and I had known each other as long as we have all had the misfortune to know him.

'So we were sitting in one of those nice steel affairs, which are of course actually made of tin. Müller was in a bad mood from the start, but for my benefit he blamed it on not being allowed to smoke on board. Yet he was the one who had insisted we should travel by plane and not by train.

'We were supposed to talk the whole scheme over once more, but it was clear from the start that this wouldn't be easy, because the noise of the propellers, three of them, was far too loud to let us talk in peace. Müller started off by bellowing across to me while they were warming up the engines, that is, while we were still on the ground, "You can't hear a word. Sickening." This from a man who had flown at least a dozen times.

'When the plane took off he stopped bellowing and sat self-absorbed in his wicker seat, his eyes fixed on the horizon. I had never flown before and was wholly wrapped up in studying this new phenomenon. So I didn't look round at Müller until we had reached an altitude of one or two hundred metres. And then it seemed to me – doubt me if you like – that Müller was scared.

'No need to tell me. I know. Müller served at the front. Shock troops and all that. The only reason he wasn't awarded the Iron Cross First Class was that he hadn't an iota of discipline in his make-up. I know. But at that point Müller was afraid, and he made no effort to conceal it. He sat staring dejectedly through the little glass porthole at the pilot, and each time the plane dropped a few metres he clung for dear life to the arms of his seat, and he was the only passenger with his safety-belt fastened from the start. Yet we all know that these big steel jobs are as safe in the air as locomotives on the ground, and we also know that this is obvious after the first couple of hundred metres.

'After about ten minutes Müller took his notebook out of his breast pocket, scribbled a few lines, breaking off now and then to check on the pilot up front, tore out the page and handed it to me.

' "Do you think that in twenty years anyone will understand how grown men could set foot in these things? Just look at the sheet metal! Would you call it heroism or just stupidity?" Signed Müller.

'When I looked up from his note he was sitting unmoved in his seat, looking out of the side window as if nothing had happened; then a few minutes later he pointed with a grin at the propeller on his side and bellowed over, "A din like an earthquake! Why doesn't a swallow kick up a racket like that?"

'And he shook his thick head as if he couldn't understand why this hadn't occurred to him right at the beginning. What he meant of course was that there had to be a serious structural fault to cause this noise, and he was probably thinking that in twenty years' time planes would not make such an unnatural din. When we landed at Hanover and were stretching our legs and smoking a cigarette on the runway while they loaded the mail and dropped some passengers and took on others, he went on to say, "Anything that makes a noise like that has to have something wrong with it."

'Then he proceeded to explain to me that it was senseless for a thing that two men could easily move to need 240 horse power to move through the air, where there was no resistance at all. He trotted out more of the same, and just before we climbed back in he rounded off his deliberations with the remark that the whole principle was wrong.

'As far as Essen he kept quite silent and contented himself with a single scornful laugh when we dropped a few metres. But in Essen, where we were on the ground for ten minutes, he told me quickly about a flight a remote acquaintance of his had been through in bad weather.

'Right there on the tarmac the three passengers were told it was doubtful whether the flight could start, since the weather over the Taunus Mountains was bad. They'd already been delayed an hour, and one of them was rather edgy because he was in a hurry and couldn't possibly be in time for an important business meeting if he had to take the train. Then the flight controller decided that the pilot should "give it a try". The passengers climbed aboard with mixed feelings.

'You have to remember that the sky above the airfield was quite blue. Just as it is here. The storm was only over the Taunus.

'Well, the flight was quite smooth at first, but then they came to the Taunus. No trace of blue sky any more. The fog around them was thick and strangely white. Like wet bed sheets or something. And the plane kept jumping like a grasshopper. The man at the controls was "giving it a try" as those bunglers put it in their jargon, but don't waste your breath, they are rank amateurs, the whole business has only been going on for a few years, did you ever hear of men flying around in hunks of tin? There is absolutely no need. Managed without it for a thousand years! So the pilot tried to break out of the storm zone, that is, he pulled up the nose of the old crate. He reached 1800 metres and when he got up there he found to his amazement that it was just the same as far down below, in other words rather bumpy, which I could have told him before he climbed.'

'You weren't there, though,' I said, disgusted at the arrogant and scornful tone in which he was telling the story.

'Well, my friend whom he took up with him could have told him. That is to say if he hadn't been thrown from side to side like a badly stowed suitcase. For that was what was happening to him. The aeroplane suddenly slipped away, out of control, down to the right. About ten metres.

'Then it picked up again, climbed a bit, then slipped away again, another ten metres just as before. My friend had put his elbow through the window the first time it slipped, so the hail could now come in at will. Hailstones, rain, everything there was out there now came in, and you can take my word for it, the people in the plane had had a basinful. They were more or less preparing slowly to meet their Maker. In a moment their whole lives flashed, etc. It was the most sensible thing for them to do. The pilot put an end to this state of affairs.

'They were at 1800 metres, and when he saw that it was just as bad up above as down below, he decided to go back down since he felt more at home down below anyhow. He cut the engine and the aeroplane just somersaulted down, nose over tail, like a walking-stick. Just imagine! You have already been through plenty up there. You are reduced to the state of a suitcase, your entire life flashing in a trice before your inner eye, then suddenly the engines cut out, the seat under you rears up, your head falls forward and down and you streak uncontrollably downwards, possibly with a female passenger screaming in your ear.

'The man brought it down from 1800 metres to 30 metres. Do you realise what that means? 30 metres is close enough to the ground to see every stone in the fields, and that is precisely what you do see, for the thing is flying upside-down and from your "seat" you look straight through the windscreen at the ground. The ground, on the other hand, rushes inexorably up at you. The two must meet soon. What is soon supposed to mean? Immediately, now, at this very moment, and it is only then, in the moment before that moment, that the engines pick up again, there is a jerk and the thing gathers itself up and opts for the horizontal in the nick of time.

'Half an hour later they were back where they had started. Their "try" at flying over the Taunus could be called a failure.

' "Yes, yes," said Müller, pulling himself up to the entrance to the cabin by the chrome handles and casting a glance at the heavens, for we were flying on, "a thing like this is a real marvel."

'On the last leg of the flight Müller, now that he had unburdened himself, seemed to feel much more lighthearted. He had, as I've said, often flown before. We landed unscathed in Cologne. (Flying is, by the way, a really pleasant and comfortable mode of travel, and not at all dangerous.) And now for the unpleasant part of the story. I will keep it short.

'We arrived at noon and were to dine with the men from the company in the evening. Then next morning we would fly back.

'The afternoon we spent strolling around town, and Müller was quite breezy. Not another word did he say about his conduct that morning, which evidently required no apology in his opinion. Well, so what, I was prepared to forget it. But then a bombshell burst when I least expected it.

'In the evening about nine o'clock, just as I was dressing for dinner, there was a knock and in came Müller in his travelling outfit, with his case in his hand. He placed the case on a chair beside my shoes, cast a look of disapproval at the disorder I had created in the room and said drily, "Well, my dear Pucher, there isn't going to be any dinner."

'I must have looked somewhat astonished, because he went on immediately, keeping it on a business footing, "As you see I haven't bothered to change, I am going straight back to Berlin. The train leaves at 11.15. If it doesn't take you too long to slip out of your glad rags you can come with me. What is the use of staying in Cologne for a pointless night?"

' "Don't be funny, Müller," I said.

' "I don't feel in the least inclined to be funny, the whole affair is extremely embarrassing for me. I admit it is annoying for you too, but not to the same extent. When all is said and done you don't know those gentlemen, but they know me. Let me tell you something. This transaction would only have made sense if we could both have worked together, right? Well, you can see that's impossible. We are not suited to each other. You realise of course I am speaking of this morning. Don't think I wasn't watching you. I am also well aware that it was the first time you had flown. No, I'd rather you didn't say anything."

' "What is that supposed to mean, 'didn't say anything'. What is the meaning of this whole thing? Are you trying to say that I was cowardly, you, who . . . I refuse to listen to such insane drivel. I think it was pretty big of me to refrain from commenting on *your* behaviour. But my God, even that has nothing to do with our business."

'I have never understood how Müller did this kind of thing, but he actually managed to seem completely astonished.

' "What? What do you mean it has nothing to do with our business? You behaved like a clown. You fly into the air in some old thing that somebody has persuaded you is safe, and you sit like an umbrella with no sign of life. Like a semi-idiot, if you will pardon the expression, who can't see what is being done to him, and I'll eat my hat if you don't call that courage. Let me tell you: a man who doesn't adopt the natural attitude in an unknown situation – in this case, alarm – such a man merely proves that he has no natural instincts. To be blunt, I am not going into business with you. Your sort are capable of taking a cheque from the rag-and-bone man. You just don't have the primitive minimum of mistrust which you will find in any animal you care to name and without which it would perish on a planet like ours." '

'Saying which, he sidled into the lift.'

NORTH SEA SHRIMPS

It is fairly well known that in November and December '18 a vast horde of men came home whose manners had suffered a little and whose habits got on the nerves of the folk they had been fighting for. You can't really blame them for this. It was considerably worse with another sort of returning soldier, of whom there were far fewer, namely, those whom the war had turned into fastidious gentlemen. Nothing can coax this sort out of their tiled bathrooms after they have spent all those years lying in muddy trenches.

Kampert of the Eighth Machine-Gun Corps was one such. He was a fine man. He lay in the mud at Arras, and he lay in the mud at Ypres, and he did everything that was asked of him. He never featured in the Lille Army Newspaper, but he always shared his tobacco with the man next to him, and when he was afraid, his fear was of the permissible sort, which is only a sign of common sense. Müller of the Eighth, my friend who is now back and an engineer in civilian life again, was at that time his lieutenant, and according to Kampert only missed promotion because he fetched the field mail himself, and was too familiar with the men. A very good sign. But then the war ended, and Kampert wrote it all off and within three weeks he had managed to forget Arras and Ypres, just as he had forgotten his birth 29 years earlier. He went back to work for A.E.G. as an engineer, and from the very moment when he stuffed his entire kit, underwear, pocket-knife, wrist-watch, even his diaries into a chest along with his lousy field-grey uniform and told the maid to get rid of it, he never deviated from his adopted line, which was that a man who had been forced to eat filthy grass and carry chamber-pots with unspeakable contents through stinking sick-bays for weeks on end had a right to sleep in eiderdown and dine in style for the rest of his life. I was recently present at an occasion when this led to total disaster.

Fatty Müller and I had heard nothing of Kampert for some time, almost nine months. We knew that in the meantime he had married and married money. We were not invited to the wedding, but a couple of weeks ago I saw him in a top-notch two-seater, all gleaming chrome with red morocco seats, in which you lay behind the wheel as if you were rocking in a bathtub, and a few days later he rang us up and said we should come over sometime, say tomorrow evening, and have a whisky with him, in very select company of course.

'Whisky,' said Müller as we climbed the stairs, 'the boy really seems to be making an effort.' And he took a nice little tin of top quality North Sea shrimps out of his jacket pocket. 'The boy was always one for fancy nosh.' I thought that was terribly nice of Müller.

Kampert himself opened the door. Müller greeted him volubly, and Kampert seemed very moved. As he impaled our hats on two very funny black enamelled iron spikes on the wall, he made excuses for the absence of the maid, who had the evening off. 'But then you aren't embassy attachés anyhow, are you,' he said good-humouredly.

'No,' said Müller, 'but I suppose there is a big crowd here?'

'Nonsense,' said he, 'not a soul. Just the three of us. A most select company.'

'You have got yourself up damned formally, old bean; that must be one of those bright, dinky little dinner suits that you're wearing?'

'Nonsense,' said Kampert, 'I just happen to like to change for dinner. It is a little foible of mine. You don't mind?'

'Not at all,' said Müller, 'Whisky is whisky.' Then Kampert settled us into two very comfortable American easy chairs in his lounge and we waited for the lady of the house.

'This is quite an exhibition hall,' said Müller after a couple of minutes of silence while we looked round the rather high room which was all done in white. Müller seemed rather tired and yawned audibly. 'Well, let's have this whisky of yours.'

Kampert crossed the room and fished a few bottles of liqueur out of a little red mahogany cabinet. 'One thing at a time,' he said smiling. 'Do you really think this room is too high?'

'Um,' said Müller, 'just a bit. Yes, it is perhaps just a wee bit high, but you don't spend your whole life in it. But these chairs are stupendous. And this curaçao is not at all bad.'

'Just try the chartreuse,' Kampert pressed us, 'What I thought was, a large hall and a couple of plain seats in it. That would be damned restful.'

'But the sun-blind is pretty,' I encouraged him, 'and quite original.'

It was a fine Japanese straw mat in front of a huge, sloping window.

He stood up and went over. Then he turned a little wooden wheel, and the whole thing rolled on to a bamboo rod at the top. 'You feel as if you were sitting in Cuba all day. The thing collects an unbelievable amount of sunshine.'

'Was the flat like this when you moved in?' asked Müller, who clearly couldn't make up his mind whether the time had come to mix the curaçao with the chartreuse.

'What do you think? We did it up of course. It was two plain bourgeois rooms. You know the kind of thing, cramped to start with and then stowed to the gunwales with furniture.

Müller decided he had better wait until he had greeted the lady of the house before he started mixing his drinks, so, holding the chartreuse up to the light, he said, 'Yes, people live like pigs, how thoughtless of them.'

At this point Kampert's wife came in. She was very pretty, very nice, and very well dressed. She shook hands and acted as if we were her friends, not his. She said the flat was not finished, but we should take a look at it. We might notice this or that. The important thing for them in furnishing it had been the overall effect. Why shouldn't one design a flat as harmoniously as one would an evening dress? Most people just lived their lives in a dreadful clutter of furniture without even realising how thoroughly they ruined their own taste by just getting up each morning. What, for instance, did we think of the lounge we were sitting in?

'Delightful,' I said.

She laughed and looked at her husband. 'I don't know if delightful is the right word. At any rate, it's not exactly what we had in mind. We wanted the lounge to be simple, almost crude, in fact I should really have liked garden chairs but they look so awful. Then some coarse matting. I drove round like mad before I found any. I looked at coarse canvas by the kilometre. But the moment I saw that mat standing somewhere at the back of the shop, I said, that's it.'

'Yes,' I said mockingly to Müller, 'and you just sit there as if you had paid at the door, acting as if it went without saying and was just accidental that we feel so much at ease here.'

Kampert seemed to notice nothing, and just asked, 'Doesn't anything strike you here – about the walls, I mean?'

'They're pretty high,' said Müller.

Kampert's wife laughed again. But Kampert said quite matter-of-factly: 'What I meant was that there are no pictures. Most people plaster their walls with them as if they were billboards. I maintain that if a man doesn't have a special room for pictures he should forget about them.'

That was the point where Müller cast his first nasty sidelong glance at me, but I have to admit that for some time I did not see what he was getting at.

Müller was not laughing as heartily as the others. He looked at the walls in some surprise. I had the impression that he would rather not have been told why he felt so comfortable.

'Come on,' said Kampert's wife, 'I'll show you the rest.' And as Kampert stood up saying, 'The whole thing really wasn't done with money, because then it would look entirely different, it just takes a little thought, and if you like, a certain skill. What we say is, we are not here for the flat's sake, it is here for ours.' I saw

Müller, who had got to his feet with surprising alacrity, fill a tumbler with curaçao and take it pointedly on his tour of the house.

We climbed an iron spiral staircase which led to the rooms upstairs, and which Müller found remarkably practical. 'It hardly takes up any space,' said Kampert. And at the top he said, 'Go on, look down, a room should be as beautiful as a landscape.' At this Müller just took a swig of curaçao from his tumbler and tried to pass me another nasty sidelong glance. But Mrs Kampert was terribly nice and showed us Kampert's bedroom.

This was a small, simply appointed room with an iron bedstead, a chair and a plain glazed washbasin. The only light came from overhead, 'so that seeing the walls of the house opposite doesn't give one the impression one is camping in the open.' On the bed was a plain camel-hair rug.

'You naturally expected a more sumptuous camping ground,' said Kampert jokingly to Müller. Müller gave him a friendly grin (he was occupied exclusively with Mrs. Kampert, to whom I noticed he had taken a great fancy) and then led the way enthusiastically to the next room, the study. This was separated from the bedroom only by a chintz curtain: the two rooms together were a little world on their own. A pine table. A hard uncomfortable chair. Pine shelves. A low, hard chaise-longue. Books.

Müller emptied his tumbler.

As we climbed back down the spiral staircase ('it saves having to do exercises each morning'), I told Kampert, since we had become a little silent, 'Your study is excellent, really. It's so spartan.'

'There should be nothing in a study that's not practical,' said Kampert simply.

Downstairs Müller waddled over to the mahogany cabinet, which had clearly impressed itself more strongly on his memory than anything else, and groped among the bottles. He said, 'The main thing is to have your whisky in the right place.'

Kampert laughed and put his hand on his arm. He brought out a large bottle, held it up to the light, and said, 'Black and White.' There is no doubt that 'Black and White' is the most highly regarded of all brands of whisky, and not without reason. But at this moment I sensed instinctively that Müller would have preferred it if something less than the right brand had been placed in the cabinet for him. He helped himself liberally. But the mere fact that he was drinking whisky (with very little soda) out of a tumbler which still undeniably had a little chartreuse in it was a bad sign; and a worse sign was that he suddenly seemed changed and demanded to be shown everything else in this carefully thought-out flat.

He stood resolutely in a lilac room in which everything was lilac, wallpaper, tables, cupboards, lamps. Pale lilac, dark lilac, violet. Of all things there was even a Bechstein grand that matched the lilac surroundings. He stumped through the cloakroom with its simple built-in cupboards in pale green, which were there for purely practical purposes, through the bathroom, which lacked for nothing, into the kitchen which was impeccably hygienic. Then he sat with us in a friendly dining-room holding his insidious peace and ate solid but delicious fare at a round oak table with no picture opposite to distract him. It was wrong of him to carry on drinking whisky out of his old tumbler between courses, taking less soda with each refill, but he needed it. He thought very highly of Kampert, who incidentally regaled us with some brilliant stories that showed he had a clear head and a sense of humour. It could not be Kampert or Kampert's wife – whom Müller liked. What irritated Müller was the flat. He was completely wrong about this. It was a very pleasant flat, not at all ostentatious. But I think Müller just could not stand the carefully contrived harmony and the dogmatic functionalism of it any longer. And I must say that I was gradually coming round to the same view.

Then Mrs. Kampert, whose naturalness had held the whole thing together and, as it were, tamed the animal in Müller, withdrew and I could see immediately that something had to give.

With a casualness which for Kampert was imperceptible but for me was quite unnatural he cunningly steered the conversation round to the subject of North Sea shrimps. But then he grew more and more outspoken and finished up by suddenly expressing a blunt desire for North Sea shrimps out of a tin. Kampert was rather startled, but he was much too good a host and took too naive a pleasure in the completeness of his household not to be genuinely embarrassed. Added to which we had both by now, like Müller, drunk rather a lot; so Kampert stood up, took his hat and promised with a laugh to procure some North Sea shrimps.

And one can only assume that just that evening Kampert's guardian angel must have gone to bed early, for before he left to satisfy his guests' ultimate wishes, his unfortunate proprietorial eye fell on a chest beside the door, an unprepossessing brown affair with iron fittings, at which, quite naively and utterly oblivious to the predicament which he had already been in for well nigh an hour, he said, 'Have you ever seen such an eyesore as that thing; it sticks out like a sore thumb in an otherwise quite decent dining room, eh, boys? But I wouldn't part with it for anything in the world, because there is nothing so irritating as having every little thing just right. It isn't necessary for *everything* to match everything else in a house, or else it would be unliveable in.' And without waiting to see the effect of his words he hurried out to get the North Sea shrimps.

Müller nodded laughingly to me. His agony had left him. He was again the good, old, drunken, humorous Müller whom I loved and feared.

We lost no time. We got down to work straightaway. Müller took off his jacket and threw it in a corner. Then he went into the lounge and fell upon the mahogany cabinet. He took out three bottles, smashed the necks off them on a groaning bamboo chair. He then poured them all into a pan which had recently had tomatoes floating in it and came back into the dining room. He imbibed a soup-ladleful of this brew, waved me aside, and strolled to one of the original American armchairs, then fell into it with a groan and sketched his plan of campaign. This took three minutes, but without it he would not have been able to do the thorough job that I was about to witness. The first thing he did was to tear down the sun-blind (My God, how firmly this thing's been fixed!), and hang it between the window catch and the spiral staircase, using some violet tassels from the drawing-room to tie it up so that he now had a giant hammock which filled the whole room (This'll cover the whole of Cuba!). Then he made a cosy corner with the lounge chairs, the dining room table and the kitchen curtains, and enthroned the ominous little mahogany cabinet in the middle of it all. (The little cabinet so there is something that doesn't match), after which, using the left-over sugar in the coffee cups, he stuck some revolting illustrations on the walls, tearing them out of magazines since he had no time to look anywhere else. Having secured the cosy corner for all eventualities, he, with a bottle in his pocket, staged what he called a Macedonian triumphal progress through the upstairs rooms, hurling himself most perilously on the bed, overturning the pine table and the washbasin. All this in total silence apart from a few statements of principle. When he got back to the lounge he looked extraordinarily triumphant. Then, swinging in his Cuban hammock, under the stimulating influence of mighty amounts of alcohol, he delivered a fulminating and memorable *Speech on Temperance*.

'Man,' he said, 'is born to fight. It is his nature to avoid the effort. But thank God there are natural powers which pep him up a little. Left to himself, in other words, Man is a miserable worm who would like to have everything matching. Pale blue, dark blue, blue-black. But on the other hand, and especially after partaking of North Sea shrimps, Man is like a terrible tornado, creating the grandiose multiplicity and admirable disharmony of all creation out of an almighty pile-up of patent American chaise-longues, common washbasins and old, venerable magazines. It is not given to man to grow up to heaven on sun-blinds and Bechstein grands. A home exists wherever a man throws his old collar in a corner. God has ordained it thus, not I, Müller. So be it. And now this *is* a home.'

And once he had said this, swinging from wall to wall in front of a huge window that gave on to the night, he climbed out of his hammock, unsteady after his unaccustomed intellectual indulgence, and proceeded with faltering steps into the lilac room to sustain himself with a modest repast. From the pocket of his jacket where it lay in a corner he extracted his tin of North Sea shrimps and opened it on the Bechstein grand with a paper-knife. And at that moment, Kampert appeared in the doorway with a paper bag in his hand.

Then suddenly Müller the terrible, Müller the guest, flushed crimson with embarrassment as he sat on the purple, polished table in Kampert's perfectly styled drawing room, eating North Sea shrimps out of a tin perched on the grand piano, swilling it down with tomato-flavoured whisky and looking with a sad, insecure, guilty expression at Kampert the hospitable. And he said, 'My home is my castle.'

His main reason for saying this, I think, was that it was totally out of place, and deep down he had this longing for all that was most ill-matched, most illogical and most natural.

'For every poison there is an antidote,' said MacBride, stretching his legs philosophically, and seemed to have something specific in mind.

I had arrived on the island that morning and promptly witnessed a rather sad little to-do, the burial of a white man whom a native or, as it later turned out, a half-caste had despatched. They buried him late that afternoon, and for me that was a stroke of luck, for it enabled me to meet a lot of people all at once and save a good deal of time. Then I was sitting on MacBride's verandah with MacBride himself, the colony's trader, and Keeny who was in charge of the telegraph, over one of those outlandish equatorial drinks made with paprika and ice, listening to the whispering of the coconut palms overhead. From time to time this pleasant sound was interrupted by another, less pleasant one, which was confused and human in origin. It came from the men who were taking the murderer to be hanged.

We could, as it happened, sit there quietly without fear of missing anything. He would be led past the front of the house when the time came, and we would be able to watch him at our leisure, thanks to MacBride's kind invitation.

MacBride had attended the trial and was still full of it. He said that the murderer, a certain Lewis, was an astonishingly placid and reasonable man, a half-caste, but more white than black, actually almost totally white, though reasonable only if regarded as coloured. Evidently MacBride was not entirely clear about him.

That morning there had been another burial, not at the same place as Smith's, not in consecrated ground, and without the participation of the community. It was a woman whom they had buried in haste in the hope of attracting as little attention as possible. She was Atua Lewis, a Papuan. Lewis, whom they were just taking out to be hanged, was both her husband and her murderer. Atua Lewis and old Fatty Smith had met their ends simultaneously in incongruous circumstances, but the murder was not a crime of jealousy.

MacBride stood up, then went to the balustrade at the edge of the verandah and listened. It sounded not so much like a lot of voices mixing and amplifying one another, as like one primitive belly voice that had disintegrated: the voice of the people. The trader spat at one of the parched bread-fruit trees that formed the corner posts of his villa, came back and said, nodding back over his shoulder, 'the voice of justice'.

It was already dark. I think his face was pale when he sat down again.

Then he told the story.

There was a time, according to MacBride, when this Lewis had a chance.

Where he had been before he arrived on the island nobody knew, or if they did they had forgotten. Probably in one of those equatorial ports where a whole section of humanity is tolerated as raw material, slaughtered when they look like competition and, otherwise, not taken too seriously. Lewis himself did not look particularly worn out, said MacBride. There was something naive about him. You can imagine how he would fare if he was naive in these latitudes.

He had a little capital with him, and traded in a small way in pearls. It is not hard to take enough off the natives to make a living in these parts. The white competition is a little tougher. But at the beginning Lewis was treated quite decently by the colony; though a half-caste, he was allowed to play poker with the men on the station and let them take his money, for he naturally did not win, his intelligence fell far short of that. They overlooked the bluish tinge of his finger-nails when he shuffled, not least because they were more interested in squinting at the cards than at his finger-nails. Lewis liked this sort of tolerance, and he never made trouble. But then in the course of business he became involved with one of the white sharks, and his parentage began to crop up in the men's conversations on various verandahs. Whenever he turned up, the men's silence would be audible all the way to the jungle. He suddenly had to pay more for whisky, and the cards disappeared from his fingers, and his nails caught the eye (they were bluish), and then there was no whisky for him at all. It is difficult in such cases to go back and sit all alone in your shop and eat your savings. And that was what Lewis did.

The interesting thing about his otherwise rather ordinary and common case was that Lewis married, in other words he tried to settle down. He picked up one of those golden-yellow, narrow-hipped natives who are judged variously according to taste, but between ourselves are far preferable to most white women on this side of the globe. Lewis appeared before the priest at the side of his golden-yellow Atua, ordered her to take her pipe out of her mouth and asked to be married in the manner customary in those parts.

Then he dropped out of the colony's sight, and the next time they heard about him, what they heard was unpleasant.

There was in the colony a trader called Smith, a fat, common fellow who was rather too good-natured for a trader, and was, it might be said, rather a greenhorn in business. That was probably why he displayed such an interest in Papuan women and was always stating loudly in male company that yellow made love better than white, and straight hips were preferable to curved ones. Now it was with this same Smith that Lewis was seen sitting deep in discussion over a glass of whisky. Smith was hardly kept uninformed. Some very plain words were spoken, but he protested that his connection with Lewis had nothing to do with business, and that he had no need of advice about his private affairs.

After that they held their discussions in Lewis's hut, and soon the whole colony was saying that Smith was having lengthy discussions even when Lewis wasn't there. He was there quite a lot.

Lewis himself could be seen regularly at this time wandering around drunk. He went on long excursions into the interior of the island. Walking is the best medicine for steadying your nerves. And yesterday, three weeks after Lewis had first been seen together with Smith, in the early hours of the morning, Lewis clubbed Fatty Smith to death with a bamboo club and while he was at it did in his golden-yellow Atua too.

So far so good. The story was an open book even without the trial. The motive was there, it was a case of adultery on the part of Fatty Smith and of murder committed out of jealousy on the part of Lewis. But Lewis's behaviour in court put paid to all that and effectively turned the tale into something much less ordinary. Lewis denied any feeling of jealousy. He admitted that he had left Mrs. Lewis alone with Smith, and not so that they could play poker either. He had also taken money from Smith, and the court was absolutely astounded when Lewis blandly declared that Smith's death had just been an unfortunate accident.

'What,' asked Lewis, 'could I have had against Smith? He gave me some money and I repaid him in a way that suited him. Between the two of us everything was in order. I believe we were fully satisfied with each other. I am really very sorry that Smith fell victim to this accident.

But Smith was dead, and Lewis had clubbed him, and with a bamboo club as thick as your arm at that.

But Lewis had not intended to kill Smith, according to Lewis; only his own wife. It was just that Mrs. Atua Lewis and Smith (speak no evil of him, for God's sake!) had been lying in such an awkward position in their sleep that Lewis had to hit Smith to get at his wife. If Lewis had had more time at his disposal he would naturally have asked Smith politely to make way so he could get in a hefty belt with his bamboo club. But Lewis had no time, because he was very angry and bent on an immediate reckoning with Mrs. Lewis, not one preceded by an exchange of more or less elaborate civilities with Smith. And the cause of his anger had not been jealousy. He would not have had to sit as he did outside his hut for an hour for that. The reason, and the only reason, as Lewis repeatedly stressed, was Mrs. Lewis's bad housekeeping, a piece of negligence on her part which had been the last straw.

To tell the whole story, it had been like this:

Smith had been in bed with Lewis's wife in the hut, and Lewis, who had come back early from an excursion into the interior, had sat down outside. In the pale light of the moon Lewis had a few cups of rice-brandy to help him sleep. He was, he admitted, annoyed that Smith had not yet gone, because Lewis was tired, and the more rice-brandy he drank the more tired he became. And it was mainly to clear the sleep out of his head – this is the contentious point, because Lewis based his entire defence on this assertion – that he wanted a drink of water to sort himself out and fight off his fatigue.

The prosecution, however, maintained he only wanted to plunge his head into water to sober himself; if indeed he bothered with the water at all.

You don't, they said, drink water out of buckets that have been standing around for a long time and are infected.

But Lewis maintained that he had indeed drunk water, or rather had meant to drink water. The whole point was that he had found filth in the bucket. The bucket had not been rinsed, and the person who had failed to rinse out the bucket was Mrs. Lewis. It was part of the housework. It was her job to fetch water; she was expected to do at least that much, whatever else she might regularly neglect. But a duty is a duty, and it happened that Lewis found dirty water in his unwashed bucket, and he was not the man to take that kind of thing from Mrs. Lewis. So he strode straight in and took his bamboo club with him and killed his wife, and unfortunately Mr. Smith too, since he chanced to be there and found himself in the midst of a domestic conflict.

Lewis could not be expected to drink dirty water. That was what he was trying to say, and that was why he based his case on the fact that he had wanted a drink and not just a wash. Because his anger seemed more justifiable if he was faced with dirty drinking water than just with dirty washing water. They had argued this point (washing water or drinking water?) at length in court, but then the judge had ruled that the distinction was immaterial, since Lewis was going to be hanged anyway, something which Lewis for his part could not comprehend.

This was MacBride's story and he had barely finished it when the shouting which MacBride had previously called the voice of justice approached, and a disorderly mob appeared among the mimosa trees. They were bringing the murderer.

He was walking amid howling natives, and rather fast at that, probably to prevent them from dragging him. He had a round, open face, and as he passed he cast a quick, cool glance at us, which, since I was new to those parts, sent the shivers through my bones.

A LITTLE TALE OF INSURANCE

A financier by the name of Kückelmann who had been on the verge of bankruptcy for years was eventually forced by the wolves baying at his heels to take a week off and try his damnedest to boost his sagging morale and come up with a money-making idea. By the end of the said week he had put the bar at the Adlon Hotel, the Bristol Bar and a number of other establishments behind him for ever, without having the slightest result to show for his efforts. He had stimulated the old brain with stiff American drinks here and soothed it with incomparable coffee there, he had whipped up his flagging vitality with all kinds of jazz, he had rushed to the Kabarett der Komiker, he had sought mental fecundation in every musical in town, and from morn to midnight twixt heaven and earth had come up with nothing that would yield the slightest profit unless you owned it before you started. He ended up in Aschinger's beer bar.

Here he had an obscure urge to tap vital springs among the common folk whose struggle for existence still took the form of actual work, to draw strength, so to speak, like Antaeus from contact with mother earth. After two exhausting hours of just sitting around, his eye lit on a beggar with a glass of beer at the next table, nothing else seemed worthy of note.

The look of this beggar was quite horrifying. Kückelmann, whose sensitivity to pictures of misery was particularly acute at that time, distinctly felt a shiver go through his bones. The man bore the mark of death. His thinness was absurd. He seemed to have been fed from childhood on no more than two water biscuits a day. Overcome by a heroic desire to confront utter poverty eyeball to eyeball, Kückelmann sat down in desperation at this fellow's table. From a safe distance behind his newspaper he examined this walking, beer-swilling skeleton with growing dismay, ordered pease pudding for him as if in a dream, and then, while the man's strength revived with surprising alacrity, engaged him in conversation. And what can one say? Kückelmann ended up taking the beggar Joseph Kleiderer to his hotel for the night.

The beggar had told him that he was in the best of health, though just a little starved; and between a greasy waiter and a silver cash-register Kückelmann saw a sudden vision in the air.

From now on he had his meals sent up to his room and shared them with Joseph Kleiderer, who, preserved for the world in all his filth, was completely restored at the end of three weeks and indeed presented an appearance of blooming health. People who had known the old Kleiderer now said they could not recognize him; that he was so fat that you were bound to drink a schnaps to his health. Kückelmann wanted nothing from him in return for all this, only a chance to take him to an insurance office since his, Kleiderer's, life was so dear to him, Kückelmann, that he wanted it to be covered for all eventualities – and Kleiderer saw the point. So Kückelmann insured Kleiderer for 100,000 marks and paid the first premium with most of the ready cash he had left. On the way home he told Kleiderer he had to buy some cigars and disappeared into a tobacconist's from which he never re-emerged. Understandably deep in the dumps, Kleiderer went to the hotel, and there, and later at the beer bar, he waited in vain.

Thereafter Kleiderer waited often in the beer bar for his benefactor who had gone to ground, and now that he had no funds his physical decline was rapid. His robust bloom lasted a few days, then he lost weight, and before five weeks had passed he was once again the same walking, beer-swilling skeleton, sitting in the beer bar, when Kückelmann appeared behind a newspaper just as he had done the last time.

Kückelmann still showed a great interest in Kleiderer, immediately ordered him something to eat, and even asked him to go along to his bank with him – wherewith Kleiderer complied.

In his banker's office Kückelmann produced Kleiderer's insurance policy, introduced Kleiderer as his brother-in-law, and asked the banker to buy the policy from him, Kückelmann. Since he was momentarily in financial straits he couldn't pay the premiums, though it could be seen at a glance that Joseph Kleiderer would not live a week, being all skin and bones, and the sum for which he was insured, 100,000 marks, would then be paid to the policy holder.

Kückelmann, looking ostentatiously downcast, sighed as he put the banknotes into a morocco leather case, steered his 'dying' brother-in-law carefully out of the door, helped him into a hansom and invited him to dine at Lauer's. In the next few days they dined either at Lauer's or at Kempinski's or at the Bristol Bar.

Kückelmann took a childish delight in Kleiderer's second blooming, and among other things proved conclusively to him that listening to classical music over coffee and imported cigars leads one to put on weight.

At the end of two amply filled weeks Kleiderer, on whom Kückelmann could now afford to lavish more than on the first occasion, was fully restored, and one day Kückelmann went along with him to his banker.

The man was aghast. Later on Kückelmann assured his business friends that no one else would have recognised the 'skeleton' in the fat, smiling Joseph Kleiderer, but the banker took in the situation at a glance. He had the keen eye of a man who has laid out 40,000 marks.

Kückelmann said excitedly that his brother-in-law had pulled through better than anyone had expected, and that a remarkable vitality seemed to run in the family. As things now stood, he could of course not expect anybody to pay premiums for thirty to forty years – for a man's life is three score years and ten, or at best four score. He fully wished to do the decent thing and, at a reasonable price, would buy back the policy, whose value had been drastically reduced by such a happy turn of events. The price which he felt he could reasonably offer was 2500 marks. The banker totted up in his mind the legal costs he would face if he yielded to his urge to smash Kückelmann in the teeth, but decided to forget it, since his birthday only came round once a year. He accepted the 2500 marks for the insurance policy and contented himself with reviewing his estimate of his own fitness for this life.

Kückelmann put the insurance policy in his morocco leather brief case and walked through the glass door in front of Joseph Kleiderer, then tilted his Borsalino slightly forward and, before Joseph Kleiderer's eyes, vanished into a taxi as into a cloud.

Kleiderer, whose second bloom was therewith at an end, did not even look for him again. A sullen uneasiness took possession of the simple soul, who failed to understand the surprising but seemingly lucrative behaviour of his quarterly benefactor. He declined speedily, and when Kückelmann quite predictably turned up, asked him to dinner again, took him to see a banker where he again sold the same insurance policy, stowed the money in his morocco leather brief case and proceeded yet again to eat with him, a mad rebellion rose within him. As he was hungry, he could not turn the food down, but he ate only enough to stave off the pangs. He ate, as it were, absently, even with a slight disgust. He listened to Kückelmann's praise of his improved appearance (for food is food and makes you fat) with a sidelong glance from beneath his eyebrows, and walked past mirrors quickly, averting his gaze. And one day when he was still far from fat he started, to Kückelmann's complete astonishment, making the rounds of the newspaper offices looking for a job. He picked the profession of newsvendor. The job was meagrely paid but it enabled him to climb countless stairs. However, before the exercise stopped him gaining weight, Kückelmann cunningly showed him the insurance policy in the course of a meal to which he had allowed himself to be seduced, and Joseph Kleiderer with eyes betraying an ocean of slimy vengeful notions, watched Kückelmann, with a look of disappointment, make a mental estimate of his, Kleiderer's, girth and then take out his leather case again.

It was in those days that Kückelmann founded the celebrated Kückelmann Jam Factory. His ship had come in, and he had little time to concern himself with Kleiderer who naturally went into total decline. Still, he looked him up, though many months later, but only because it was his principle to finish any job he started. And when he found Kleiderer, who had now sunk totally into the morass, he was in for a surprise. The man whom he had repeatedly dragged out of that morass, whom he had clothed and fed, not to say stuffed – this man, who should have thanked him for the few moments in his poor and uneventful life in which his health and fortunes had bloomed – had the gall to respond to his friendly invitation to a meal for old time's sake with a negative and quite unprintable answer.

FOUR MEN AND A POKER GAME
or
TOO MUCH LUCK IS BAD LUCK

They sat on cane chairs in Havana and let the world go by. When it got too hot they drank iced water; in the evenings they danced the Boston at the Atlantic Hotel. All four of them had money.

The newspapers called them great men. They read it three times and chucked the paper into the sea. Or they held the paper between their hands and pierced it with their toecaps. Three of them had broken swimming records in front of ten thousand people, and the fourth had brought all ten thousand to their feet. When they had beaten the field and read the papers they boarded ship. They were headed back to New York with good money in their pockets.

To tell this story properly really calls for jazz accompaniment. It is sheer poetry from A to Z. It begins with cigar smoke and laughter and ends with a corpse.

For one of them, it was generally agreed, could coax salmon out of a sardine tin. He was what they call fortune's child. His name was Johnny Baker. Lucky Johnny. He was one of the best short-distance swimmers in either hemisphere. But the ridiculous luck he enjoyed threw a shadow over all his triumphs. For when a man can't unfold a paper napkin without finding a dollar bill, people begin to wonder whether he is good at his business, even if his name is Rockefeller. And wonder they did.

He had won in Havana just like the two others. He had won the 200 yard crawl by a length. But once again it was an open secret that his strongest opponent couldn't stand the climate and hadn't been fit. Johnny of course said they would try to pin something like that on him and go on about his 'luck' whatever happened, no matter how well he had been swimming. When he said it the other three just smiled.

This was the state of play when the story began, and it began with a little game of poker. The ship was a bore.

The sky was blue and so was the sea. The drinks were good, but they always were. The cigars smoked as well as any other cigars. In short, sky, sea, drinks and cigars were no good at all.

They thought a little game of poker might be better. It wasn't far short of the Bermudas when they began to play. They settled themselves comfortably for the game; each of them used two chairs. They agreed like gentlemen about the seating arrangements. One man's feet lay by another's ear. Thus, not far short of the Bermudas, they began to work their own downfall.

Since Johnny was feeling insulted by certain insinuations, they were only three to start with. One won, one lost, one held his own. They were playing with tin chips, each standing for five cents. Then the game got too boring for one of them and he took his feet out of the game. Johnny took his place. After that, the game wasn't boring any more. That is, Johnny began to win. If there was one thing Johnny couldn't do, it was play poker: but winning at poker was something he could do.

When Johnny bluffed, the bluff was so ridiculous that no poker player in the world would have dared go along with it. And when anybody who knew Johnny would have suspected a bluff, Johnny would innocently lay a flush on the table.

Johnny himself played stone cold for a couple of hours. The two others were het up. When the fourth man came back after watching potatoes being peeled in the galley for two hours, he observed that the tin chips were standing at a dollar.

This little increase had been the only way Johnny's partners could hope to get back some of their money. It was quite simple: they were to recoup in greenbacks what he had won in cents. Responsible family men could not have played with more caution in this situation. But it was Johnny who raked in the spondulicks.

They played six hours at a stretch. At any time during those six hours they could have left the game and lost no more to Johnny than the prize-money they had won in Havana. After those six hours of worry and effort they no longer could.

It was time for dinner. They polished off the meal in double-quick time. Instead of forks they felt straights between their fingers. They ate their steaks thinking of royal flushes. The fourth man ate much more slowly. He said he was really beginning to feel like taking a hand, since a little life seemed to have crept into their dreary diddling.

After dinner they were a foursome again. They played for eight hours. When Johnny counted their money about three in the morning they had left the Bermudas behind.

They slept rather badly for five hours and started again. By then three of them were men who, whatever happened, would be in hock for years. They had one more day ahead of them; at midnight they would arrive in New York. In the course of that day they had to make sure they were not going to be ruined for life. For among them was a lousy poker player who was sucking the marrow from their bones.

In the morning, when the appearance of several ships showed that the coast was near, they began to stake their houses. On top of everything else Johnny won a piano. Then they took two hours off at noon before squaring up to play for the shirts on their backs. At five in the afternoon they saw no choice but to go on. The man who had waited till after the Bermudas to take a hand and who was still eating calmly when the others had forgotten what their forks were for, offered to play Johnny for his girl. That is to say, if Johnny won, he would have the right to take a certain Jenny Smith to the male voice choir's Widows' Ball in Hoboken, but if he lost he would have to give back everything he had already won from the others. And Johnny took him up.

First of all he got his facts straight.

'And you won't be coming along?'

'Wouldn't dream of it.'

'And you won't hold it against me?'

'I won't hold it against you.'

'Or against her?'

'What do you mean, against her?'

'Well, the girl, you won't hold it against her?'

'Godammit no, I won't hold it against her either.'

And then Johnny won.

When you place a bet, win, pocket your winnings, raise your hat and leave, it means you have been in danger and emerged unscathed. But if you have too big a heart and give your partners another chance, then, unless you end in the poorhouse, your partners will be on your back for the rest of your life. They will eat your liver like vultures. When playing poker you have to be as hard-hearted as in any other form of expropriation.

From the moment when Johnny joined the game because another player left the table, he had let the others call the shots. They had forced him to look at several thousand cards, they had robbed him of his sleep, they had made him wolf down his meals in record time. They would really have preferred him to carry on playing and every six hours snatch the odd mouthful from a steak dangling on a string above the card-table. Johnny found it all distasteful.

When he got up from the table after playing for the girl – which so far as he was concerned had topped everything – he had in his naive way thought they had had enough. They had taken him on knowing how lucky he was, because they thought he knew as little about poker as a traindriver knows about geography. But trains have rails which know their geography: a guy goes from New York to Chicago and nowhere else. That was exactly the system with which he had won, and the only thing left was for him to return his winnings without mortally offending them. Johnny's weakness was his heart. He had too much tact.

He said straight out not to worry, it had all been in fun. They didn't answer. They sat there as they had since the previous day and watched the seagulls, which were now more plentiful.

Johnny concluded from this that, so far as they were concerned, more than 24 hours of poker was no joke.

Johnny stood by the railing and thought. Then it came to him. He suggested that they should first of all have a meal with him that evening to restore their spirits. At his expense naturally. What he had in mind was a grand function, a blow-out, a really slap-up meal. He himself would mix drinks that would loosen their tongues. In view of the circumstances no expense need be spared. He even had caviare in mind. Johnny expected big things of this meal.

They didn't say no.

They took this without exactly showing enthusiasm, but at any rate they agreed to go along with him. It was time to eat anyhow.

Johnny went off and did the ordering. He went into the kitchen and ingratiated himself with the chef. He wanted a meal dished up for himself and his friends, a banquet which would outdo anything of its kind ever produced by any first class ship's galley between Havana and New York. Johnny felt a lot better after this conversation with the chef.

During this half-hour not a single word was spoken on deck.

Johnny set the table himself downstairs. Beside his own place he put a little serving table on which he arranged the drinks. No need for him to stand up to mix. He had the chef bring his guests down. They came with a look of indifference and sat down as if it were an ordinary meal. It was all a bit flat.

Johnny had thought that they would open up during the meal. People usually unbutton when they are eating, and this meal was excellent. They tucked in but they did not seem to be enjoying it. They ate the fresh vegetables as if they were porridge, and the roast chicken as if it were cafetaria ham. They seemed to have ideas of their own about Johnny's meal. At one point one of them reached for a beautifully glazed little porcelain pot and asked 'Is this caviare?' And Johnny answered truthfully. 'Yes, the best that a leaky old tub like this has to offer.' The man nodded and emptied the pot with a spoon. Right after that another pointed out to his neighbour a little, specially packed speciality in mayonnaise. And then they smiled. Neither this nor several other aspects of their behaviour escaped their host.

But it was only over the coffee that it dawned on Johnny what a piece of impertinence it had been for him to invite them to a meal. They didn't seem to appreciate his desire to apply some of the money he had won to the common good. It seemed as if they only realised the extent of their losses once they were forced to watch their money being spent on such senseless titbits. It is more or less the same with a woman who wants to leave you. When you read her nice little parting letter, you may understand, but it is only when you see her getting into a taxi with another man that it really hits you. Johnny was quite taken aback.

It was eight in the evening. Outside you could hear the tugs hooting. It was four hours to New York.

Johnny had a vague feeling that it would be intolerable to sit in this cabin with these ruined men for four hours. But it didn't look as if he would be able simply to get up and go. Given the situation, Johnny realised that he only had one chance. He suggested playing again for the whole pot.

They put down their coffee cups, pushed the half-empty cans to one corner of the table and dealt the cards.

They played for money with the same tin chips as they had

done at the beginning. It struck Johnny that the other three were unwilling to go beyond a certain stake. So they were taking the game seriously again.

At the very first hand Johnny was dealt yet another straight. Nonetheless he dropped out in the second round and threw in his hand. He had definitely learnt a thing or two.

In the second hand and in the third when the stakes were raised he bluffed and strung them along as far as he could. But then one of them calmly looked him straight in the eye and said, 'Play the game.' Whereupon he played a few hands as he had done previously, and won as before. Then he had a curious desire to play it by ear and follow his luck where he saw it. Then he saw their faces again and noticed that they scarcely looked at their cards before throwing them in, and at that he lost his nerve. He wanted to start deliberately losing, but each time he had a chance to pull a fast one he felt them watching him so closely that he drew back. And when he played badly out of sheer ignorance they played even worse, because the only thing they believed in was his luck. They took his total uncertainty for sheer malice. More and more they came to think that he was just playing cat and mouse with them.

When once again he had collected all the chips in front of him the other three all got up, and he was left sitting alone without a thought in his head, amid the cards and the cans. It was eleven o'clock, one hour out of New York.

Four men and a poker deck in a cabin between Havana and New York.

They still had a little time. Since the air in the cabin was hot and stuffy they decided to go up on deck. They thought the fresh air would help. The idea of fresh air seemed to improve their spirits. They even asked Johnny whether he wanted to go on deck with them.

Johnny didn't want to go on deck.

When the other three saw that Johnny didn't want to go on deck they began insisting.

It was then that Johnny lost his head for the first time and made the mistake of not standing up immediately. This probably gave them a prolonged glimpse of fear on his face. And this in turn made up their minds.

Five minutes later, without uttering a word, Johnny went on deck with them. The steps were wide enough for two. It just happened that one of them went up ahead of Johnny, one behind him and one at his side.

When they reached the top the night was cool and foggy. The deck was damp and slippery. Johnny was glad to be in the middle.

They passed a man at the wheel who paid no attention to them. When they had gone four paces beyond him Johnny had a distinct feeling that he had missed a chance. But by then they were heading for the stern railings.

When they reached the railings Johnny wanted to put his plan into effect and give a loud shout. But he abandoned this idea, oddly enough because of the fog; for when people have trouble seeing, they think no one can hear them.

From the railings they heaved him into the sea.

Then they sat in the cabin for a while eating what was left in the half-empty cans. They consolidated what was left of the drinks, three men and a poker deck on the way from Havana to New York, and asked one another whether Johnny Baker who was no doubt swimming behind the ship as its red navigation light disappeared into the night, was as good at swimming as he was at winning poker games.

But *nobody* can possibly swim well enough to save himself from his fellow men if he has too much luck in this world.

BARBARA

I wondered for a long time what this story should be called. But then I realised it had to be 'Barbara'. I admit that Barbara herself only comes into it right at the beginning and is presented in an unflattering light throughout, but it's a story that can only be called 'Barbara'.

Edmund, known as Eddy, 200 pounds of melancholy, made a bad move one evening at nine o'clock, when, just because we had downed a couple of cocktails on the Kurfürstendamm together and his Chrysler was standing outside the bar, he took me up to see Barbara at 53 Lietzenburger Strasse, although he should have known that Barbara would have 'a very important appointment with a man who ran a cabaret.'

We rang, went in, hung up our coats, saw Barbara bearing down on us in a rage, heard her scream, 'You'll drive me mad with your idiotic jealousy,' then a door banged and we found ourselves down in front of Eddy's Chrysler again. We climbed straight in.

Eddy drove at a tidy pace. He whistled between two passing trams like the wind, flashed under the nose of an old lady, round a policeman and over the Halensee bridge at full throttle.

And he talked the whole time. It was as if a ball of fat with a little, stiff black hat for a head, had a little black gear-lever right in its middle, and between this and the hat, all carefully padded with fat, a sizeable steering wheel, and was travelling terribly fast and getting faster all the time as it headed for deeper and deeper forests.

Moreover, as I told you, the ball of fat was talking the whole time.

'You know,' he said, 'that was just a little thing. A bit of rudeness due to nerves. But you know, to be candid, it's just these little things. I've had more than enough of them. What does she mean by jealousy? If there is one man who isn't jealous, doesn't know the feeling, never has known it, it's me. Naturally I'm not struck on cabaret johnnies, that would be too much to ask. Naturally she has every right to entertain a guy like that at nine o'clock at night in her pyjamas, and if there is anybody who respects people's rights, of every kind, right up to the hilt, it's me. It's just that it was thoughtless of Barbara. That's all I'm saying, no more. Jealousy!

'I can't tell you how mad I get when I see a man's ulster on Barbara's coatstand. It's not the coat of course, I don't know what it is really, but I've got a thing about coats with fur linings. Even my own, the one I wear myself, makes me puke. I've long since given up expressing my own opinions. But all I can say is, that's got to end now. For good.'

This is how Eddy was talking as we crossed the Halensee bridge. In the Grunewald he went further. It was a gloomy night with a nasty fog and I would rather have been at home. But Eddy still had plenty to say.

He clearly intended to let me have the benefit of his views on life. He told me what he thought of the world, in full. He told it straight from the shoulder, travelling at fifty on a road which didn't exist except in his imagination. He was weak on philosophy and an excellent driver, but his driving was a lot more dangerous than his philosophy.

He said people were poorly constructed, a bad job which had not been properly tested, the kind of thing put on the market by firms who don't take enough time and then conceal their shoddy workmanship with nifty aluminium coachwork. But I was watching the pines flash by with the feeling that we were going much too fast.

Eddy pressed the pedal to get up more speed, and told me what he thought of women. Eddy considered women, when he had touched sixty-five, to be such trash that he couldn't really understand why they were always rated above other domestic animals which were far more reliable. They were far too flimsy, jerry-built. He really seized on this word 'jerry-built' as applied to women. He blurted it out repeatedly and added that they should be forbidden by the fire regulations as unsafe, and with that in mind he hit seventy.

I couldn't concentrate on Eddy's anti-woman arguments in the rush (seventy miles an hour!) but the pines I could see flashing by seemed immensely solid and quite permanent.

The strange thing was that Eddy's *Weltschmerz* had one foot on the accelerator. There being no way of moving the foot I had to try to do something about the *Weltschmerz*.

Consequently in the middle of the night on an unlit road between Wannsee and Potsdam, in the Grunewald forest, etc., I began to expound the merits of our planet to that raving ball of fat. I told him that in the circumstances I couldn't go into detail, but that, in simple terms, everything was relative, although I couldn't help observing that our speed was absolute. There was no way the speed at which we were racing towards our deaths could be termed 'relatively' fast. As I broached the theme of 'the silver lining to every cloud' we were careering down a wooded slope, and when we reached the bottom we bumped across a meadow, so my discourse on 'women having their good sides too' could scarcely have had much effect. Eddy spotted the road again and quickly got the car up to a speed commensurate with his despair.

I was totally exhausted. I could see us lying by some hitherto unblemished milestone, in the grey light of dawn, us being the remains of a car, the remains of a lunatic, and the remains of the lunatic's victim. I felt terribly bitter.

We drove for a while, at least half an hour, in stony silence, but at unrelenting speed. Then Eddy drove down a gravel slope again and I said curtly and harshly, 'you're a lousy driver!'

This statement, which I meant seriously, had a powerful impact on Eddy. He had the reputation of being an excellent driver. Driving was the one thing he could do.

A muffled sound came from his shapeless body. It sounded like the wail of a mastodon that had been told it was too weak to pull up a blade of grass.

Eddy accelerated to seventy-five.

We had just reached a stretch with a lot of bends. Eddy went into every bend on full throttle. There wasn't much light, only a few glimmers here and there in the villages, from cow-sheds, etc. In one of these I glimpsed Eddy's phiz; he had a thin, scornful smile on his babyface, which was no longer of this world.

But in the middle of a wood that was black as sin the engine coughed.

Then Eddy pressed the accelerator.

Then the car slowed down.

Then Eddy declutched and stepped on the accelerator.

Then the car stopped.

It was out of petrol.

Eddy climbed out and glared at the tank, looked into his spare can, shook it and sat down on the running board, broken. It was a wood with no beginning and no end, a wood that certainly was not on the map. It must have been quite a long way east, because it was as cold as a hole in the ice.

And that to all intents and purposes is the end of my story. All that remains is to say that towards morning two men were seen in a remote village shoving a Chrysler along, and one of them, the thin one, was telling the other what he thought of him and a few other things to boot, while the other, a battered ball of fat, shoved and panted and occasionally laughed.

But it was happy, childlike laughter.

THE GOOD LORD'S PACKAGE – A CHRISTMAS TALE

Draw your chairs up to the fire, and don't forget to lace your tea with rum. It is best to be nice and warm when you are telling a tale about the cold.

Many people, especially a particular sort of man with a thing against sentimentality, find Christmas quite repugnant. But there is at least one Christmas in my life which I recall with genuine pleasure. It was Christmas Eve 1908 in Chicago.

I had arrived in Chicago at the beginning of November, and when I enquired about the general situation there they told me straight away that it was going to be the hardest winter even that city – which was unpleasant enough at the best of times – could come up with. I asked what were the chances for a boilermaker and was told that a boilermaker had no chance at all, and when I went looking for a half-way decent place to lay my head, everything turned out to be too expensive. This was a lesson many were to learn in that winter of 1908 in Chicago, whatever their trade.

And the wind howled horribly across Lake Michigan the whole of December, and towards the end of that month a whole succession of meat-packing firms closed down and threw a flood of unemployed men out on the freezing streets.

All day long we trudged round various districts looking desperately for work, and we were happy if we could find a seat in the evening near the abattoirs in one of the little bars full of exhausted people. There at least it was warm and we could sit in peace. And we sat as long as we possibly could over a single glass of whisky, and we saved up all day for that glass of whisky which came complete with noise, warmth and comradeship, all that we could hope for by then.

And that is where we were sitting on Christmas Eve that year. The bar was even more crowded than usual, and the whisky more watery, and the customers more desperate. Obviously neither customers nor landlord will be in festive mood when the customers' main object is to get through the evening on a single glass and the landlord's main object is to eject anybody sitting with an empty one.

However, about ten o'clock three fellows rolled in who had, God knows how, a few dollars in their pockets. And since it was Christmas and sentimentality was in the air they asked for doubles to be put up for the entire company. Five minutes later the whole bar was unrecognisable.

Everybody fetched himself a fresh whisky (and saw to it that he was given good measure), the tables were pushed together and a frozen-looking girl was asked to dance the cake-walk, during which the entire festive company clapped their hands. But what can I say – the Devil may have had a hand in it, but there was no way to break the ice.

In fact things took a nasty turn from the outset. I think it was having to accept other people's generosity that got on everyone's nerves. The men who were footing the bill for all this Christmas spirit were not viewed with a friendly eye. Right after the first free whiskies it was decided to organise Christmas presents for everybody, no mean feat, you might say.

Since there wasn't much giftware to hand, the idea was that people would look less for articles of intrinsic value, and more for those that were appropriate for the recipient and might even have a deeper significance.

So the landlord's present was a bucket of dirty, melted snow from outside where there was plenty, *to help him make his old whisky last into the new year*. To the waiter we gave an old, opened tin can, *to give him one decent utensil to serve from*, and to a girl who worked in the bar, a pocket knife with a broken blade, *to scrape off at least one layer of last year's powder with*.

All these presents were greeted with provocative applause by everybody present, with the possible exception of those who received them. Then came the biggest joke of the evening.

You see, there was a man among us who clearly had something to hide. He sat there every evening and people who knew about these things stated categorically that, unconcerned though he might wish to appear, he must have an insurmountable fear of anything that had to do with the police. On the other hand anybody could see that he was ill at ease.

For this man we thought out something special. With the landlord's permission we tore three pages out of an old street directory which had nothing but addresses of police stations on them, wrapped them carefully in newspaper and handed the package to our man.

When we handed it to him there was a long silence. The man took the thing hesitantly in his hand and looked up at us from under his eyebrows with a rather wan smile. I noticed that he felt the parcel with his fingers to find out what was inside even before opening it.

And then something very remarkable happened. The man was fiddling with the string with which his 'present' was tied when his eye, quite idly it seemed, fell on the newspaper in which those interesting pages from the street directory were wrapped. From that moment there was nothing idle about his eyes. His whole thin body (he was very tall) curled round the newspaper and he bent his face deep down into it and read. Never, either before or since have I seen anybody read like that. He quite simply devoured what he read. And then he looked up. And again I have never, neither before nor since, seen a man look so radiant as that man then.

'I have just read in this paper,' he said with a rusty voice which he was having difficulty keeping calm, and which contrasted ludicrously with his beaming face, 'that the whole affair was cleared up long ago. Everybody in Ohio knows I had nothing to do with it.' And then he laughed.

And all of us, who had been standing by astonished, expecting something quite different, and could only guess that the man had been under some kind of suspicion but had in the meantime, as he had just discovered from this newspaper, been rehabilitated, suddenly started to laugh in sympathy with almost as much heart as belly, and that broke the ice at last, our bitterness was quite forgotten, and it turned out to be an excellent Christmas that lasted into the morning and left everybody happy.

And amid the general satisfaction it was of course quite irrelevant that it was not we who had sought out that sheet of newsprint but God.

THE MONSTER

Just how many constructions can be put on a man's behaviour was shown recently by an incident at the Russian Mezhrabpom film studios. It may have been insignificant and it had no consequence, but there was something horrible about it. While *The White Eagle* – a film about the pre-war pogroms in south Russia, which pilloried the attitude of the police at the time – was being shot in the studio, an old man turned up and asked for a job. He forced his way into the porter's box at the street entrance and told the porter he would like to take the liberty of drawing the company's attention to his extraordinary resemblance to the notorious governor Muratov. (Muratov had instigated the bloodbath at the time. His was the leading role in the aforesaid film.)

The porter laughed in his face, but since he was an old man he did not eject him straight away, and that is how the long, thin fellow came to be standing, hat in hand, with a faraway look amid the hubbub of extras and studio technicians, seemingly still nursing a faint hope of earning bread and shelter for a couple of days on the strength of his resemblance to the notorious killer.

For almost an hour he stood there, constantly stepping aside to let people go by until he ended up hemmed in behind a desk, and there he was at last suddenly noticed. There was a break in the shooting and the actors headed for the canteen or stood around chatting. Kochalov, the famous Moscow actor playing Muratov, went into the porter's box to make a phone call. As he stood by the phone he was nudged by the grinning gatekeeper and when he turned he saw the man behind the desk, whereupon peals of laughter rang out all around him. Kochalov's make-up was based on historical photographs, and the extraordinary resemblance that the old man behind the desk had been telling them about was obvious to everybody.

Half an hour later the old man was sitting with the directors and cameramen like the twelve-year-old Jesus in the temple, discussing his contract with them. The negotiations were greatly facilitated by the fact that Kochalov had from the outset not been very keen to risk his popularity by playing an out and out monster. He was all for giving the 'double' a screen test.

It was not unusual for the studios to cast historical figures with suitable types rather than actors. The directors have special methods for handling these people: they simply outlined to the new Muratov the bald historical facts of the incident being enacted and asked him to play the said Muratov for the tests just as he imagined him. It was hoped that his manner would match his physical resemblance to the real Muratov.

They chose the scene in which Muratov receives a deputation of Jews who implore him to call a halt to the murders. (Page 17 of the script: 'Deputation waits. Enter Muratov. Hangs cap and sabre on a peg on the wall. Goes to his desk. Glances through the morning paper', etc.) Lightly made up, wearing the uniform of an Imperial Governor, the 'double' stepped on to the set, part of which was an authentic historical mock-up of the office in the governor's palace, where he proceeded to play Muratov 'as he imagined him' to the entire production team. He played him as follows:

('Deputation waits. Enter Muratov.') The 'double' came in quickly at the door. Hands forward in his pockets, bad, drooping posture. ('Hangs cap and sabre on a peg on the wall.') The 'double' had apparently forgotten this stage direction. He sat down at the desk straight away without taking off his cap or sabre. ('Glances through the morning paper.') The 'double' did this quite absent-mindedly. ('Opens the hearing.') He did not even look at the bowing Jews. He put the paper aside hesitantly, seemingly unsure just how to switch his attention to the business with the Jews. Simply froze and cast an agonized look at the team of directors.

The team of directors laughed. One of the assistants stood up with a grin, sauntered on to the set with his hands in his pockets, sat down beside the 'double' at the desk and tried to help him along.

'Now comes eating the apple', he said encouragingly. 'Muratov's apple-eating was famous. His governorship, apart from his bloodthirsty decrees, consisted mainly of eating apples. He kept his apples in this drawer. Look, here are the apples.' He opened the drawer to the left of the 'double'. 'The deputation now approaches and as soon as the first man opens his mouth you eat your apple, my lad.'

The 'double' had listened to the young man with the keenest attention. The apples seemed to have made a big impression on him.

When shooting resumed Muratov did in fact slowly take an apple out of the drawer with his left hand, and as he began to scrawl characters on some paper with his right he ate the apple, not with any great zest, but more out of habit as it were. By the time the deputation came to the point he was wholly engrossed in the apple. After a short time, during which he had not listened to a word, he made a casual gesture with his right hand to a Jew in mid-sentence and brought the matter to an instant end.

Then the 'double' turned enquiringly to the directors and muttered, 'Who is going to see them out?'

The head director stayed in his seat. 'Have you finished, then?'

'Yes, I thought they would be taken away now.'

The head director looked around with a grin and said: 'With monsters it's not that simple. You'll have to try a little harder.' At that he stood up and began to run through the scene again.

'No monster ever behaves like that,' he said, 'That is how a little clerk behaves. You see, you have to think about it. You can't do it without giving it some thought. You have to try to imagine this killer for yourself. You have to get right into his skin. Now come back on.'

He began to construct the scene anew on dramatic principles. He built up details and developed the characterisation. The 'double's' efforts were not without skill. He did all that they told him, and not at all badly either. He seemed just as capable of acting the monster as anybody else. All he lacked, it seemed, was a little imagination of his own. After they had worked on it for half an hour the scene looked like this:

('Enter Muratov.') Shoulders back, chest out, jerky movements of the head. As he came in at the door he cast a hawk-like look at the deeply bowing Jews. ('Hangs his cap and sabre on the peg on the wall.') His coat fell as he did this and he left it lying. ('Goes to the desk. Glances through the morning paper.') He looked for the theatre notices on the arts page. He tapped the rhythm of a hit song with his hand. ('Opens the hearing.') Meanwhile he moved the Jews back three metres with an unceremonious gesture with the back of his hand.

'You won't understand, but what you are doing there won't do', said the head director. 'It's just ham acting. A villain of the old school, my dear chap, is not how we picture a monster in this day and age. That's not Muratov.'

The team of directors stood up and addressed themselves to Kochalov who had been watching it all. They were all talking at the same time. They broke up into groups, exploring the nature of the monster.

On General Muratov's authentic chair the 'double' sat clumsily slumped forward, staring into space but listening nonetheless. He followed each conversation closely. He made great efforts to grasp the situation. The actors playing the Jewish deputation also took part in the discussion. At one point everybody listened to two extras, both Old Jews from the city who had been members of that deputation at the time. These old men had been taken on to give the film character and authenticity. Curiously enough they found the way the 'double' had played the part at the outset had not been bad at all. They could not say how it affected others, people who had not been involved, but at the time it was precisely the routine, bureaucratic way in which everything was done that made the experience so terrifying. The 'double' had got this side of it pretty accurately. And the way he ate the apple during the first take, quite mechanically – during their interview, by the way, Muratov had not eaten an apple. The assistant director could not accept this. 'Muratov always ate apples,' he said sharply, 'Are you sure you were really there?'

The Jews, who had no wish to be suspected of not being among the candidates for execution at the time, took fright at this and conceded that Muratov might perhaps have eaten an apple just before or just after he received them.

At this point there was a movement in the group around Kochalov and the head director. The 'double' had pushed his way through the group till he was face to face with the director. He began to talk insistently to him with an avid, hasty look on his gaunt physiognomy. He seemed to have understood what people wanted of him and the fear of losing his bread and butter had brought illumination to him – now he wanted to make a suggestion.

'I think I know what you have in mind. He is supposed to be a monster. Look, I tell you what we can do with the apples. Just try to imagine: I take an apple, and I hold it right in front of a Jew's nose. "Eat", I say. And while he' – 'now, you listen to this,' he said, turning to the actor playing the spokesman of the deputation – 'while you are eating the apple you have to remember, you must realise, that the fear of death naturally makes it stick in your throat, and yet you have to eat the apple if I, the governor, give it to you. It's a friendly gesture on my part towards you, is it not?' and he turned to the director, 'Then I could just sign the death warrant, quite offhand. And the man eating the apple sees me do it.'

The head director stared at him raptly for a moment. The old man stood stooping before him, thin, excited and yet burnt-out, a full head taller than himself, so that he could see over his shoulder; and for a moment the director thought the old man was mocking him, for he seemed to detect a passing, almost intangible scorn, something quite contemptuous and unseemly in his flashing eyes.

Kochalov had listened avidly to the apple scene suggested by the 'double', and it had sparked off his artistic imagination. Pushing the 'double' aside with a brutal movement of the arm he said to the team, 'Brilliant. This is what he means.' And he began to act the scene in a fashion that froze the blood in your veins. The entire studio burst into applause as Kochalov, sweat streaming down his face, signed the death warrant.

The lights were rigged. The Jews were told what was to happen. The cameras were set up. The take began. Kochalov played Muratov. It had been shown yet again that mere physical resemblance to a killer means nothing, and that it takes art to convey an authentically monstrous impression.

Former Imperial Governor Muratov collected his cap from the porter's box, said a humble farewell to the porter and dragged himself off into the cold October day towards the town, where he disappeared into the slum quarters. That day he had managed to eat two apples and lay his hands on a little money, enough for a bed for the night.

THE JOB
or BY THE SWEAT OF THY BROW SHALT THOU FAIL
TO EARN THY BREAD

In the decades after the Great War unemployment and the oppression of the lower orders went from bad to worse. An incident which took place in Mainz shows better than any peace treaty, history book or statistical table the barbaric condition to which the great European countries had been reduced by their inability to keep their economies going except by force and exploitation. One day in 1927, a poverty-stricken family in Breslau called Hausmann, consisting of husband, wife and two small children, received a letter from a former workmate of Hausmann's offering him his job, a position of trust which he was giving up because of a small legacy in Brooklyn. The letter caused feverish excitement in the family which three years of unemployment had brought to the verge of desperation. The man (who was down with pneumonia) rose at once from his sick-bed, asked his wife to put a few essentials in his old case and several cardboard boxes, took his children by the hand, told his wife how she was to close down their miserable home, and in spite of his weakened condition, went to the station. (He hoped that, whatever happened, taking the children with him would confront his friend with a fait accompli.) Slumped in his compartment with a high fever, he was glad to let a young fellow traveller, a housemaid who had been sacked and was on her way to Berlin, take care of his children, supposing him to be a widower. She even bought them a few little things that she paid for out of her own money. In Berlin his condition was so bad that he had to be taken almost unconscious to hospital. There he died five hours later. The housemaid, a certain Fraülein Leidner, had not foreseen this eventuality, so she had not left the children but taken them with her to cheap lodgings. She had paid all sorts of expenses for the dead man and his children, and she was sorry for the helpless little mites, so, without due consideration perhaps, for it would doubtless have been better to send word to Frau Hausmann, asking her to come, she went back to Breslau the same evening with the children. Frau Hausmann took the news with the terrible blank placidity that you sometimes find in people who have long forgotten what a peaceful, normal existence is like. For the whole of the next day the two women were busy buying cheap mourning clothes on hire-purchase. Meanwhile they set about clearing out the house, though this now of course made no sense at all. Standing in the empty rooms, laden with cases and cardboard boxes, the woman was struck just before their departure by a terrible thought. The job which was lost when she lost her husband had not been out of her mind for a minute. The only thing that mattered was to salvage it at all costs: Fate could not be expected to make such an offer a second time. At the last moment she adopted a plan that was as bold as her situation was desperate: she aimed to stand in for her husband and take the job as nightwatchman – for that is what it was – disguised as a man. No sooner had she settled this in her own mind than she tore the black rags from her body, undid the cord of the suitcase, pulled out her husband's Sunday suit and clumsily put it on before her children's eyes, with the help of her new-found friend who had almost instantaneously understood what she was up to. Thus it was a new family that travelled to Mainz to renew the assault on the promised job, and one that consisted of no more mouths than before. Even so do fresh recruits fill the gaps caused by gunfire in the ranks of decimated battalions.

The date by which the current holder of the job had to join his ship in Hamburg did not permit the women to leave the train at Berlin for Hausmann's funeral. While he was being moved, unaccompanied, from the hospital to be lowered into his grave, his wife was being shown round the factory in his very clothes with his papers in her pocket by his former workmate with whom she had quickly come to an arrangement. She had spent an extra day in the workmate's flat – all this incidentally in front of the children – practising her husband's walk, his way of sitting and eating, and his manner of speech under the eyes of his workmate and her new friend. Little time elapsed between the moment when Hausmann was committed to the grave and the moment when she took the promised job.

Brought back to life – that is to say, to the process of production – by a combination of fortune and fate, the two women led their new life in the most orderly and circumspect fashion as Herr and Frau Hausmann with their children. The job of nightwatchman in a big factory is not undemanding. The nightly round of the yards, workshops and stores calls for reliability and courage, qualities that have from time immemorial been called *manly*. The fact that Hausmann's widow was equal to these demands – she even received a public commendation from the management for having caught and secured a thief (a poor devil who was trying to steal some wood) proves that courage, physical strength and presence of mind can be shown by anybody, man or woman, who really needs a job. In a few days the woman became a man, in the same way as men have become men over the millennia: through the production process.

For four years, the little family with its growing children lived in relative security while all around them unemployment increased. Thus far the Hausmanns' domestic situation had aroused no suspicion in the neighbourhood. But then came an incident which had to be smoothed over. The caretaker of the block often sat in the Hausmanns' flat of an evening. The three of them played cards. The 'nightwatchman' sat there with legs apart, in shirtsleeves, a tankard of beer in front of her (a picture later to be given prominence in the illustrated magazines). Then the nightwatchman went on duty, leaving the caretaker sitting with the young wife. Intimacy was unavoidable. Now whether Fraülein Leidner let the cat out of the bag, or whether the caretaker saw the nightwatchman changing through a half-open door, suffice it to say that a point came when the Hausmanns began to have trouble with him. He was a drinking man whose job provided him with a free flat but not much else, and from then on they had to make payments to him. Things got particularly difficult when the neighbours began to notice Haase's – that was his name – visits to the Hausmann flat, and Frau Hausmann's habit of taking leftovers and bottles of beer to the caretaker's office became a subject of gossip in the neighbourhood. Rumours about the nightwatchman's indifference to the indecent goings-on in his flat even reached the factory and for a time shook the management's confidence in him. The three were forced to stage a break in their friendship for public consumption. Of course, however, the caretaker's exploitation of the two women did not stop, but got even worse. An accident at the factory put an end to the whole thing and brought the catastrophic affair to a conclusion.

When one of the boilers blew up one night, the nightwatchman was injured, not seriously, but badly enough to be carried away unconscious. When Frau Hausmann woke up, she found herself in a hospital for women. She was unspeakably outraged. With wounds in her legs and back, swathed in bandages, racked by nausea, but gripped by a fear even greater than could be caused by wounds whose full extent she did not know, she dragged herself through a ward full of sleeping women patients to the head nurse. Before the nurse could say a word – she was still dressing and, grotesque as it may seem, the spurious nightwatchman had to overcome her acquired embarrassment at seeing a partially dressed woman, something only permitted to members of the same sex – Frau Hausmann overwhelmed her with pleas not to report the disastrous state of affairs to the management. It was not without pity that the sister told the desperate woman, who twice fainted but insisted on going on with the interview, that the papers had already gone to the factory. What she did not tell her was that the incredible story had also gone through the town like a brushfire.

The hospital released Frau Hausmann in men's clothes. She came home in the morning, and from noon on the whole quarter gathered in the hall and on the pavement outside to wait for the male impersonator. That evening the police took the unfortunate woman into custody to put an end to the uproar. She was still in men's clothes when she got into the car. She no longer had anything else.

She continued to fight for her job while in custody, needless to say without success. It was given to one of the countless thousands waiting for any vacancy, one whose legs chanced to have between them the organ recorded on his birth certificate. Frau Hausmann, who cannot be accused of leaving any stone unturned, is thought to have worked as a waitress in a suburban bar, amid photographs (some of which she had posed for *after* being found out) showing her in shirtsleeves playing cards and drinking beer as a nightwatchman and to have been regarded as resident freak by the skittle players. Thereafter she probably sank without trace into the ranks of that army of millions who are forced to earn their modest bread by selling themselves, wholly, in part, or to one another, shedding in a few days century-old habits which had almost seemed eternal and, as we have seen, even changing sex, generally without success – who are in short lost and, if we are to believe the prevailing view, lost forever.

Stories Written in Exile (1933–1948)

SAFETY FIRST

At a stag party the conversation came round to cowardice. Having had plenty to drink we were brimming over with wisdom. We served up almost every episode in our lives when our behaviour had been 'somehow cowardly'. We realised how bad it was when others found this weakness in us, but that it was ten times worse when we discovered cowardice in ourselves. At that point somebody told the following story.

Mitchell was captain of one of those colossal ships that ply between Brazil and England, a so-called floating hotel. You must not, of course, picture these captains as the rough old sea-dogs of our grandparents' days, standing on the bridge amid spray and towering waves, and bellowing orders. Mitchell was a big, powerful fellow, but in a drawing room nobody would have taken him for a sailor, more likely an engineer, which he in fact was. Or perhaps a hotel manager.

Now something very remarkable happened to him. Towards the end of a voyage, not far off Scotland, his ship struck a small fishing boat in fog – through no fault, by the way, of Mitchell or his men. But the giant ship, she was called the *Astoria*, sprang a leak and shipped water. The gentlemen on the bridge took stock of the damage and decided to send out an SOS. They estimated the time she would stay afloat as no more than an hour, and every cabin in the ship was occupied.

SOS messages were sent and two ships responded. To them the passengers were transferred.

While in London the passengers' relatives were falling upon each other's necks, Mitchell was having a rough time in the Transatlantic Company's offices. He and his officers and crew had stayed aboard the *Astoria* which surprisingly, in spite of the forecasts, had not sunk. Nor did she sink in the hours that followed, but reached port without further incident.

Mitchell viewed the behaviour of his craft with mixed feelings, to say the least. He followed the state of the old tub and the progress of that water in the hull with real desperation. He was quite disgusted that the goddamned ship wouldn't sink.

When he docked, his own family was on the quay to meet him – his father and his sisters, one of them with her fiancé. They had been worried to death when the papers reported the SOS from the *Astoria*. He was their support. Now they were very happy, and also very proud. They bored him to tears with their questions. How did you manage to nurse the ship home? Etc. Being laymen they believed he had performed an heroic feat.

The next day he went to face the music.

His hopes were not exactly high when he reached the Transatlantic Company's offices. He had called for assistance from other ships too soon and without necessity, very expensive assistance too. But the reception that awaited him was worse than anything he had anticipated.

The owner of the Transatlantic Company was the great J. B. Watch, and he received Mitchell personally. He was by his own lights a lover of the truth and accordingly felt entitled to shout what he thought of people like Mitchell so loud that the whole office could hear. And coward was the word that came through the walls to the clerks, and from there it passed effortlessly on to the offices of other shipping companies, and to the bars and ship's chandlers and wherever there were people who had anything to do with ships. Nor did J. B. Watch confine himself to shouting – what he said in a muted voice on the telephone about his man Mitchell was even worse.

Mitchell was sacked. The reason given for his sacking was cowardice, and this was tantamount to sacking him from the entire American shipping industry, not just the Transatlantic Company. No matter where he went in the next days and then weeks, nobody had a command for him. None of the shipping lines had any desire to take on a man who called expensive doctors, in other words ships, to ships that were not quite dead, instead of having the courage to soldier on and try at least to reach port in one piece under his own steam. For public consumption the reason for Mitchell's sacking was that 'he had lost his head and caused unnecessary anxiety to our esteemed passengers'.

The papers carried the story in this form, and it was read by Mitchell's family.

To start with, as I told you, the family had taken an optimistic view of the affair. Mitchell naturally did not mention the row at the Transatlantic Company at home. The family had no inkling of his sacking and continued to live in some style. His older sister was preparing to get married, an expensive affair. Then the news-papers came out with the story and his younger sister's friends teased her about her brother. Her fiancé likewise got wind of the matter and his concern showed on his face. He had not, as he informed his bride-to-be, been blessed with the goods of this world.

Of course it was not as if the family now suddenly adopted a new attitude to its former breadwinner. They had always idolised him. But they could not really get over what had happened. They could not take it in, so to speak. They were having to watch their expenditure now too. Their tactfulness got on Mitchell's nerves.

He had other unpleasantness to contend with.

He was half engaged to a young widow who ran a boarding house for sailors of the rank of petty officer and above, a certain Beth Heewater. She was fond of Mitchell, but unfortunately her work brought her into contact with seamen who took a dim view of Mitchell. They all had much to put up with from shipowners, so they might have had some understanding for Mitchell. After all, he had put the welfare of his passengers above his company. But unfortunately these people did not think like that, but rather as competitors. They thought they'd have a little fun with him when he came to visit Beth Heewater and went into the saloon to wait for her.

The ringleader was Tommy White, the captain of the *Surface* who had taken a few weeks' leave because his ship was going into dock. He had an eye on Beth Heewater and he was behind the prank body and soul.

White got Beth to agree not to see Mitchell when he called, but to ask him to wait in the saloon on the pretext that she was visiting her mother. There he was joined by a few guests who commiserated with him over his bad luck and Beth's protracted visit to her mother.

Meanwhile Tommy was up in Beth's room setting the stage. He knocked over a couple of chairs, kicked the carpet aside, poured some red ink on it and told his mate Harry Biggers to sprawl on it, face down. On the dressing-table he threw the little silver Brown-ing that Mitchell had given Beth for her birthday. While he was about it – this was not in the agreement with Beth – he took Mitchell's photograph from the dressing-table, tore it up and threw it in the wastepaper basket. Then he fired the Browning into the fireplace and laid it back on the dressing-table.

When he stumbled into the saloon 'with every appearance of horror' Mitchell was sitting gloomily in a corner. But he quickly got up when he heard that 'something had happened to Mrs. Heewater'. The men went upstairs and took a look at Mrs. Heewater's room and then went to Tommy's room to put their heads together.

Pouring out whiskies all round, Tommy explained that Harry Biggers had bailed Heewater out to the tune of a tidy sum during his lifetime. Now that business was booming he had asked for his money back. But Beth had not been keen to pay up. It looked as though she had chosen to shoot him instead. At any rate they had to make up their minds what to do. As he said this he looked at Mitchell. Mitchell said he was for bringing Beth back and discussing with her what they should tell the police. They could say that the mate had tried to get fresh with her, for instance.

As soon as he said that he saw them all smile. It was a very unpleasant smile.

'Are you suggesting that we should bring in the police?' Tommy asked, giving the others a look.

'No, I was suggesting that we should try to bring Beth back,' said Mitchell.

'You know, I thought we might perhaps take care of this business for Beth,' said Tommy with a show of contempt. 'I mean, we men could do something for her.'

'That makes it my pigeon,' said Mitchell. 'What do you suggest?' Mitchell was no longer quite sober. He had been downing drinks steadily as he waited for Beth in the saloon. It was not too difficult to impress a few points on him. Tommy said the worst of it was, as his mate had told him, that there was a letter somewhere which Harry Biggers had received from Beth. She had asked him in this letter to come and see her. They had to get hold of it.

They all went up to Beth's bedroom and looked for the letter. Harry Biggers did not have it in his pocket, and it was not in the waste-paper basket. What there was in the basket was a torn-up photograph and Mitchell fished it out. Understandably, he did nothing to draw attention to it, but just slipped it casually into his pocket. This he was to regret.

In Tommy's room they all sank a few whiskies. Then Tommy suddenly decided that little Jane, the 'mite with the glasses' who was often in Harry Biggers's company, might have it. He remembered having seen the two of them together in the hall. Mitchell was sent to fetch her.

In the Heewater boarding house there was a young girl called Jane Russell who helped out in the kitchen and bedrooms, an unprepossessing creature with a long apron, thick stockings, glasses and very little of what is known as sex-appeal.

Mitchell was almost alone among the guests in sometimes treating her civilly. When the men in the boarding-house decided to prove to Beth Heewater that her fiancé was a coward, little Jane with her crush on Mitchell was given the central role in their plan of campaign.

Mitchell took the girl into a vacant room and questioned her. She told him straight out that she did not even know Biggers, nor had any letter been passed to her by him. Mitchell had plenty of drink in him by this time, but he could still see that she was telling the truth. With Jane Russell that was not hard to tell.

When he told the gentlemen that Jane did not have the letter, he again saw that fatal smile. Then Tommy said suddenly. 'And what about that letter you have in your pocket?'

Mitchell was slightly taken aback. He did in fact feel in his trouser pocket, and there of course was the torn-up photograph. He could not bring himself to produce it. They smiled again.

Then they brought a car round, loaded Harry Biggers into it and put Mitchell behind the wheel while the chauffeur was having a whisky in the bar. Mitchell was to put the body aboard the *Surface*, Tommy White's ship. He knew where she was lying and drove off.

But when he got there he found a police car at the foot of the gangway. No wonder. Tommy had phoned the police while Mitchell was questioning Jane and had told them that paraffin had been found in the coal bunker of the *Surface* and arson was suspected.

Mitchell nonetheless stumbled out of the car and went to the water's edge. He saw policemen on the *Surface* and turned unsteadily. When he got back to the car the body was gone. He took fright and drove to Beth's boarding house by a roundabout route.

Meanwhile back at the house something had happened to Jane. Since her cross-examination by Mitchell she had been keeping her eyes open and watching everything that happened in the house. She knew that Mrs. Heewater was confined to the room where the linen was kept. She saw Mr. White and Mr. Mitchell carry the seemingly drunk figure of Harry Biggers down the stairs, and she saw Mr. Mitchell drive off with him. Then she heard Mr. White talking to the chauffeur and telling him that a guest had made off with the car, while Mrs. Heewater stood by. She saw the man go to the phone and she heard him call the police.

This was when she stepped in. She went up to the chauffeur and told him that the man who had taken his car was a gentleman, and that the whole thing was a joke and no concern of the police. Beth Heewater interrupted her curtly and even tried to drag her away. But at this point little Jane went wild and fought with Beth Heewater in the hall, whereupon she was sacked. However Mitchell was at least spared the ordeal of being questioned by the police in a situation where he would not have been able to say anything.

There was something else which he was *not* spared.

He opened the saloon door and thought he was not seeing right. In a corner were Beth, Tommy and the others, ensconced behind glasses of whisky, and beside Beth, grinning, was Harry Biggers. And Beth, Tommy and the others were grinning too.

'You were going to tell us you had got rid of Harry?' said Tommy White to greet him, and there was nothing Mitchell could say. He stumbled out again and stood for a time in front of the house.

After a while he noticed that there was someone standing beside him, and that it was Jane Russell with tears in her eyes and suitcases in her hands. He discovered that Beth had thrown her out 'because she had assaulted Mrs. Heewater on Mitchell's behalf'. She had no relatives in London and did not know where to turn, and it was getting late. Mitchell told her she could come back with him and that was how he came to bring her home in the early hours. He gave her his own room and lay down on the living room sofa, still very drunk.

In the morning an awkward situation arose. His sister to her great surprise found little Jane in his bedroom. Mitchell sputtered incoherently, especially when he noticed a distinct coolness as his sister listened to him. He did however manage to make it clear that Jane was a servant, so she was given breakfast in the kitchen. This was not entirely what he would have wished, and, worse still, he then had to talk to Jane in the presence of the family. He put on a friendly face and asked her about her intentions, agreeing that it would be best for her to go into a certain home where servants were boarded cheaply. Unfortunately he had spoken with Jane about this very same home as they were returning in the night. She had said that it was very bad and too expensive for her anyhow, at best a last resort for two or three days.

When Jane had left with her cases Mitchell had the feeling for the first time that he was a coward.

In the next few days he pursued his search for a new appointment with renewed zeal. His family played ostrich and simply took no notice of the change in the situation. His sister even bought a piano on hire purchase just at that time.

He found no new appointment. They seemed to have heard all about him everywhere. There were not too many commands for captains of luxury liners, even courageous ones.

Preoccupied as he was, he even forgot to enquire about Jane at the home for three days. On the fourth his sister asked him about her and he went along. She had moved out after two days. But that evening he was offered a command.

Down by the East India Docks was a firm run by two brothers which had an extremely bad reputation. These two sent word that they might have something for him. He went along and was told there was a chance for him to take a collier to Holland for them.

'You've had bad luck of late, Mitchell,' said one of the brothers, grinning, 'but this is just the job to get you out of the rut. You won't put out another SOS in a hurry, will you?'

Mitchell swallowed this and went to look at the collier with them. It was the oldest, dirtiest, most battered old tub he had ever seen. There was no way in which a hulk like this could ever make Rotterdam. Nor did the brothers want it to. It was a clearcut case of an insurance swindle, nothing else.

Mitchell's good name and his sense of responsibility (which is after all only the reverse side of cowardice) made him the ideal captain for the trip.

He felt a certain gut reaction, but he fought it down and did not say no. He asked for time to think it over and turned on his heel. From time to time he stopped in front of a shop window and talked to his own reflection.

'Are you a coward?' he asked, and Mitchell in the mirror shrugged his shoulders.

'Have you always been one?' he asked, and Mitchell in the mirror shook his head.

Then he met Jane. She was standing in a doorway waiting for something. He thought the worst and did not dare to walk past her. So it was from the other side of the road that he watched a man, who no doubt thought the same as him, accost her. But she appeared to reject his approaches very vigorously. Then Mitchell went across to her and invited her into a café. She replied that would be fine, provided she could sit at the window and watch the street. She was expecting a friend who knew of a job.

During those twenty minutes in the café Mitchell's life touched rock bottom.

In an effort to be friendly he opened the conversation by remarking that she looked well.

That surprised her, she said, looking him straight in the eye. She was no coward. And without turning a hair she ate up all the cakes that he pushed towards her. She had no objection to letting him see that she had not eaten.

In some confusion he then went over to telling her that she would have to do something about her appearance if she wanted another job. He criticised her hair-do and even took off her glasses. She had beautiful eyes.

She replied that she would rather not have the kind of job where she had to look pretty. Though she feared that the job her girl-friend had heard of was one such.

Thereupon he began, to his own astonishment, to press her not to take that kind of job. He even went so far as to suggest that she should accept money from him and live off that until such times as she found something better.

To his annoyance she did not seem to take his offer seriously at all. For at this juncture she saw her girl-friend (the one with the bad job), stood up and hurried out. He just managed to get her address.

After this little experience he should have been completely shattered, but in fact he was rather cheered. He now knew that something had to happen to put an end to the whole sad tale. He went into a bar and drank several whiskies, rather more than he could hold. It was only when he realised that he was no longer seeing *one* glass where there was only one that he left.

He went straight home.

His father and his younger sister were sitting in the living room. They were listening to *Traviata* on the wireless. He turned off the music and told them without beating about the bush that they would have to move out of their eight-room flat into a two-room flat, and that his sisters would have to find office jobs, since the company had thrown him out for reasons that need not concern them.

Then he slept like a log, and in the morning he took his sisters, including the elder one, to an employment agency. They were quite cowed. It was clear to him that some of their lost respect for him was returning. There was not even any protest from his elder sister when he told her to give her fiancé his marching orders if he seemed dissatisfied with his prospective brother-in-law.

The second thing he did was to ring the brothers with the collier boat. He said he would sign up with them and asked them to have the papers ready. He fixed the day of departure with them. They were to come aboard the collier the evening before and hand over the papers. He meanwhile would muster a crew. The evening in question was to be a Tuesday.

The third thing he did was to ring up a goodly number of people and invite them for Tuesday to a little supper aboard the *Almaida*. Among them were the gentlemen from the boarding-house, among them was Beth Heewater, among them was even his former owner. They all accepted, even J. B. Watch. Outwardly Mitchell's relations with his colleagues and with his former boss had remained just as they had been before the 'incident'. They still slapped him on the back when they met him anywhere. The only thing now was that all of them had that damned smile which Mitchell did not like, not one little bit.

Then he sent an invitation to a reporter of his acquaintance, ordered an excellent supper from the Savoy with waiters to serve it on board the *Almaida*, and addressed himself on the Tuesday morning to point four.

Point four was Jane.

He managed to find her in a crummy boarding-house, still without a job. There was only one subject in this doss-house that he viewed with pleasure, and that was his (torn) photograph. She had managed to get hold of it on that decisive evening and there it was on the dressing-table. Jane made no effort to conceal it.

'Don't you want to hide it from me at least?' he asked, but she shook her head. This being the case everything else was comparatively simple. There was a certain conflict when he took off her glasses ('I will be your guide and see for both of us'), and as he combed her hair into a new style ('Beth doesn't think hair combed over your forehead is pretty').

On the *Almaida* everything was ship-shape. The waiters raised an eyebrow at the room in which they were to set up their classy and expensive things. Keynes, the reporter, was there already and they had a good laugh over what was to come.

About nine the first guests rolled up. By a quarter to ten the whole lot were there. Jane had done the honours, and Beth's face showed that she registered this as a courageous move on Mitchell's part. Mitchell stood up and made a short speech.

He explained that he had decided, at the behest of Messrs. Knife (he bowed to the brothers), to take this ship to Rotterdam. He was doing this because making a fresh start showed courage, and certain doubts had been cast on his courage of late. To ensure that everybody who had recently taken an interest in his courage would have the chance to see that courage in action, he would take the liberty of inviting them along in this little voyage.

At that moment the ship began to vibrate as ships do when they put to sea, and the engines started up so that everybody could hear them.

The surprise was quite striking.

In the improvised dining room there was absolute panic. The men made for the door. The door was locked. The women screamed: then Mitchell went on.

'Ladies and gentlemen,' he said, 'if you were familiar with the state of the deck of my *Almaida*, you wouldn't rush around on it like that. The door you are heaving at is more or less the only sound piece of wood on the ship, it won't give. The state of the ship is the reason why it was so highly insured, am I right, Messrs. Knife? Given the uncertainty of her making her destination, she had to be insured. Of course it takes no little courage to take a thing like this out on the high seas, but that courage I have. You will be pleased to hear this, and I fancy there will be one or two things you will wish me to forgive. You too, Beth, doubted whether I would have the courage to do away with something nobody wanted to see again. Well this ship, the *Almaida*, is just such a thing. And I will get rid of it, fear not! And you, Watch, need not fear that I will call for the assistance of another ship before this one has gone to the bottom. I did so once and I will not do it again. Cowardice needs to be resisted, does it not?'

I shall cut it short. There were a few more rather unworthy scenes. Most of those present were most regrettably lacking in courage. J. B. Watch even offered his former captain his old job back, before witnesses. Tommy White behaved like a madman. And Harry Biggers almost died in earnest.

Mitchell, disgusted and at the same time satisfied with the results of his experiment, let his guests tread dry land again before too long. When the door was opened it became apparent that Mitchell had just let the ship ride on steel hawsers in the current to make it move. His guests' cars were visible from the ship.

Keynes promised Mitchell that he would sit on the story, at least for the time being.

'You see, I'm certainly not such a coward as to turn down J. B. Watch's offer,' said Mitchell gaily. 'So long as he sticks by it,' added Jane, pressing close to him.

'He will,' said Keynes cynically.

THE SOLDIER OF LA CIOTAT

After the First World War, during a fête to celebrate the launching of a ship in the small port town of La Ciotat in the South of France, we saw in a public square the bronze statue of a French soldier with a crowd pressing round it. We went closer and found that it was a living man standing there in a dun-coloured greatcoat, a tin hat on his head, his bayonet fixed, motionless on a plinth in the hot June sun. His face and hands were coated with bronze paint. He did not move a muscle, not even his eyelashes flickered.

At his feet a piece of cardboard was propped against the plinth with the following legend:

HUMAN STATUE
(L'Homme Statue)

I, Charles Louis Franchard, private in the . .th regiment, have acquired as a result of being buried alive at Verdun, the unusual faculty of remaining as motionless *as a statue* for any desired length of time. This skill of mine has been tested by many professors and described as an inexplicable disease. Please contribute a small donation to the unemployed father of a family.

We threw a coin into the plate which stood by the placard and walked away, shaking our heads.

So here he stands, we thought, armed to the teeth, the indestructible soldier of the long millennia, he with whom history was made, he who enabled Alexander, Caesar and Napoleon to perform those great deeds we read about in school text-books. This is he. He does not flicker an eyelash. This is Cyrus's archer, Cambyses's scythe-wheeled charioteer whom the sands of the desert could not bury for all eternity, Caesar's legionary, Jenghis Khan's mounted lancer, Louis XIV's Swiss Guard, Napoleon I's grenadier. His is the faculty – not, after all, so unusual – of not betraying his feelings when every conceivable instrument of destruction is tried out on him. He remains (he says) like a stone, without feeling, when he is sent to his death. Pierced by spears of every possible age – stone, bronze, iron – mown down by the chariots of war, those of Artaxerxes and those of General Ludendorff, trampled underfoot by Hannibal's elephants and Attila's horsemen, smashed to pieces by flying metal from the ever-improved guns of many centuries, though also by flying stones from catapults, riddled by rifle bullets as big as pigeons' eggs, as small as bees, he stands indestructible, ever commanded anew in diverse tongues, but never knowing why or wherefore. It was not he who took possession of the lands he conquered, just as the mason does not live in the house he has built. Nor indeed did the territory he defended belong to him. Not even his weapon or his equipment belongs to him. But he stands under the rain of death from aircraft and burning pitch from city walls, mine and pitfall beneath his feet, pestilence and mustard gas around him, there he stands, flesh-and-blood quiver for javelin and arrow, target, tank pulp, gas inhaler, with the enemy in front of him and the General behind.

The untold hands that wove the jacket, forged the armour, cut the boots for him! The untold pockets that were filled by him! The immeasurable clamour in *every* language in the world that urged him on! No god who did not bless him. He who is afflicted by the hideous leprosy of patience, sapped by the incurable disease of imperviousness.

What sort of burying alive is this, we thought, to which he owes this disease, this frightful, monstrous, supremely infectious disease?

Might it not, we asked ourselves, be curable after all?

A MISTAKE

Karl Krucke, a small, thickset lathe operator from Halle an der Saale who had come to France in 1936 because the Gestapo were showing too much interest in him, was found lodgings by friends in the house of a French metalworker in the Paris *banlieue*. He did not speak a word of French, but he knew what *Front Populaire* meant and that the things they said to him when sharing that lovely French bread were friendly. He lived quietly with these people, went regularly to the *mairie* and to meetings arranged by German friends where they held discussions and were able to read the newspapers. But after a few weeks he began to look yellow and to complain of stabbing pains on the right side of his belly, so friends gave him a note with the address of a good specialist who was prepared, they said, to examine him free of charge on the following Friday at seven o'clock. They urged him to be punctual, since the doctor was a very busy man.

This was unnecessary since Krucke was always punctual, and his pains were giving him a great deal of trouble.

He rose early that Friday, wrapped one leg of an old pair of drawers tightly round his middle and set out to walk to Paris.

He was not quite without cash, but he thought he would save the fare, for he had unlimited time, far too much time indeed.

It was April and still dark on the streets. For a while he did not meet a soul. The road ran through open fields and was in bad repair, full of holes, but there was no wind and it was not particularly cold. From time to time he would pass a farmhouse and a dog would bark. He could see neither the fields nor the farms because of the darkness. Yet this did not make them seem any less foreign. It was undoubtedly not Germany.

Thank God he was walking on a main road, so there were no decisions to be made at crossroads, otherwise he might have had problems with signposts. On the other hand he could ask people; it would suffice to say Paree in a questioning tone. That was what they called Paris in those parts.

After he had been walking for an hour he heard a horse and cart rattling behind him. He stopped and let it go by. The cart was loaded high with cabbages. A wizened old man nodded when he said Paree in a questioning tone. But he did not ask him to climb aboard, though he did look round again ten metres further on as if he were still contemplating such an invitation.

When the next cart passed him, carrying a load of milk churns and driven by a plump woman, he produced a few gestures to ask whether he could get on. But the woman did not stop. He decided that she did not trust the stout stick which he had carved himself out of a young willow. For the going was bad with the pains in his side.

These two experiences put the little man off making further attempts to get a lift in a cart, although the carts began to come along more and more frequently. The famous giant convoys of vegetables, milk and fruit were beginning to converge on the city in the hours after first light from every point in the fertile countryside.

For a while the tramping and rattling was constant. He had to keep stepping aside, for the peasants did not bother to keep to the right since hardly any vehicles were coming in the opposite direction. Paris was asleep and had nothing to offer the country in the early hours.

At one time the lathe operator walked along a railway line. When the train thundered by he stood still. He could not read the destination boards on the coaches, the train was going far too fast, but the train could not be coming from Germany, for he was to the south of the city.

About half past four the sky became light. The region had changed its appearance, the fields had been left behind, these were the suburbs.

Small houses with gardens and fine trees. Streets of houses with a café already open here and there. Sleepy waiters with dirty aprons and brilliantine on their hair were putting wicker chairs on the pavement. At the counter drivers were downing their coffee and cognac.

Then more stretches with nurseries, greenhouses, walls covered with posters, notices from the *mairie*. A cement works.

By now the cartloads of provisions had probably reached the markets. Only a few stragglers were still driving their horses on. But there were now more cars. They could start later. They were the type of car that had a coffin-shaped bonnet, mostly blue.

Then came the belt of buses and trams, packed with workers.

The thickset little man from Halle an der Saale walked with even strides, somewhat tired, with rather more pains in his belly. Now as he passed the cafés he looked more often at the white clocks behind the bar. He had to be at the Boulevard Saint Michel at seven o'clock sharp.

By about five it was fully light, and half an hour later he could feel the sun. He had crossed the city boundary.

Walking became harder on the stone and asphalt. And there was traffic here too. Mainly workers carrying billy-cans. And a big water-cart whose fan of jets sent people jumping. The city was being cleaned and tidied up. For the daily grind that brought in the dinner, rent, children's school money, *gauloises*, the city had to be clean.

For all these people, all the Frenchmen worked and struggled and lived. The lathe operator from Halle an der Saale understood that, because he too had worked, struggled and lived in Germany.

In fact he was still struggling, of course, and in a sense he was still working too, and wasn't he living as well? Dead men did not have pains in the belly.

His march to the Boulevard Saint-Michel was an act in the struggle. And he had allies, friends who had given him the note, and the Front Populaire, a mighty support!

The question was now, 'Boulvahr Sang Meeshell?'

Then it was a side street, number 123. A tall, narrow, distinctive house. It was half past six.

Half past six is not seven. There were few signs of life in the house. So now he'd have to wait.

The lathe operator took up his position opposite. Once a servant came out of the house, once a maid in a bonnet, once a portly man with a red face stepped out on to the pavement and looked round. Then a *flic*, a policeman, walked down the street, and he had to move on to the next corner so that it wouldn't look as if he was up to no good. Policemen the world over require this, it doesn't vary.

Then it was seven o'clock.

The thickset little man crossed the street and went up the stairs. The red balloon face he had seen before appeared at the window in the hallway. The con-syersh! Krucke showed him the note with the doctor's name. The con-syersh said something with much gesticulation which did not do much to explain matters. He ended with a violent shrug and the way was clear.

You climbed the stairs on a red coconut runner. The house was damned posh. He must be a good doctor.

There was his brass plate. All you have to do is ring the bell.

A maid opened the door. The lathe operator pronounced the doctor's name. The French workmate with whom he lodged had taught him how to say it the previous evening.

But the girl shook her head in astonishment. She too said a good deal in that damned language, and once again the accompanying gestures did nothing to clarify the matter. What was the use of pointing into the flat with his stick and at his belly where the pain was with his finger? The girl simply shut the door.

Only one of her gestures had made sense. She had pointed to the brass plate where he could read 5–8. These were of course the consulting hours. But he was to be taken outside of hours, naturally enough, since he could not pay! That was why it was fixed for seven in the morning, unusual though the hour was, so he could be taken before the doctor's real business started. As he had understood it, the doctor was doing overtime for him so to speak, because he was busy later, a specialist for whom every minute means money, in a house with coconut runners and servants, all of which cost money and more money.

At such a moment it would help to speak French.

He had stood outside the closed door. But down on the landing balloon-face appeared, redder than ever. He was probably suspicious. The stick alone must look suspicious. And his trousers were not the newest.

The lathe operator went down the stairs again, past the consyersh and out of the door. There was nothing else to do.

Probably the doctor had forgotten to say that he was coming and was to be let in early. Such people have a lot on their mind. And the examination was free.

It was also possible that the doctor had been called out to an operation. In that case a new time would have to be arranged, before or after his consulting hours. There was nothing to be gained from a rash move. On Sunday evening he was meeting his friends. The next move could be discussed then.

The little man sat on a stone pillar in a niche in the wall of the house, unpacked the provisions his host had given him and chewed the white bread.

Then he set out slowly for the outskirts. He would get there in the afternoon.

When the French doctor, a friendly and helpful man, asked a few days later why the patient had not turned up and was told that the German had assumed seven o'clock to mean seven a.m. – since he never expected to get free treatment in regular consulting hours, he was dumbfounded.

GAUMER AND IRK

To fell Irk was easy. He was very busy, and he looked after many but not after himself. Gaumer had beaten him to death before he noticed how extraordinarily hard it was to bury him.

He was lying on the floor of the office, and Gaumer first tried to take him on his shoulders. But that of course was impossible. Gaumers cannot carry Irks.

So Gaumer took him by the left leg and pulled him with all his might towards the door. Irk's other leg wedged itself so firmly against the doorpost that Gaumer had to drag the corpse back into the office, this time by the head which did not afford a good grip. Gaumer was glad to get Irk back in the room where he had been lying before. Covered with sweat, he sat down on a chair and breathed deeply.

Gaumer began to ponder. He pondered more deeply than he had ever pondered before. Irk ought to be pulled head first through the door. That was the solution. There was always a solution if you only pondered fearlessly. So Irk had always said.

While pulling Irk to the door by his head Gaumer twice fell because he lost his grip on Irk's head. No wonder; that head had not been designed as a handle. All the same, the corpse was now lying on the landing and its own (excessive) weight ought to take it down the stairs. A kick from Gaumer sufficed. Of course the banister at the foot of the stairs fell to pieces under the impact. The thing was rotten, Irk had always said they ought to have had it replaced. Pity that Gaumer had never agreed to this. Now people would see it when they came to work next morning.

Anyhow Irk was now downstairs, and that was progress. At least it would be progress when he was moved on, for there he was more likely to be discovered than up in the office.

And now things took a very nasty turn. Gaumer realised after struggling desperately with the body for two hours that he would never get it outside on his own. The space between the stairs and the door was too narrow and the door opened inwards. Gaumer could not open the door and lift the body at the same time. He could not even turn it on to its side and that was what he would have to do. It had to be turned at all costs.

Gaumer saw that there was nothing for it but to fetch his nephew and explain all. That was terrible. That lazy, spoilt lout would make him pay dearly for his help. Of course if he had not been lazy and spoilt Gaumer would not have been able to turn to him in such a matter. After tonight he would be entirely in the fellow's hands, which meant that he would have to do away with him. That was a fine prospect.

True enough, his nephew looked at him rather more than curiously when he told him his story. All the same he came along straight away. Gaumer had the impression that he came rather too easily. He could scarcely contain his delight, it seemed. The two of them managed to open the door and drag the body through the doorway. And then suddenly they could not move it another step.

What was wrong? There was nothing in the way and there were two of them. The main part of the job seemed to be done. It took some time for them to work out what had happened. At first it seemed to Gaumer that his eyesight had suddenly begun to fail. As he held Irk's feet together, his nephew, who was pulling Irk by the head, struck him as strangely far away. Then his nephew suddenly said, 'He's growing.'

Yes indeed, that was it. Irk in his lifetime had not been much bigger than Gaumer, at least in Gaumer's eyes. After the murder, in the office, hard as he had proved to carry, he had still retained his more or less natural dimensions. But now in the open air he was inconceivably big. His legs seemed like two pillars and his head was like a spherically pruned laurel tree. And he was still growing.

While the two of them stood there looking at him in horror, the uncle from the foot, the nephew from the head, the body grew longer and fatter at amazing speed. It was no longer a man, it was a giant.

How was this colossal heap of flesh and bones to be buried, how was this mountain to be put underground?

Gaumer did all he could to fight down his panic. They would have to get ropes immediately, or better still steel cables. If they put a truck in front of Irk and towed him they might still just manage to get him down to the canal that flowed past the factory. Lucky that Gaumer carried all the keys and had such things as trucks and cables at his disposal.

He proceeded to the sheds with leaden steps.

In backing the truck out of the shed he ran over Irk's leg. It was as if he had run over a block of granite; the springs groaned and one of them snapped.

Irk's body was now a good five metres long and one and a half metres in diameter. To raise one foot so as to put a cable round it they had to use a jack. That bent as well. In the end the whole contraption broke down.

Climbing into the lorry, Gaumer caught a glance from his

nephew which troubled him deeply. The man was clearly afraid of him. That made him very dangerous. He plainly realised now that Gaumer would have to do away with him once the job was done, and he was no doubt mulling over plans to beat his uncle somehow to the punch. Gaumer would have to do him in at the first possible opportunity, but only after the job was done, that went without saying.

The cable slipped off Irk's foot twice, then the engine turned out to be short of power and simply stalled. The driver ought to have been cut into little pieces. Why didn't he keep his engine in proper running order? Or was there some dark purpose behind it?

Gaumer ran into the second shed in a sweat.

They now had two lorries harnessed to the body with the uncle driving the front one and the nephew driving the one behind. So they could not see what was happening to the body. First the vehicles faltered, then there was a jerk, and the rear lorry ran into the one in front. Gaumer climbed out cursing. The body had been dragged a short way forward, but the radiator of the second truck had been bashed in by its collision with the one in front.

They tried again. From a certain point the yard sloped down towards the canal. There they began to skid and the body now developed the impetus of a loaded truck on its own and stepped up their speed tremendously. And in addition the bad light made it hard to drive properly. Too bad they could not have done the job by daylight . . .

With a crash that must have been heard for miles Gaumer's lorry thundered into the canal with its brakes full on, and behind him the same thing happened to his nephew.

When Gaumer emerged from the muddy water and reached the edge, he heard splashing and saw his nephew swimming towards the embankment. The two lorries had disappeared completely into the canal. But Irk's body, although it was right in the canal, was not covered by the water. Huge, gigantic, so vast he could never be hidden, Irk's head and knees jutted out of the black waters.

Madness in his eye, Gaumer trampled on the fingers with which his nephew was clinging to the embankment as he tried to clamber out of the water.

SOCRATES WOUNDED

Socrates, the midwife's son, who was able in his dialogues to deliver his friends of well-proportioned thoughts so soundly and easily and with such hearty jests, thus providing them with children of their own, instead of, like other teachers, foisting bastards on them, was considered not only the cleverest of all Greeks but also one of the bravest. His reputation for bravery strikes us as quite justified when we read in Plato how coolly and unflinchingly he drained the hemlock which the authorities offered him in the end for services rendered to his fellow-citizens. Some of his admirers, however, have felt the need to speak of his bravery in the field as well. It is a fact that he fought at the battle of Delium, and this in the light infantry, since neither his standing, a cobbler's, nor his income, a philosopher's, entitled him to enter the more distinguished and expensive branches of the service. Nevertheless, as you may suppose, his bravery was of a special kind.

On the morning of the battle Socrates had primed himself as best he could for the bloody business by chewing onions which, in the soldiers' view, induced valour. His scepticism in many spheres led to credulity in many others; he was against speculative thought and in favour of practical experience; so he did not believe in the gods, but he did believe in onions.

Unfortunately he felt no real effect, at least no immediate one, and so he traipsed glumly in a detachment of swordsmen who were marching in single file to take up their position in a stubble field somewhere. Behind and ahead stumbled Athenian boys from the suburbs, who pointed out that the shields from the Athenian arsenals were too small for fat people like him. He had been thinking the same thing, but in terms of *broad* people who were less than half covered by the absurdly narrow shields.

The exchange of views between the man in front of him and the man behind on the profits made by the big armourers out of small shields was cut short by the order: 'Fall out'.

They dropped on to the stubble and a captain reprimanded Socrates for trying to sit on his shield. He was less upset by the reprimand than by the hushed voice in which it was given. Apparently the enemy were thought to be near.

The milky morning haze completely obscured the view. Yet the noise of tramping and of clanking arms indicated that the plain was peopled.

With great disquiet Socrates remembered a conversation he had had the previous evening with a fashionable young man whom he had once met behind the scenes and who was a cavalry officer.

'A capital plan!' the young puppy had explained. 'The infantry just waits drawn up, loyal and steadfast, and takes the brunt of the enemy's attack. And meanwhile the cavalry advances in the valley and falls on him from the rear.'

The valley must lie fairly far to the right, somewhere in the mist. No doubt the cavalry was advancing there now.

The plan had struck Socrates as good, or at any rate not bad. After all, plans were always made, particularly when your strength was inferior to the enemy's. When it came to brass tacks, it was simply a matter of fighting, that is, slashing away. And there was no advance according to plan, but merely according to where the enemy let you.

Now, in the grey dawn, the plan struck Socrates as altogether wretched. What did it mean: the infantry takes the enemy's attack? Usually one was glad to evade an attack, now, all of a sudden, the art lay in taking the brunt of it. A very bad thing that the general himself was a cavalryman.

The ordinary man would need more onions than there were on the market.

And how unnatural it was, instead of lying in bed, to be sitting here on the bare ground in the middle of a field so early in the morning, carrying at least ten pounds of iron about your person and a butcher's knife in your hand. It was quite right to defend the city if it was attacked, for otherwise you would be exposed to gross inconveniences; but why was the city attacked? Because the shipowners, vineyard proprietors and slave-traders in Asia Minor had put a spoke in the wheel of Persian shipowners, vineyard proprietors and slave-traders. A fine reason!

Suddenly everyone sat up.

Through the mist on the left came a muffled roar accompanied by the clang of metal. It spread fairly rapidly. The enemy's attack had begun.

The detachment stood up. With bulging eyes they stared into

the mist before them. Ten paces away a man fell on his knees and gibbered an appeal to the gods. Too late, in Socrates' view.

All at once, as if in answer, a fearful roar issued from further to the right. The cry for help seemed to have merged into a death-cry. Socrates saw a little iron rod come flying out of the mist. A javelin.

And then massive shapes, indistinct in the haze, appeared in front: the enemy.

Socrates, with an overpowering sense that perhaps he had already waited too long, turned about awkwardly and took to his heels. His breastplate and heavy greaves hampered him a good deal. They were far more dangerous than shields, because you could not throw them away.

Panting, the philosopher ran across the stubble. Everything depended on whether he could get a good enough start. If only the brave lads behind him were taking the attack for a bit.

Suddenly a fiendish pain shot through him. His left sole stung till he felt he simply could not bear it. Groaning, he sank to the ground, but leapt up again with another yell of pain. With frantic eyes he looked about him and realised what was up. He had landed in a field full of thorns.

There was a tangle of low undergrowth with sharp thorns. A thorn must have stuck in his foot. Carefully, with streaming eyes, he searched for a spot on the ground where he could sit down. He hobbled a few steps in a circle on his sound foot before lowering himself for the second time. He must pull the thorn out at once.

He listened intently to the noise of battle: it extended pretty far on both sides, though straight ahead it was at least a hundred paces away. However, it seemed to be coming nearer, slowly but unmistakably.

Socrates could not get his sandal off. The thorn had pieced the thin leather sole and was deeply embedded in his flesh. How dared they supply soldiers, who were supposed to defend their country against the enemy, with such thin shoes? Each tug at the sandal was attended by searing pain. Exhausted, the poor man's massive shoulders drooped. What now?

His dejected eye fell on the sword at his side. A thought flashed through his mind, more welcome than any that ever came to him in debate. Couldn't the sword be used as a knife? He grabbed it.

At that moment he heard heavy footsteps. A small squad broke through the scrub. Thank the gods, they were his own side! They halted for a few seconds when they saw him. 'That's the cobbler,' he heard them say. Then they went on.

But now there was a noise from the left too. And there orders in a foreign language rang out. The Persians!

Socrates tried to get to his feet again, that is, to his right foot. He leant on his sword, which was only a little too short. And then, to the left, in the small clearing, he saw a cluster of men locked in combat. He heard heavy groans and the impact of dull iron on iron or leather.

Desperately he hopped backwards on his sound foot. Twisting it he came down again on the injured one and dropped with a moan. When the battling cluster – it was not large, a matter of perhaps twenty or thirty men – had approached to within a few paces, the philosopher was sitting on his backside between two briars looking helplessly at the enemy.

It was impossible for him to move. Anything was better than to feel that pain in the ball of his foot even once more. He did not know what to do and suddenly he started to bellow.

To be precise it was like this: he heard himself bellowing. He heard his voice roaring from the mighty barrel of his thorax: 'Over here, Third Battalion! Let them have it, lads!'

And simultaneously he saw himself gripping the sword and swinging it round him in a circle, for in front of him, appearing from the scrub, stood a Persian soldier with a spear. The spear was knocked sideways, tearing the man down with it.

And Socrates heard himself bellowing again and saying:

'Not another step back, lads! Now we've got them where we want them, the sons of bitches! Crapolus, bring up the Sixth! Nullus, to the right! If anyone retreats I'll tear him to shreds!'

To his surprise he saw two of his own side standing by gaping at him in terror. 'Roar!' he said softly, 'for heaven's sake, roar!' One of them let his jaw drop with fright, but the other actually started roaring something. And the Persian in front of them got up painfully and ran into the brush.

A dozen exhausted men came stumbling out of the clearing. The yelling had made the Persians turn tail. They feared an ambush.

'What's going on here?' one of his fellow-countrymen asked Socrates, who was still sitting on the ground.

'Nothing,' he said. 'Don't stand about like that gaping at me. You'd better run to and fro giving orders, then they won't realise how few we are.'

'We'd better retreat,' said the man hesitantly.

'Not one step!' Socrates protested. 'Have you got cold feet?'

And as a soldier needs to have not only fear, but also luck, they suddenly heard from some way off, but quite clearly, the trampling of horses and wild shouts, and these were in Greek! Everyone knows how overwhelmingly the Persians were routed that day. It finished the war.

As Alcibiades at the head of the cavalry reached the field of brambles, he saw a group of foot soldiers carrying a stout man shoulder high.

Reining in his horse, he recognised Socrates, and the soldiers told him how, by his unflinching resistance, he had made the wavering battle-line stand firm.

They bore him in triumph to the baggage-train. There, despite his protests, he was put on one of the forage wagons and, surrounded by soldiers streaming with sweat and shouting excitedly, he made his return to the capital.

He was carried shoulder high to his little house.

Xantippe, his wife, made bean soup for him. Kneeling at the hearth and blowing at the fire with puffed out cheeks, she glanced at him from time to time. He was still sitting on the chair where his comrades had set him down.

'What's the matter with *you*?' she asked suspiciously.

'Me?' he muttered, 'nothing.'

'What's all this talk about your heroic deeds?' she wanted to know.

'Exaggeration,' he said. 'It smells first class.'

'How can it smell when I haven't got the fire going yet? I suppose you've made a fool of yourself again,' she said angrily. 'And tomorrow when I go for the bread I shall find myself a laughing-stock again.'

'I've not made a fool of myself at all. I gave battle.'

'Were you drunk?'

'No. I made them stand firm when they were retreating.'

'You can't even stand firm yourself,' she said, getting up, for the fire had caught. 'Pass me the salt-cellar from the table.'

'I'm not sure,' he said slowly and reflectively, 'I'm not sure if I wouldn't prefer on the whole not to eat anything. My stomach's a little upset.'

'Just as I said; you're drunk. Try standing up and walking about the room a bit. We'll soon see.'

Her unfairness exasperated him. But in no circumstances did he intend to stand up and show her that he could not put his foot to the ground. She was uncannily sharp when it came to nosing out something discreditable to him. And it would be discreditable if the underlying reason for his steadfastness in battle came to light.

She went on busying herself round the stove with the pot and in between let him know her mind.

'I haven't any doubt that your fine friends found you some funk-hole again, well in the rear, near the cookhouse. It's all a fiddle.'

In torment he looked out of the little window on to the street where a lot of people with white lanterns were strolling about, for the victory was being celebrated.

His grand friends had tried to do nothing of the sort, nor would he have agreed to it; at all events, not straight off.

'Or did they think it quite in order for the cobbler to march in the ranks? They won't lift a finger for you. He's a cobbler, they say, and let him stay a cobbler. Otherwise we shouldn't be able to visit him in his filthy dump and jabber with him for hours on end and hear the whole world say: what do you think of that, he may be a cobbler, but these grand people sit about with him and talk philersophy. Filthy lot!'

'It's called philerphoby,' he said equably.

She gave him an unfriendly look.

'Don't keep on correcting me. I know I'm uneducated. If I weren't you wouldn't have anybody to bring you a tub of water now and again to wash your feet.'

He winced and hoped she had not noticed it. On no account must there be any question of washing his feet today. Thank the gods, she was off again on her harangue.

'Well, if you weren't drunk and they didn't find a funk-hole for you either, then you must have behaved like a butcher. So there's blood on your hands, eh? But if I squash a spider, you start shouting. Not that I believe you really fought like a man, but you must have done something crafty, something a bit under-hand or they wouldn't be slapping you on the back like this. I'll find out sooner or later, don't you worry.'

The soup was now ready. It smelled enticing. The woman took the pot and, holding the handles with her skirt, set it on the table and began to ladle it out.

He wondered whether, after all, he had not better recover his appetite. The thought that he would then have to go to the table restrained him just in time.

He did not feel at all easy. He was well aware that the last word had not yet been said. There was bound to be a lot of unpleasantness before long. You could hardly decide a battle against the Persians and be left in peace. At the moment, in the first flush of victory, no one, of course, gave a thought to the man responsible for it. Everyone was fully occupied proclaiming his own glorious deeds from the housetops. But tomorrow or the day after, everyone would wake up to the fact that the other fellow was claiming all the credit, and then they would be anxious to push him forward. So many would be able to score off so many others if the cobbler were proclaimed the real hero in chief. They couldn't stand Alcibiades as it was. What pleasure it would give them to throw in his teeth: Yes, you won the battle, but a cobbler fought it.

And the thorn hurt more savagely than ever. If he did not get his sandal off soon, it might mean blood-poisoning.

'Don't smack your lips like that,' he said absentmindedly.

The spoon remained stuck in his wife's mouth.

'Don't do what?'

'Nothing,' he hastened to assure her in alarm. 'I was miles away.'

She stood up, beside herself, banged the pot down on the stove and went out.

He heaved a deep sigh of relief. Hastily he levered himself out of the chair and hopped to his couch at the back, looking round nervously. As she came back to fetch her wrap to go out she looked suspiciously at the way he lay motionless on the leather-covered hammock. For a moment she thought there must be something the matter with him after all. She even considered asking him, for she was very devoted to him. But she thought better of it and left the room sulkily to watch the festivities with the woman from next door.

Socrates slept badly and restlessly and woke up feeling worried. He had got his sandal off, but had not been able to get hold of the thorn. His foot was badly swollen.

His wife was less sharp than usual this morning.

She had heard the whole city talking about her husband the evening before. Something really must have happened to impress people so deeply. That he had held up an entire Persian battle-line she certainly could not accept. Not him, she told herself. Yes, hold up an entire public meeting with his questions, he could do that all right. But not a battle-line. So what had happened?

She was so uncertain that she brought him in goat's milk in bed.

He made no attempt to get up.

'Aren't you going out?' she asked.

'Don't feel like it,' he growled.

That is not the way to answer a civil question from your wife, but she thought that perhaps he only wanted to avoid being stared at and let the answer pass.

Visitors began arriving early: a few young men, the sons of well-off parents, his usual associates. They always treated him as their teacher and some of them even made notes while he talked, as though it were something quite special.

Today they told him at once that Athens resounded with his fame. It was an historic date for philosophy (so she had been right after all: it was called philersophy and not something else). Socrates had demonstrated, they said, that the great thinker could also be the great man of action.

Socrates listened to them without his usual mockery. As they spoke he seemed to hear, still far away, as one hears a distant thunderstorm, stupendous laughter, the laughter of a whole city, even of a whole country, far away, but drawing nearer, irresistibly approaching, infecting everyone: the passers-by in the streets, the merchants and politicians in the market-place, the artisans in their little workshops.

'That's all rubbish what you're saying,' he said with a sudden resolve. 'I didn't do anything at all.'

They looked at each other and smiled. Then one of them said: 'That's just what we said. We knew you'd take it like that. What's this hullabaloo all of a sudden, we asked Eusopulos outside the gymnasium. For ten years Socrates has been performing the greatest intellectual feats and no one so much as turned his head to look at him. Now he's won a battle and the whole of Athens is talking about him. Don't you see how disgraceful it is, we said.'

Socrates groaned.

'But I didn't win it at all. I defended myself because I was attacked. I wasn't interested in this battle. I neither trade in arms nor do I own vineyards in the area. I wouldn't know what to fight battles for. I found myself among a lot of sensible men from the suburbs, who have no interest in battles, and I did exactly what they all did, at the most, a few seconds before them.'

They were dumbfounded.

'There you are!' they exclaimed, 'that's what we said too. He did nothing but defend himself. That's his way of winning battles. With your permission we'll hurry back to the gymnasium. We interrupted a discussion on this subject only to wish you good morning.'

And off they went, in deeply savoured discussion.

Socrates lay propped up in his elbows in silence and gazed at the smoke-blackened ceiling. His gloomy forebodings had been right.

His wife watched him from a corner of the room. Mechanically she went on mending an old dress.

All of a sudden she asked softly: 'Well, what's behind it all?'

He gave a start. He looked at her uncertainly.

She was a worn-out creature, flat-chested as a board and sad-eyed. He knew he could depend on her. She would still be standing up for him when his pupils would be saying: 'Socrates? Isn't that the vile cobbler who repudiates the gods?' He'd been a bad bargain for her, but she did not complain – except to him. And there had never yet been an evening without some bread and a bit of bacon for him on the shelf when he came home hungry from his rich pupils.

He wondered whether he should tell her everything. But then he realised that before long, when people, like those just now, came to see him and talked about his heroic deeds, he would have to utter a whole lot of lies and hypocrisies in her hearing, and he could not bring himself to do that if she knew the truth, for he respected her.

So he let it be and just said: 'Yesterday's cold bean soup is stinking the whole place out again'.

She only shot him another suspicious look.

Naturally they were in no position to throw food away. He was only trying to find something to sidetrack her. Her conviction that there was something wrong with him grew. Why didn't he get up? He always got up late, but simply because he went to bed late. Yesterday he had gone to bed very early. And today, with victory celebrations, the whole city was on the go. All the shops in the street were shut. Some of the cavalry that had been pursuing the enemy had got back at five o'clock in the morning, the clatter of horses' hoofs had been heard. He adored tumultuous crowds. On occasions like this he ran round from morning till night, getting into conversation with people. So why wasn't he getting up?

The threshold darkened and in came four officials. They remained standing in the middle of the room and one of them said in a businesslike but exceedingly respectful tone that he was instructed to escort Socrates to the Areopagus. The general, Alcibiades himself, had proposed that a tribute be paid to him for his martial feats.

A hum of voices from the street showed that the neighbours were gathering outside the house.

Socrates felt sweat breaking out. He knew that now he would have to get up and, even if he refused to go with them, he would at least have to get on his feet, say something polite and accompany these men to the door. And he knew that he would not be able to take more than two steps at the most. Then they would look at his foot and know what was up. And the enormous laughter would break out, there and then.

So, instead of getting up, he sank back on his hard pillow and said cantankerously:

'I require no tribute. Tell the Areopagus that I have an appointment with some friends at eleven o'clock to thrash out a philosophical question that interests us, and therefore, much to my regret, I cannot come. I am altogether unfitted for public functions and feel much too tired.'

This last he added because he was annoyed at having dragged in philosophy, and the first part he said because he hoped that rudeness was the easiest way to shake them off.

The officials certainly understood this language. They turned on their heels and left, treading on the feet of the people standing outside.

'One of these days they'll teach you to be polite to the authorities,' said his wife angrily and went into the kitchen.

Socrates waited till she was outside. Then he swiftly swung his heavy body round in the bed, seated himself on the edge of it, keeping a wary eye on the door, and tried with infinite caution to step on the bad foot. It seemed hopeless.

Streaming with sweat he lay back again.

Half an hour passed. He took up a book and read. So long as he kept his foot still he felt practically nothing.

Then his friend Antisthenes turned up.

He did not remove his heavy coat, remained standing at the foot of the couch, coughed in a rather forced way and scratched his throat with its bristly beard as he looked at Socrates.

'Still in bed? I thought I should only find Xantippe at home. I got up specially to enquire after you. I had a bad cold and that was why I couldn't come along yesterday.'

'Sit down,' said Socrates monosyllabically.

Antisthenes fetched a chair from the corner and sat down by his friend.

'I'm starting the lessons again tonight. No reason to interrupt them any longer.'

'No.'

'Of course, I wondered whether they'd turn up. Today there are the great banquets. But on the way here I ran into young Phaeston and when I told him that I was taking algebra tonight, he was simply delighted. I told him he could come in his helmet. Protagoras and the others will hit the ceiling with rage when it's known that on the night after the battle they just went on studying algebra at Antisthenes'.'

Socrates rocked himself gently in his hammock, pushing himself off the slightly crooked wall with the flat of his hand. His protuberant eyes looked searchingly at his friend.

'Did you meet anybody else?'

'Heaps of people.'

Socrates gazed sourly at the ceiling. Should he make a clean breast of it to Antisthenes? He felt pretty sure of him. He himself never took money for lessons and was therefore not in competition with Antisthenes. Perhaps he really ought to lay the difficult case before him.

Antisthenes looked with his sparkling cricket's eyes inquisitively at his friend and told him:

'Giorgius is going about telling everyone that you must have been on the run and in the confusion gone the wrong way, that's to say, forwards. A few of the more decent young people want to thrash him for it.'

Unpleasantly surprised, Socrates looked at him.

'Rubbish,' he said with annoyance. He realised in a flash what trumps his opponents would hold if he declared himself.

During the night, towards morning, he had wondered whether he might not present the whole thing as an experiment and say he had wanted to see just how gullible people were. 'For twenty years I've been teaching pacifism in every back street, and one rumour was enough for my own pupils to take me for a berserker,' and so on and so on. But then the battle ought not to have been won. Patently this was an unfavourable moment for pacifism. After a defeat even the top dogs were pacifists for a while; after a victory even the underdogs approved of war, at any rate for a while, until they noticed that for them there wasn't all that difference between victory and defeat. No, he couldn't cut much ice with pacifism just now.

There was a clatter of horses in the street. The riders halted in front of the house and in came Alcibiades with his buoyant step.

'Good morning, Antisthenes, how's the philosophy business going? They're in a great state,' he cried, beaming. 'There's an uproar in the Areopagus over your answer, Socrates. As a joke I've changed my proposal to give you a laurel wreath to the proposal to give you fifty strokes. Of course, that annoyed them, because it exactly expressed their feelings. But you'll have to come along, you know. We'll go together, on foot.'

Socrates sighed. He was on very good terms with young Alcibiades. They had often drunk together. It was very nice of him to call. It was certainly not only his wish to rile the Areopagus. And that wish itself was an honourable one and deserved every support.

At last he said cautiously as he went on rocking himself in his hammock: 'Haste is the wind that blows the scaffolding down. Take a seat.'

Alcibiades laughed and drew up a chair. Before he sat down he bowed politely to Xantippe, who stood at the kitchen door wiping her wet hands on her skirt.

'You philosophers are funny people,' he said a little impatiently. 'For all I know you may be regretting now that you helped us win the battle. I daresay Antisthenes has pointed out to you that there weren't enough good reasons for it.'

'We've been talking about algebra,' said Antisthenes quickly and coughed again.

Alcibiades grinned.

'Just as I expected. For heaven's sake, no fuss about a thing of this sort, what? Now to my mind it was sheer bravery. Nothing remarkable, if you like; but what's so remarkable about a handful of laurel leaves? Grit your teeth and go through with it, old man. It'll soon be over, and it won't hurt. And then we can go and have one.'

He looked searchingly at the broad powerful figure, which was now rocking rather violently.

Socrates thought fast. He had hit on something that he could say. He could say that he had sprained his foot last night or this morning. When the men had lowered him from their shoulders for instance. There was even a moral to it: the case demonstrated how easily you could come to grief through being honoured by your fellow-citizens.

Without ceasing to swing himself, he leant forward so that he was sitting upright, rubbed his bare left arm with his right hand and said slowly:

'It's like this. My foot . . .'

As he spoke the word his glance, which was not quite steady – for now it was a matter of uttering the first real lie in this affair; so far he had merely kept silence – fell upon Xantippe at the kitchen door.

Socrates' speech failed him. All of a sudden he no longer wanted to produce his tale. His foot was not sprained.

The hammock came to a standstill.

'Listen, Alcibiades,' he said forcefully and in a quite different voice, 'there can't be any talk of bravery in this matter. As soon as the battle started, that's to say, as soon as I caught sight of the first Persian, I ran for it and, what's more, in the right direction – in retreat. But there was a field full of thorns. I got a thorn in my foot and couldn't go on. Then I laid about me like a savage and almost struck some of our own men. In desperation I yelled something about other units, to make the Persians believe there were some, which was absurd because of course they don't understand Greek. At the same time they seem to have been a bit nervous themselves. I suppose they just couldn't stand the roaring at that stage, after all they'd had to go through during the advance. They stopped short for a moment and at that point our cavalry turned up. That's all.'

For a few seconds it was very quiet in the room. Alcibiades stared at him unblinkingly. Antisthenes coughed behind his hand, this time quite naturally. From the kitchen door, where Xantippe was standing, came a loud peal of laughter.

Then Antisthenes said drily:

'And so of course you couldn't go to the Areopagus and limp up the steps to receive the laurel wreath. I can understand that.'

Alcibiades leant back in his chair and contemplated the philosopher on the couch with narrowed eyes. Neither Socrates nor Antisthenes looked at him.

He bent forward again and clasped one knee with his hands. His narrow boyish face twitched a little, but it betrayed nothing of his thoughts or feelings.

'Why didn't you say you had some other sort of wound?' he asked.

'Because I've got a thorn in my foot,' said Socrates bluntly.

'Oh, that's why?' said Alcibiades. 'I see.'

He rose swiftly and went up to the bed.

'Pity I didn't bring my own wreath with me. I gave it to my man to hold. Otherwise I should leave it here for you. You can take my word for it, I think you're brave enough. I don't know anybody who in this situation would have told the story you've just told.'

And he went out quickly.

As Xantippe was bathing his foot later and extracting the thorn she said acrimoniously:

'It could have meant blood-poisoning.'

'Or worse,' said the philosopher.

THE EXPERIMENT

The public career of the great Francis Bacon ended like a crude illustration of the specious maxim 'Crime doesn't pay'. As the highest judicial functionary of the realm he was found guilty of corruption and thrown into gaol. With all the executions, the granting of obnoxious monopolies, the decreeing of arbitrary arrests and the passing of prescribed verdicts, the years of his Lord Chancellorship rank among the darkest and most shameful in English history. After his exposure and confession it was his world renown as a humanist and philosopher that made his offences known far beyond the frontiers of the realm.

He was an old man when he was allowed to leave prison and return to his estate. His body was weakened by the exertion it had cost him to bring about other people's ruin and by the sufferings other people had inflicted when they ruined him. But no sooner did he reach home than he plunged into the most intensive study of the natural sciences. He had failed in mastering men. Now he dedicated his remaining strength to investigating how best mankind could win mastery over the forces of nature.

His researches, devoted to practical matters, led him constantly out of the study into the fields, the gardens and to the stables on the estate. For hours on end he discussed with the gardeners the possibilities of grafting fruit trees, and told the dairymaids how to measure the milk yield of each cow. In this way a stableboy came to his notice. A valuable horse had fallen ill and the lad reported on its condition twice a day to the philosopher. His zeal and his powers of observation delighted the old man.

But one evening as he came into the stables he saw an old woman with the boy and heard her say:

'He's a bad man; look out! He may be a great lord, he may have made his pile, but he's bad for all that. He's your master, so do your work conscientiously, but always bear in mind he's bad.'

The philosopher did not hear the boy's answer, for he turned about at once and went back into the house, but he found the lad's attitude towards him the next morning unchanged.

When the horse was well again he let the boy accompany him on many of his rounds and entrusted him with minor tasks. Little by little he fell into the habit of talking to him about various experiments. In doing this he did not bother to choose words that grown-ups commonly believe suited to the understanding of children, but spoke to him as to an educated man. In the course of his life he had associated with the greatest minds and had seldom been understood: not because he did not make himself clear, but because he made himself too clear. So he was not put out by the boy's difficulties; nevertheless, he patiently corrected him when the boy himself tried out the unfamiliar words.

The lad's main duty consisted in having to describe the objects he saw and the processes he observed. The philosopher taught him how many words there were and how many were needed to describe the behaviour of a certain thing in such a way that it was more or less recognisable from the description and, above all, that it could be dealt with in accordance with the description. There were also some words that it was better not to use since, strictly speaking, they meant nothing: words like 'good,' 'bad,' 'beautiful,' and so on.

The boy soon realised that there was no sense in calling a beetle 'ugly'. Even 'quick' was not good enough; you had to state how quickly it moved compared with other creatures of its size and what this enabled it to do. You had to put it on an inclined surface and on a flat one and make noises so that it ran away; or set out little scraps of prey towards which it could advance. You had only to busy yourself with it long enough and it 'quickly' lost its ugliness.

Once he had to describe the piece of bread that he was holding in his hand when the philosopher came upon him.

'Now here you may safely use the word "good",' said the old man, 'for bread is made for people to eat and can be good or bad for them. It is only in the case of larger substances created by nature and not, on the face of it, created for specific purposes and, above all, not purely for the use of man, that it is foolish to be satisfied with such words.'

The boy thought of his grandmother's remarks about his lordship.

He made rapid progress in grasping things, inasmuch as it was always something quite tangible that had to be grasped: that the horse recovered as a result of the treatment applied, or a tree withered as a result of the treatment applied. He grasped, too, that there must always remain a reasonable doubt as to whether the observed changes could really be owed to these measures. The boy scarcely took in the scientific significance of the great Bacon's mode of thought, but the manifest utility of all these undertakings fired him with enthusiasm.

This was how he understood the philosopher: a new era had dawned for the world. Mankind was enlarging its knowledge almost daily. And all knowledge was for the advancement of well-being and of human happiness. Science was the leading force. Science investigated the universe, everything that existed on earth – plants, animals, soil, water, air – so that greater use could be extracted from it. The important thing was not what you believed, but what you knew. People believed far too much and knew far too little. So one had to test everything, oneself, with one's hands, and speak only of things seen with one's own eyes and that could be of some use.

That was the new teaching and ever more people turned towards it, ready and eager to undertake the new tasks.

Books played a big part in this, even though there might be many bad ones. It was quite clear to the boy that he must find his way to books if he wanted to be among those who were undertaking the new tasks.

Naturally he never came within reach of the library in the house. He had to wait for his lordship at the stables. The most he could do, if the old man had not appeared for several days, was to come across him in the park. Nevertheless, his curiosity about the study, where every night a lamp burnt late, waxed ever greater. From a hedge facing the room he could catch a glimpse of bookshelves.

He decided to learn to read.

That was by no means easy. The parish priest, to whom he

went with his request, eyed him as though he were a spider on the breakfast table.

'Do you want to read the gospel of the Lord to the cows?' he asked irately. And the lad was lucky to get away without a thrashing.

So he had to adopt a different way.

There was a missal in the vestry of the village church. If you volunteered to pull the bell-ropes, you could get in. Now, if you could determine which passages the priest was singing at mass, it ought to be possible to find a connecton between the words and the letters.

At all events, at mass the boy began to learn by heart the Latin words which the priest intoned, or at least some of them. It must be admitted that the way the priest articulated the words was uncommonly indistinct, and all too often he did not read the mass.

All the same, after a while the boy could repeat some introits sung by the priest. The head groom surprised him at this exercise behind the barn and thrashed him, for he thought the boy was trying to parody the priest. So he got his thrashing after all.

He had not yet succeeded in finding the place in the missal with the words which the priest sang when a great catastrophe occurred, putting an end for the time being to his efforts to learn to read. His lordship fell mortally ill.

He had been ailing all the autumn and had not recovered by the winter when he drove in an open sledge to an estate a few miles off. The boy was allowed to accompany him. He stood on the runners at the back next to the coachman's box.

The visit was paid, the old man was plodding back to the sledge, escorted by his host, when he saw a frozen sparrow lying on the path. Halting, he turned it over with his stick.

'How long has it been lying here do you think?' the boy, trotting behind him with a hot-water bottle, heard him ask his host.

The answer was: 'Anything from an hour to a week or more.'

The little old man walked on deep in thought and took a very abstracted farewell of his host.

'The flesh is still quite fresh, Dick,' he said, turning round to the boy as the sledge drove off.

They made their way at a good pace, for dusk was falling over the snow-covered fields and it was rapidly growing colder. Thus it came about that, as they turned into the gates of the courtyard a chicken, having apparently escaped from the coop, was run over. The old man followed the coachman's attempts to avoid the stiffly flapping chicken and made a sign to stop when the manoeuvre failed.

Working his way out of his rugs and furs, he left the sledge and, his arm supported by the boy, he went back to the spot where the chicken lay, despite the coachman's warnings of the cold.

It was dead.

The old man told the lad to pick it up.

'Take out the entrails,' he ordered.

'Can't it be done in the kitchen?' asked the coachman, seeing his master standing so frail in the cold wind.

'No, it's better here,' he said. 'I am sure Dick has a knife on him and we need the snow.'

The boy did as he was told and the old man, who had evidently forgotten his illness and the cold, himself stooped down and, with an effort, picked up a handful of snow. Carefully he stuffed the snow inside the chicken.

The boy understood. He, too, gathered up snow and handed it to his teacher till the chicken was entirely filled with snow.

'It should keep fresh like this for weeks,' said the old man with animation. 'Put it on cold flagstones in the cellar.'

He walked the short distance to the door, a trifle exhausted and leaning heavily on the boy who carried the snow-stuffed chicken under his arm.

As he stepped into the hall he shivered with the cold.

The next morning he lay in a high fever.

The boy trailed about dejectedly and tried wherever he could to pick up news of his teacher's condition. He learnt little. The life of the great estate went on unchanged. Things took a turn only on the third day: he was called to the study.

The old man lay on a narrow wooden bed under many rugs, but the windows stood open, so it was cold. Nevertheless, the sick man seemed aglow. In a tremulous voice he enquired after the state of the snow-filled chicken.

The lad told him it looked as fresh as ever.

'That's good,' said the old man with satisfaction. 'Give me further news in two days' time.'

As he went away the boy regretted that he had not brought the chicken with him. The old man did not seem to be as ill as they made out in the servants' hall.

Twice a day he changed the snow. putting in fresh, and the chicken was still unblemished when he made his way again to the sickroom.

He met with quite extraordinary obstacles.

Doctors had come from the capital. The corridor buzzed with whispering, commanding and obsequious voices and there were unfamiliar faces everywhere. A servant, who was carrying a dish covered with a large cloth, rudely turned him away.

Several times throughout the morning and afternoon he made vain attempts to reach the sickroom. The strange doctors appeared to be trying to settle down in the great mansion. They seemed to him like huge black birds settling on a sick man who was now defenceless. Towards evening he hid in a closet in the corridor where it was very cold. He shivered all the time, but considered this a good thing, since the chicken must be kept cold at all costs in the interests of the experiment.

During the dinner hour the black tide receded a little and the boy was able to slip into the sickroom.

The invalid lay alone; everyone was at dinner. A reading lamp with a green shade stood by the small bed. The old man's face was peculiarly shrivelled and as pale as wax. The eyes were closed, but the hands moved restlessly on the stiff covers. The room was very hot; they had shut the windows.

The boy took a few steps towards the bed, clutching the chicken as he held it out. and said in a low voice several times: 'My lord!' He got no answer. The invalid did not, however, seem to be asleep, for his lips moved every now and again, as though he were speaking.

The boy decided to rouse his attention, convinced of the importance of further instructions for the experiment. But even before he could tweak the covers – he had had to lay the chicken in its box on a chair – he felt himself seized from behind and pulled away. A fat man with a grey face glared at him as if he were a murderer. He tore himself free with great presence of mind and, in one bound, caught up the box and made off through the door.

In the corridor he fancied a manservant coming up the stairs had seen him. That was bad. How was he to prove that he had come at his lordship's bidding, in the conduct of an important experiment? The old man was completely in the doctor's power; the closed windows in the room showed it.

And now he saw a servant crossing the courtyard on his way to the stables. So he went without his supper and, after he had put the chicken into the cellar, crept into the forage loft.

The enquiry hanging over him made his sleep uneasy. It was with fear that he emerged from his hiding-place the next morning.

No one paid any attention to him. There was a terrible coming and going in the courtyard. His lordship had died towards morning.

All day the boy went about as though stunned by a blow on the head. He felt he would never get over the loss of his teacher. As he went into the cellar with a bowl of snow in the late afternoon, his grief at the loss turned into grief for the unfinished experiment and he shed tears over the box. What would become of the great discovery?

Returning to the courtyard – his feet seemed to him so heavy that he looked back to see whether his footprints were not deeper than usual – he found that the London doctors had not yet left. Their carriages were still there.

Despite his aversions, he made up his mind to confide the discovery to them. They were learned men and would be bound to recognize the significance of the experiment. He fetched the little box with the frozen chicken and stood behind the well, concealing himself until one of the gentlemen came by, a dumpy fellow, not too awe-inspiring. He stepped forward, holding out the box. At first his voice stuck in his throat, but he did at last manage to bring out his request in disjointed sentences.

'His lordship found it dead six days ago, your excellency. We stuffed it with snow. His lordship believed it might keep fresh. See for yourself; it has kept fresh.'

The dumpy fellow gazed into the box with perplexity.

'And what of it?' he asked.

'It hasn't gone bad,' said the boy.

'Oh,' said the dumpy fellow.

'See for yourself,' urged the lad.

'I see,' said the dumpy fellow and shook his head. Still shaking his head, he walked on.

The boy stared after him flabbergasted. He could not understand the dumpy fellow. Had not the old man brought on his death by going out in the cold for the sake of the experiment? He had gathered up snow from the ground with his own hands. That was a fact.

The boy went slowly back to the cellar door, but stopped short outside it, then turned about smartly and ran to the kitchen.

He found the cook very busy, as funeral guests from the neighbourhood were expected for dinner.

'What are you doing with that bird?' growled the cook testily. 'It's completely frozen.'

'That doesn't matter,' said the lad. 'His lordship said it doesn't matter.'

The cook gazed at him in an absentminded way for a moment, then went importantly to the door with a big pan in his hand, presumably to throw something out.

The boy followed him eagerly with the box.

'Couldn't you try it?' he entreated.

The cook lost patience. He grabbed at the chicken with his enormous hands and sent it spinning into the yard.

'Haven't you anything better to think about?' he yelled, beside himself. 'And his lordship lying dead!'

Angrily the boy picked up the chicken from the ground and slunk off with it.

The next two days were filled with the funeral ceremonies. He had a lot to do, harnessing and unharnessing horses, but though almost asleep with his eyes open he went out at night to put fresh snow into the box. Everything seemed to him hopeless and the new era at an end.

But on the third day, the day of the burial, well washed and in his best clothes, he felt a change of mood. It was fine bright winter weather and the bells pealed out from the village.

Filled with new hope, he went into the cellar and gazed long and attentively at the dead fowl. He could discern no speck of decay on it. He carefully packed the creature in its box, filled it with clean white snow, put it under his arm and set off for the village.

Whistling merrily he stepped into his grandmother's lowly kitchen. His parents had died young, so she had brought him up and enjoyed his confidence. Without at first showing her what was in the box, he gave the old woman, who was just dressing for the funeral, an account of his lordship's experiment.

She heard him out patiently.

'But everybody knows that,' she said at the end. 'They go stiff in the cold and keep for a bit. What's so remarkable about it?'

'I believe you could still eat it,' answered the lad, trying to appear as casual as possible.

'Eat a chicken that's been dead for a week? Why it's poisonous!'

'If it hasn't changed at all since it died why should it be? And it was killed by his lordship's carriage so it was quite healthy.'

'But inside, inside, it's gone bad,' said the old woman, growing slightly impatient.

'I don't believe it,' said the lad stoutly, his bright eyes on the chicken. 'It's had snow inside the whole time. I think I'll cook it.'

The old woman got cross.

'You're coming along to the funeral,' she said with finality. 'I should have thought you'd had enough kindness from his lordship for you to walk decently behind his coffin.'

The boy did not reply. While she tied her black woollen kerchief round her head he took the chicken out of the snow, blew off the last flakes and laid it on two logs in front of the stove. It had to thaw out.

The old woman took no further notice of him. As soon as she was ready, she took him by the hand and went resolutely out of the door with him.

He went along obediently for quite a stretch. There were other people, men and women, also on their way to the funeral. Suddenly he gave a cry of pain. One of his feet was stuck in a snowdrift. He pulled it out with a grimace, hobbled to a milestone and sat down, rubbing his foot.

'I've sprained it,' he said.

The old woman looked at him suspiciously.

'You can walk all right,' she said.

'I can't,' he said sullenly. 'But if you don't believe me, you can sit down with me till it's better.'

The old woman sat down next to him without a word.

A quarter of an hour went by. Villagers still kept passing, though fewer all the time. The two of them squatted stubbornly by the roadside.

Then the old woman said gravely: 'Didn't he teach you not to lie?'

The boy made no answer. The old woman got to her feet, groaning. It was getting too cold for her.

'If you don't follow in ten minutes,' she said, 'I'll tell your brother and he'll tan your backside.'

And she waddled on, in great haste not to miss the funeral oration.

The boy waited until she had gone far enough and got up slowly. He turned back, but looked round several times and also went on limping for a while. Only when a hedge hid him from the old woman's view did he walk normally again.

In the cottage he sat down by the chicken and looked at it expectantly. He would boil it in a pot of water and eat a wing. Then he would know whether it was poisonous or not.

He was still sitting there when three cannon shots were heard in the distance. They were fired in honour of Francis Bacon, Baron Verulam, Viscount St Alban, former Lord High Chancellor of England, who filled not a few of his contemporaries with loathing, but also many of them with enthusiasm for the practical sciences.

THE HERETIC'S COAT

Giordano Bruno, the man from Nola, whom the tribunals of the Roman Inquisition sent to the stake in the year 1600 to be burnt for heresy, is generally held to be a great man, not only by virtue of his bold and, as was subsequently proved, correct hypotheses concerning the movements of the stars but also by virtue of his spirited bearing in face of the Inquisition, to which he said: 'You pronounce sentence upon me with greater fear, it may be, than I hear it.' When one reads his writings and also takes a glance at reports of his demeanour in public, there is indeed every reason to call him a great man. And yet there is a story which may even heighten our respect for him.

It is the story of his coat.

You must first know how he fell into the hands of the Inquisition.

A patrician of Venice, one Mocenigo, invited the man of learning to stay in his house to instruct him in natural philosophy and mnemonics. He gave him hospitality for a few months and in return was given the agreed instruction. But instead of the tuition in black magic for which he had hoped, he received only that in natural philosophy. At this he was most disgruntled as, of course, it was of no use to him. He deplored the expense to which his guest had put him. Again and again he solemnly exhorted him to yield up the secret and lucrative knowledge of which so famous a man must surely be possessed; and as this did no good, he denounced him in a letter to the Inquisition. He wrote saying that this wicked and ungrateful man had spoken ill of Christ in his hearing, had said that the monks were asses who stultified the people and, besides, asserted that, contrary to what stood in the Bible, there was not only one sun but untold numbers, and so on and so on. Therefore he, Mocenigo, had locked him into his attic and requested that he be taken away by the authorities without delay.

The authorities did, in fact, arrive in the middle of the night between Sunday and Monday and took the man of learning to the prison of the Inquisition.

This occurred on Monday the 25th of May 1592, at three o'clock in the morning, and from that day until he went to the stake on the 17th of February 1600, *il Nolano* never came out of prison again.

Throughout the eight years which the terrible trial lasted, he fought unremittingly for his life; but the fight he waged against his extradition to Rome during the first year in Venice was perhaps the most desperate.

The story about his coat belongs to that period.

In the winter of 1592, while still living in an hotel, he had been measured for a thick overcoat by a tailor named Gabriele Zunto. When he was arrested the garment had not yet been paid for.

On hearing of the arrest the tailor rushed to Signor Mocenigo's house near to St. Samuele to present his bill. He was too late. One of Signor Mocenigo's servants showed him the door. 'We've spent enough on that impostor,' he shouted so loudly from the porch that several passers-by looked round. 'Perhaps you'd like to go to the tribunal of the Holy Office and let them know that you've had dealings with that heretic.'

The tailor stood aghast in the street. A bunch of guttersnipes had overheard everything, and one of them, a pimply urchin in tatters, threw a stone at him. And although a poorly dressed woman came out of her door and boxed his ears, Zunto, an old man, had a distinct hunch that it was dangerous to be someone who 'had dealings with that heretic'. Looking furtively behind him, he turned the corner and made for home by a very indirect way. He said nothing to his wife about his trouble, and for a whole week she was puzzled by his depressed mood.

But on the first of June, when she was writing out the bills, she discovered that there was a coat unpaid for by a man whose name was on everyone's lips, for *il Nolano* was the talk of the town. The most appalling rumours of his wickedness went about. He had not merely dragged matrimony through the mud, both in books and in conversation, but he had called Christ Himself a charlatan and said the most insane things about the sun. It was all in keeping that he had not paid for his coat. The good woman had not the least inclination to be the loser. After a furious row with her husband, the seventy-year-old woman went to the seat of the Holy Office in her Sunday clothes and, with an angry face, demanded the thirty-two *scudi* owed her by the imprisoned heretic.

The official she spoke to wrote down her claim and promised to pursue the matter.

Before long, indeed, Zunto received a summons and, shaking in his shoes, presented himself at the dread building. To his astonishment he was not interrogated but simply informed that his claim would be borne in mind when the prisoner's financial affairs were settled. Of course, the official intimated, this would not lead to much.

The old man was so glad to get off thus lightly that he humbly expressed his thanks. But his wife was not satisfied. To make good the loss it was not enough for her husband to forgo his evening beer and stitch late into the night. There were debts to the cloth merchant that had to be paid. She shouted in the kitchen and all over the courtyard that it was a disgrace to take a criminal into custody before he had paid his debts. If need be, she would go to the Holy Father himself in Rome to get her thirty-two *scudi*. 'He doesn't need a coat at the stake,' she screamed.

She told her father confessor what had happened to them. He advised her to ask that at least the coat be returned to them. Taking this as an admission on the part of an ecclesiastical authority that she had a legitimate claim, she declared that she would not by any means be satisfied with the coat, which had certainly been worn already and, besides, had been made to measure. She must have the money. Since she became a trifle noisy in her vehemence, the priest threw her out. This brought her to her senses a bit and for some weeks she kept quiet. Nothing further was heard from the seat of the Inquisition about the case of the imprisoned heretic. But it was whispered everywhere that the interrogations were bringing monstrous iniquities to light. The old woman listened greedily to all this tattle. It tormented her to hear that the heretic's case looked so black. He would never be released and never be able to pay his debts. She no longer slept at night and in August, when the heat played havoc with her nerves, she began to air her grievance with great volubility in the shops where she made her purchases and to the customers who came for fittings. She insinuated that the priests were committing a sin in dismissing so lightly the rightful claims of a small artisan. Taxes were oppressive and bread had just recently gone up again.

One morning an official called for her and took her to the seat of the Holy Office where she was urgently cautioned to cease her mischievous chatter. She was asked if she were not ashamed of herself, letting her tongue wag about very grave ecclesiastical proceedings for the sake of a few *scudi*. She was given to understand that there were all sorts of ways of dealing with people of her stamp.

That had an effect for a while, even though every time she thought of the phrase 'for the sake of a few *scudi*' coming from the mouth of an overfed friar her face flushed with anger. But in September it was said that the Grand Inquisitor in Rome had demanded the extradition of *il Nolano*. The matter was being debated in the Signoria.

The citizens heatedly discussed this request for extradition and, by and large, feelings were against it. The guilds would not tolerate Roman tribunals over them.

The old woman was beside herself. Were they really going to let the heretic go off to Rome without settling his debts? That was the last straw. She had barely heard the incredible news before, without even stopping to put on a better dress, she was on her way to the seat of the Holy Office.

This time she was received by a higher official and, strangely enough, he was far more accommodating than the former officials had been. He was almost as old as herself and listened quietly and attentively to her complaint. When she had finished he asked her, after a little pause, whether she would care to speak to Bruno.

She assented at once. A meeting was arranged for the following day.

That morning, in a tiny room with grated windows, a small slight man with a thin dark beard came towards her and asked her courteously what he could do for her.

She had seen him at the time when he had been measured and since then had kept his face clearly in her memory, but she did not now immediately recognize him. The excitements of the interrogations must have changed him.

She blurted out: 'The coat. You haven't paid for it.'

He looked at her in amazement for a few seconds. Then he recollected and asked her in a low voice: 'What do I owe you?'

'Thirty-two *scudi*,' she said. 'Surely you had the bill?'

He turned to the big fat official who was supervising the interview and asked him whether he knew how much money had been handed in to the Holy Office together with his belongings. The man did not know, but promised to find out.

'How is your husband?' asked the prisoner, turning again to the old woman, as though, the business having thus been set in train, normal relations had been established and this was now an ordinary visit.

And the old woman, disconcerted by the little man's friendliness, mumbled that he was well and even added something about his rheumatism.

It was not until two days later that she went to the Holy Office building again, as it seemed only proper to allow the gentleman time to make his enquiries.

She was, in fact, given permission to speak to him once more. True, she had to wait over an hour in the tiny room with the grated windows, because he was being interrogated.

When he appeared, he seemed exhausted. As there was no chair, he leant against the wall a little. But he came to the point at once.

He told her in a very weak voice that unfortunately he was unable to pay for the coat. No money had been found amongst his belongings. Yet she need not give up all hope. He had been thinking it over and remembered that in the city of Frankfurt a man who had printed his books must still have some money laid by. If it was allowed, he would write to him. He would apply for permission the very next day. At today's audience it had struck him that the prevailing atmosphere was not particularly favourable. So he had not liked to ask and risk spoiling everything.

The old woman watched him searchingly with her sharp eyes as he spoke. She knew the subterfuges and hollow promises of debtors. They didn't give a damn for their obligations and when you cornered them they went on as though they were moving heaven and earth.

'Why did you need a coat if you hadn't the money to pay for it?' she asked stubbornly.

The prisoner nodded to show that he was following her train of thought. He answered:

'I've always earned money, with books and teaching, And I thought, I'm still earning money now. I had the idea that I needed a coat because I believed I should still be walking about outside.'

He said that without any bitterness, simply, it was plain, in order not to deny her an answer.

The old woman looked him up and down again wrathfully, but with the feeling that he was inaccessible, and, not uttering another word, she turned and hurried from the room.

'Who would dream of sending money to a man on trial by the Inquisition?' she exclaimed angrily to her husband as they lay in bed that night. His mind had now been set at rest about the ecclesiastical authorities' attitude towards him, but he still disapproved of his wife's tireless efforts to exact the money.

'I dare say he's got other things to think about now,' he growled.

She said no more.

Nothing new happened about this sorry matter during the following months. At the beginning of January it was said that the Signoria was entertaining the idea of complying with the Pope's wish and surrendering the heretic. And then the Zuntos received a fresh summons to the seat of the Holy Office.

No definite time had been stated and Signora Zunto went along one afternoon. Her arrival was inopportune. The prisoner was awaiting the visit of the Procurator of the Republic who had been invited by the Signoria to draw up an expert opinion on the question of extradition. She was received by the higher official who had earlier arranged her first interview with *il Nolano*, and the old man told her that the prisoner had wanted to talk to her, but that she should reflect whether this was the right moment, since the prisoner was about to attend an interview of the highest importance to him.

She said curtly, why not ask him?

An official went out and returned with the prisoner. The meeting took place in the presence of the higher official.

Before *il Nolano* – who smiled at her as he entered the door – could say anything, the old woman rapped:

'Why do you go on like this if you want to walk about outside?'

For an instant the little man seemed bewildered. In the past three months he had answered a great many questions and hardly remembered the end of his last conversation with the tailor's wife.

'No money has come,' he said at last. 'I've written for it twice, but it hasn't come. I was wondering whether you would take the coat back.'

'I knew it would come to this all along,' she said contemptuously. 'And it's made to measure and too small for most people.'

He looked at the old woman with distress.

'I hadn't thought of that,' he said and turned to the cleric. 'Couldn't all my belongings be sold and the money handed over to these people?'

'That won't be possible,' broke in the official who had escorted him, the big fat one. 'Signor Mocenigo has put in a claim for it. You lived at his expense for a long while.'

'He invited me,' replied the man from Nola wearily.

The old man raised his hand.

'That's really neither here nor there. I think the coat should be returned.'

'What are we supposed to do with it?' said the old woman obstinately.

The old man's face grew slightly red. He said with deliberation:

'My good woman, a little Christian forbearance would not be unbecoming to you. The accused is about to go to an interview which may mean life or death for him. You can hardly expect him to take overmuch interest in your coat.'

The old woman looked at him uncertainly. She suddenly recollected where she was. She was considering whether she should leave when she heard the prisoner behind her say in a quiet voice:

'In my view she can expect just that.'

And, as she turned towards him, he added:

'You must forgive all this. Don't think for a moment that your loss is a matter of indifference to me. I shall draw up a petition about it.'

At a nod from the old man the big fat official had left the room. Now he came back, spread out his arms and said: 'The coat was never handed in at all. Mocenigo must have held on to it.'

Bruno was plainly dismayed. Then he said firmly:

'That's not right. I shall sue him.'

The old man shook his head.

'Better give your mind to the conversation you will be holding in a few minutes. I cannot allow this squabble over a few *scudi* to go on any longer.'

The old woman's blood rushed to her head. While *il Nolano* was speaking she had kept quiet and stared sullenly into a corner of the room. But now she lost all patience again.

'A few *scudi*!' she shouted. 'That's a month's earnings. It's easy for you to show forbearance. It's not your loss!'

At that moment a tall monk entered the door.

'The Procurator has arrived,' he said in an undertone and gazed with surprise at the frail old woman screaming.

The big fat man took *il Nolano* by the sleeve and led him out. The prisoner looked back over his shoulder at the woman until he was led over the threshold. His thin face was very pale.

Perturbed, the old woman went down the stone steps of the building. She did not know what to think. After all, the man was doing his best.

She did not go into the workshop when, a week later, the big fat man brought the coat. But she listened at the door and heard the official say: 'The fact is that he busied himself with the coat throughout the last days. He petitioned twice, between interrogations and his interviews with the city authorities, and several times he asked for an interview with the Nuncio on the matter. He got his way. Mocenigo had to surrender the coat. Incidentally, he could have made good use of it now, for he is being extradited and will be going to Rome this very week.'

That was so. It was the end of January.

LUCULLUS'S TROPHIES

At the beginning of the year 63 A.D. Rome was full of unrest. In a series of protracted campaigns Pompey had conquered Asia for the Romans, and now they were filled with fear as they waited for the victor to return. Following his victory of course not only Asia but Rome too was his to do what he liked with.

On one of those days of tension, a short, thin man issued from a palace situated in the vast gardens along the Tiber and walked as far as the marble steps to meet a visitor. He was the former general Lucullus, and his visitor (who had come on foot) was the poet Lucretius.

In his time the old general had launched the Asiatic campaign, but thanks to a variety of intrigues Pompey had managed to ease him out of his command. Pompey knew that in many people's eyes Lucullus was the real conqueror of Asia, and so the latter had every reason to view the victor's arrival with alarm. He was not receiving all that many visits in those days.

The general greeted the poet warmly and led him into a small room where he could take some refreshment. The poet however ate nothing but a few figs. His health was poorly. His chest troubled him, he could not stand the spring mists.

At first the conversation contained no reference to political matters, not one word. There was some airing of philosophical questions.

Lucullus expressed reservations about the treatment of the gods in Lucretius's didactic poem *On the Nature of Things*. He considered it was dangerous simply to write off religious feeling as superstition. Religious feeling and morality were the same. Renouncing the one meant renouncing the other. Such superstitious notions as are refutable are bound up with other notions whose value cannot be proved but which are none the less needed etc., etc.

Lucretius naturally differed and the old general tried to support his views by describing a dream which he had had during one of his Asiatic campaigns – in point of fact the last. 'It was after the battle of Gasiura. Our position was pretty desperate. We had been counting on some quick victories. Triarus, my deputy at that time, had led his reserves into an ambush. I was forced to extricate him at once or all would have been lost. This at the very moment when the army was becoming dangerously infected with insubordination due to prolonged holdups over pay.

'I was shockingly overworked, and one afternoon I nodded off over the map and had a dream which I will now recount to you.

'We had established our camp by a big river, the Halys, which was in full spate, and I dreamed that I was sitting in my tent at night working on a plan which would definitely destroy my enemy Mithridates. The river was then impassable, and in my dream it split Mithridates's army in two. If I went ahead and attacked the part on our side of the river it would get no help from the part on the other side.

'Morning came. I paraded the army and saw that the proper sacrifices were carried out before my legions. Since I had had a word with the priests the omens proved exceptionally favourable. I made a great speech in which I referred to our unusually good opportunity to destroy the enemy, to the backing given us by the gods who had filled the river, to the splendidly propitious omens which proved that the gods were looking forward to the battle etc., etc. As I spoke a strange thing happened.

'I was standing fairly high up and had a good view of the plain behind our ranks. Not all that far away I could see the smoke going up from Mithridates's camp fires. In between the two armies lay fields; the corn in them was already quite tall. To one side, close by the river, was a farm that was about to get flooded. A peasant family was engaged in rescuing its household possessions from the low house.

'Suddenly I saw the peasants waving in our direction. Some of my legionaries apparently heard them shouting and turned round. Four or five men began moving towards them, at first slowly and uncertainly, then breaking into a run.

'But the peasants pointed in the opposite direction. I could see what they meant. A wall of earth had been banked up to our right. The water had undermined it and it was threatening to collapse.

'All this I saw as I went on speaking. It gave me an idea.

'I thrust out my arm and pointed at the wall so that all eyes were turned towards it, raised my voice and said: "Soldiers, this is the hand of the gods! They have ordered the river to break down the enemy's dyke. In the gods' name, charge!"'

'My dream of course was not entirely clear, but I distinctly remember that moment as I stood in the middle of the whole army and paused for effect while they watched the crumbling dyke.

'It was very brief. Suddenly, with no transition, hundreds of soldiers began running towards the dyke.

'Likewise four or five who had already hastened to the peasants' assistance started shouting back to us as they helped the family drag the cattle from their stalls. All I could hear was "the dyke! the dyke!".

'And now there were thousands running that way.

'Those standing behind me ran past me till finally I was swept along too. It was a stream of men, rolling forward against a stream of water.

'I called to the nearest bystanders – by-runners, more like – "On to glory!" "Right, on to the dyke!", they enthusiastically yelled back as if they had not understood me. "How about the battle?" I yelled. "Later!" they assured me.

'I stood in the way of one disorganised cohort.

'"I command you to halt", I shouted peremptorily.

'Two or three of them actually halted. One was a tall fellow with a twisted chin, and to this day I have not forgotten him even though I only saw him in a dream. Turning to his comrades he said "Who's this?". And it was not mere insolence; he honestly meant it. And equally honestly, as I could see, the others replied "No idea". Then they all ran on towards the dyke.

'For a short while I stood there alone. Beside me the sacrifices still smouldered on the field altars. But even the priests were following the soldiers down to the river, I saw. A bit more slowly of course, on account of their being fatter.

'Yielding to a preternaturally strong impulse I decided that I too would examine the dyke. Vaguely I felt the thing would have to be organised. I walked along, a prey to conflicting feelings. But soon I broke into a run because I was worried that the operation might be badly directed and the dyke still collapse. This, I suddenly realised, would mean the loss not only of the farm buildings but also of the fields with the half-grown corn. I had, you see, already been infected by everyone else's feelings.

'When I got there however everything was under control. The fact that our legionaries were equipped with spades for revetting the camp perimeter was a great help. No one thought twice about sticking his sword into the fascines to reinforce them. Shields were used for bringing up earth.

'Seeing me standing there with nothing to do, a soldier grabbed me by the sleeve and handed me a spade. I started digging as directed by a centurion. A man beside me said, "Back home in Picenum there was a dyke burst in 82. The harvest was a total loss." Of course, I realised, most of them were peasants' sons.

'Just once, so I remember, the idea of the enemy again crossed my mind. "Let's hope the enemy doesn't take advantage of this," I told the man beside me. "Nonsense," he said mopping his forehead, "it's not the moment." And true enough when I looked up I could see some of Mithridates's soldiers further downstream working on the dyke. They were working alongside our men, making themselves understood by nods and gestures since of course they spoke a different language – which shows how exact the details of my dream were.'

The old general broke off his story. His little yellow shrivelled-up face bore an expression somewhere between cheerfulness and concern.

'A fine dream,' said the poet placidly.

'Yes. Eh? No.' The general's look was dubious. Then he

laughed. 'I wasn't too happy about it,' he said quickly. 'When I woke up I felt disagreeably disturbed. It seemed to me evidence of great weakness.'

'Really?' asked the poet, taken aback. There was a silence. Then Lucretius went on, 'What did you conclude from your dream, at the time?'

'That authority is an extremely shaky business, of course.'

'In the dream.'

'Yes, but all the same . . .'

Lucullus clapped his hands and the servants hastened to clear the dishes. These were still full. Nor had Lucullus eaten anything. In those days he had no appetite.

He proposed to his guest that they should visit the blue room, where some newly acquired *objets d'art* were on display. They walked through open colonnades to a lateral wing of the great palace.

Striking the marble paving hard with his stick, the little general continued:

'What robbed me of victory was not the indiscipline of the common man but the indiscipline of the great. Their love of their country is just love of their palaces and their fishponds. In Asia the Roman tax-farmers banded together with the big local landowners to oppose me. They swore they would paralyse me and my army. In return the landowners handed the peasantry of Asia Minor over to them. They found my successor a better proposition. "At least he's a real general," they said. "He takes." And they weren't only referring to strongpoints. There was one king in Asia Minor on whom he imposed a tribute of fifty millions. As the money had to be paid into the state treasury he "lent" him that sum, with the result that he now draws forty per cent interest each year. That's what I call conquests!'

Lucretius was scarcely listening to the old man, who had not done all that badly out of Asia himself – witness this palace. His thoughts were still focused on the dream, which struck him as an interesting counterpart to a true incident that had occurred during the capture of Amisus by Lucullus's troops.

Amisus, a daughter city of glorious Athens and full of irreplaceable works of art, had been looted and set on fire by Lucullus's soldiers even though the general – reputedly in tears – had besought the looters to spare the art works. There too his authority had not been respected.

The one event had been dream, the other reality. Should it be said that authority, having forbidden the troops the one, could not deny them the other? That was what Lucullus seemed to have felt, though hardly to have acknowledged.

The best of the new *objets d'art* was a little earthenware figure of Nike. Lucretius held it delicately in his skinny hand and looked at it, smiling.

'A good artist,' he said. 'That carefree stance and that delicious smile! His idea was to portray the goddess of victory as a goddess of peace. This figure must date from before those peoples were first defeated.'

Lucullus looked mistrustfully at him and took it in his hand too.

'The human race,' he said abruptly, 'tends to remember the abuses to which it has been subjected rather than the endearments. What's left of kisses? Wounds however leave scars.'

The poet said nothing, but in turn gave him a peculiar look.

'What's the matter?' asked the general. 'Did I surprise you?'

'Slightly, to be honest. Do you really fear you'll get a bad name in the history books?'

'No name at all, perhaps. I don't know what I fear. Altogether this is a month of fear, isn't it? Fear has become rampant. As always after a victory.'

'Though if my information is correct you should be fearing fame these days more than oblivion.'

'True enough. Fame is dangerous for me. More than anything. And between you and me, that's a strange business. I'm a soldier and I must say death has never scared me. But there has been a change. The lovely sight of the garden, the well cooked food, the delicious works of art bring about an extraordinary weakness in me and even if I still don't fear death I fear the fear of death. Can you explain that?'

The poet said nothing.

'I know,' said the general a little hurriedly. 'That passage from your poem is very familiar to me; in fact I think I even know it by heart, which is another bad sign.'

And he began in a rather dry voice to recite Lucretius's famous lines about fear of death:

'Death, then, is nothing to us, it is not of the slightest import-
    ance.
So when you see some man resenting his own destination
Either, when dead, to rot where his mortal body is buried
Or be destroyed by flames or by the jaws of predators
Then you can tell he's a fraud whose heart is surely affected
By some latent sting, however he may keep denying
Any belief that death does not deprive one of feeling.
That which he claims to admit, he does not admit, nor its basis
Nor does he tear out his roots and hurl himself from this
    existence
But he makes something survive of himself, though he doesn't
    know it.
For if someone who lives can see himself enter a future
Where when he's dead wild beasts and birds will mangle his
    body
Then he pities himself, for he can't see the thing with detach-
    ment
Nor can he stand back enough from the body that he has
    rejected;
Rather he stands beside it, infecting it with his own feelings.
So he fills with resentment at having been born a mere mortal
Failing to see true death can allow no new self to be, which
Living, could tell itself how much it regrets the deceased and
Standing, lament that, prone, either wounding or fire will
    consume it.'

The poet had listened carefully while his verses were recited.
though he had to struggle slightly not to cough. This night
air . . . However he could not resist the temptation to acquaint
his host with a few lines which he had cut from the work so as
not to depress his readers unduly. In them he had set out the
reasons for this same effort to cling to what is disappearing. In a
hoarse voice, very clearly, slowed down by the need to remember,
he spoke these verses:

'When they complain their life has been stolen from them,
    they're complaining
Of an offence both practised on them and by themselves
    practised

For the same life that they've lost was stolen by them in the
first place.
Yes, when the fisherman snatches his fish from the sea, then the
traders
Snatch it in turn from him. And the woman who's hoping to
fry it
Ruefully eyes the bottle and pours the oil with reluctance
Into the waiting pan. O fear of a shortage! The risk of
Never replacing what's gone! The awful prospect of robbery!
Violence suited our fathers. And once their inheritance passes
See how their heirs will stoop to criminal acts to preserve it.
Trembling, the dyer will keep his lucrative recipe secret
Fearful of leaks. While in that circle of roistering writers
One will bite off his tongue on betraying some new inspiration.
Flattery serves the seducer to wheedle his girl into bed with
Just as the priest knows tricks to get alms from penurious
tenants
While the doctor finds industrial disease is a goldmine.
Who in a world like this can confront the concept of dying?
"Got it" and "drop it" alone determine how life will develop.
Whether you snatch or you hold, your hands begin curving
like talons.'

'You know the answer, you versifiers,' said the little general
pensively. 'But can you explain to me why it is only now, in these
particular days, that I again start hoping that not everything I've
done will be forgotten – even though fame is hazardous for me
and I am not indifferent towards death?'

'Perhaps your wish for fame is at the same time fear of death?'
The general seemed not to have heard. He looked nervously round
and motioned the torchbearer to withdraw. When he was a few
paces away he asked half-ashamedly, in something like a whisper:

'Where do you think my fame might lie?'

They started walking back. A gentle puff of wind broke the
evening stillness that lay over the garden. The poet coughed and
said, 'The conquest of Asia perhaps?' He realised that the general
was holding him by the sleeve and gazing round in alarm, and
hastily added, 'I don't know. Perhaps also the delicious cooking of
the victory banquet.'

After saying this casually he came to a sudden stop. Extending his finger he pointed at a cherry tree which stood on a small rise, its white blossom-covered branches waving in the wind.

'That's something else you brought back from Asia, isn't it?'

The general nodded.

'That could be it,' said the poet intensely. 'The cherry tree. I don't suppose it will recall your name to anyone. But what of that? Asia will be lost once more. And it won't be long before the general poverty forces us to give up cooking your favourite dishes. But the cherry tree. . . . There might all the same be one or two people who would know it was you that brought it. And even if there aren't, even if every trophy of every conqueror has crumbled to dust, this loveliest trophy of yours, Lucullus, will still be waving each spring in the wind of the hillsides; it will be the trophy of an unknown conqueror.'

THE UNSEEMLY OLD LADY

My grandmother was seventy-two years old when my grandfather died. He had a small lithographer's business in a little town in Baden and there he worked with two or three assistants until his death. My grandmother managed the household without a maid, looked after the ramshackle old house and cooked for the menfolk and children.

She was a thin little woman with lively lizard's eyes, though slow of speech. On very scanty means she had reared five of the seven children she had borne. As a result, she had grown smaller with the years.

Her two girls went to America and two of the sons also moved away. Only the youngest, who was delicate, stayed in the little town. He became a printer and set up a family far too large for him.

So after my grandfather died she was alone in the house.

The children wrote each other letters dealing with the problem of what should be done about her. One of them could offer her a home, and the printer wanted to move with his family into her house. But the old woman turned a deaf ear to these proposals and would only accept, from each of her children who could afford it, a small monetary allowance. The lithographer's business, long behind the times, was sold for practically nothing, and there were debts as well.

The children wrote saying that, all the same, she could not live quite alone, but since she entirely ignored this, they gave in and sent her a little money every month. At any rate, they thought, there was always the printer who had stayed in the town.

What was more, he undertook to give his brothers and sisters news of their mother from time to time. The printer's letters to my father, and what my father himself learnt on a visit and, two years later, after my grandmother's burial, give me a picture of what went on in those two years.

It seems that, from the start, the printer was disappointed that my grandmother had declined to take him into the house, which was fairly large and now standing empty. He had four children and lived in three rooms. But in any case the old lady had only very casual relations with him. She invited the children for coffee every Sunday afternoon, and that was about all.

She visited her son once or twice in three months and helped her daughter-in-law with the jam-making. The young woman gathered from some of her remarks that she found the printer's little dwelling too cramped for her. He, in reporting this, could not forbear to add an exclamation mark.

My father wrote asking what the old woman was up to nowadays, to which he replied rather curtly: going to the cinema.

It must be understood that this was not at all the thing; at least, not in her children's eyes. Thirty years ago the cinema was not what it is today. It meant wretched, ill-ventilated premises, often converted from disused skittle-alleys, with garish posters outside displaying the murders and tragedies of passion. Strictly speaking, only adolescents went or, for the darkness, courting couples. An old woman there by herself would certainly be conspicuous.

And there was another aspect of this cinema-going to be considered. Of course, admission was cheap, but since the pleasure fell more or less into the category of self-indulgences it represented 'money thrown away'. And to throw money away was not respectable.

Furthermore, not only did my grandmother keep up no regular association with her son in town, but she neither invited nor visited any of her other acquaintances. She never went to the coffee-parties in the little town. On the other hand, she frequented a cobbler's workshop in a poor and even slightly notorious alley where, especially in the afternoon, all manner of none too reputable characters hung about: out-of-work waitresses and itinerant craftsmen. The cobbler was a middle-aged man who had knocked about the world and never made much of himself. It was also said that he drank. In any case, he was no proper associate for my grandmother.

The printer intimated in a letter that he had hinted as much to his mother and had met with a very cool reply. 'He's seen a thing or two,' she answered and that was the end of the conversation. It was not easy to talk to my grandmother about things she did not wish to discuss.

About six months after my grandfather's death the printer wrote to my father saying that their mother now ate at the inn every other day.

That really was news! Grandmother, who all her life had cooked for a dozen people and herself had always eaten up the leavings, now ate at the inn. What had come over her?

Shortly after this, my father made a business trip in the neighbourhood and he visited his mother. She was just about to go out when he turned up. She took off her hat again and gave him a glass of red wine and a biscuit. She seemed in a perfectly equable mood, neither particularly animated nor particularly silent. She asked after us, though not in much detail, and wanted principally to know whether there were cherries for the children. There she was quite her old self. The room was of course scrupulously clean and she looked well.

The only thing that gave an indication of her new life was that she did not want to go with my father to the churchyard to visit her husband's grave. 'You can go by yourself,' she said lightly. 'It's the third on the left in the eleventh row. I've got to go somewhere.'

The printer said afterwards that probably she had had to go to her cobbler. He complained bitterly.

'Here am I, stuck in this hole with my family and only five hours' badly-paid work, on top of which my asthma's troubling me again, while the house in the main street stands empty.'

My father had taken a room at the inn, but nevertheless expected
to be invited by his mother, if only as a matter of form; however,
she did not mention it. Yet even when the house had been full,
she had always objected to his not staying with them and spending
money on an hotel into the bargain.

But she appeared to have finished with family life and to be
treading new paths now in the evening of her days. My father,
who had his fair share of humour, found her 'pretty sprightly'
and told my uncle to let the old woman do what she wanted.

And what did she want to do?

The next thing reported was that she had hired a brake and
taken an excursion on a perfectly ordinary Thursday. A brake
was a large, high-sprung, horse-drawn vehicle with a seating
capacity for whole families. Very occasionally, when we grand-
children had come for a visit, grandfather had hired a brake.
Grandmother had always stayed behind. With a scornful wave of
the hand she had refused to come along.

And after the brake came the trip to K., a larger town some two
hours' distance by train. There was a race-meeting there and it was
to the races that my grandmother went.

The printer was now positively alarmed. He wanted to have a
doctor called in. My father shook his head as he read the letter,
but was against calling in a doctor.

My grandmother had not travelled alone to K. She had taken
with her a young girl who, according to the printer's letter, was
slightly feeble-minded: the kitchen-maid at the inn where the old
lady took her meals every second day.

From now on this 'half-wit' played quite a part.

My grandmother apparently doted on her. She took her to the
cinema and to the cobbler – who, incidentally, turned out to be a
Social Democrat – and it was rumoured that the two women
played cards in the kitchen over a glass of wine.

'Now she's bought the half-wit a hat with roses on it,' wrote
the printer in despair. 'And our Anna has no Communion dress!'

My uncle's letters became quite hysterical, dealt only with the
'unseemly behaviour of our dear mother' and otherwise said
nothing. The rest I know from my father.

The innkeeper had whispered to him with a wink: 'Mrs. B's
enjoying herself nowadays, so they say.'

As a matter of fact, even in these last years my grandmother did not live extravagantly in any way. When she did not eat at the inn, she usually took no more than a little egg dish, some coffee and, above all, her beloved biscuits. She did, however, allow herself a cheap red wine, of which she drank a small glass at every meal. She kept the house very clean, and not just the bedroom and kitchen which she used. All the same, without her children's knowledge, she mortgaged it. What she did with the money never came out. She seems to have given it to the cobbler. After her death he moved to another town and was said to have started a fair-sized business in hand-made shoes.

When you come to think of it, she lived two lives in succession. The first one as daughter, wife and mother; the second simply as Mrs. B, an unattached person without responsibilities and with modest but sufficient means. The first life lasted some sixty years; the second no more than two.

My father learnt that in the last six months she had permitted herself certain liberties unknown to normal people. Thus she might rise in summer at three in the morning and take walks in the deserted streets of the little town, which she had entirely to herself. And, it was generally alleged, when the priest called on her to keep the old woman company in her loneliness, she invited him to the cinema.

She was not at all lonely. A crowd of jolly people forgathered at the cobbler's, it appears, and there was much gossip. She always kept a bottle of her red wine there and drank her little glassful whilst the others gossiped and inveighed against the town officials. This wine was reserved for her, though sometimes she provided stronger drink for the company.

She died quite suddenly on an autumn afternoon, in her bedroom, though not in bed but on an upright chair by the window. She had invited the 'half-wit' to the cinema that evening, so the girl was with her when she died. She was seventy-four years old.

I have seen a photograph of her which was taken for the children and shows her laid out.

What you see is a tiny little face, very wrinkled, and a thin-lipped, wide mouth. Much that is small, but no smallness. She had savoured to the full the long years of servitude and the short years of freedom and consumed the bread of life to the last crumb.

A QUESTION OF TASTE

We were sitting on straw-plaited chairs in the dining-room in one of those delightful old country houses near Paris. A long narrow window reached down to the stone floor, through which we could hear every now and again the clatter of a passing train or the blast of a motor-car horn; the reflection of the logs in the open fire-place flickered gently on the greenish wallpaper; our host the painter, known as Mountain on account of his girth, was roasting a massive piece of beef on an iron spit set upon a tripod. Standing at a small polished table, his wife was making the salad in a huge bowl with those attractive movements which delighted her audience on the Boul' Miche every evening when she served them one of her saucy songs. From his chair the small lean art dealer kept his eye on her, and each time she reached for one of the carafes of oil or vinegar she first waited for his nod of approval. The responsibility was too great for so small a person.

What with the large joint of beef and the dripping fat, the conversation revolved around materialism in German philo-sophy. Mountain was not at all pleased with it.

'They really did a proper job, those Germans,' he said indig-nantly, 'they spiritualised it to such an extent that only the ghost of anything material inhabits their systems. Of course it was to be expected that once they had got hold of it materialism wouldn't survive as a way of life, they just don't know how to live, the whole point of their philosophy is to teach people the best way of not living. From the start they excluded base materialism from their meditations and turned towards higher things which have nothing to do with the delights of eating because they have nothing to do with anything at all.'

I lodged a half-hearted protest but Mountain was in full swing.

'Materialism and six days without meat! Take Love, for example. For the Germans it's a movement of the soul. There's hardly any other movement involved. Couples just want to feel cosy. Love has got to be armless.'

I was somewhat astonished until I realised he meant harmless. We were speaking German. In French you simply can't say 'feel cosy'.

This put the art dealer on his guard.

'For God's sake, Jean, don't get so excited,' he exclaimed,

'you're turning the spit too quickly. You'll put paid to German materialism all right, but you're also destroying our own matter, the beef. Of course there's something in what you say. I love the Germans. You can't say they have no taste. Just think of their music. They can even afford somebody like that ghastly Wagner. Not that he affects the issue. It's just that their culture is perhaps a little too spiritual, wouldn't you say? You've got to have spirit, but you need the body too. What good would the spirit be without it? And really, after they've put something through the refiner, there isn't much left. Once they've refined it, their love is rather sexless, as you can see from their literature. They can't enjoy nature without premonitions of death. They have beautiful feelings, but rather deep down inside, so it seems. The sixth sense is there all right, but where are the other five? Bread, wine, the chair, your arms, Yvette – all the basic materials evaporate so easily for them. They pay no attention to fundamentals. For a start, they probably exaggerate the difference between man and animals. They only cultivate man, not the animal in him as well, they leave out too much. For them, spirit has too little to do with roast beef. Their taste for art is too remote from their taste for food: when it comes to the more bodily functions their sense of beauty lets them down.'

'Every sentence an insult,' I said laughing.

'Ah,' he said contentedly, 'we are a race of gluttons. Once food is involved you have to take us seriously.'

The salad was ready. With his longhandled scoop Mountain ladled the fat in the pan over the joint of beef, which quickly turned brown.

'I like the Germans too,' Yvette said dreamily, 'they take you seriously.'

'That's the worst thing that's been said about us so far,' I protested. 'Be thankful my reaction is purely spiritual and that I'm not throwing this stool at anybody. Nice table manners you have here. The joint is roasted, the salad's delicious, the guest is warned. He's going to be tested to see if he's capable of enjoying them. Woe betide him if he doesn't smack his lips!'

Yvette seemed dismayed.

'Oh, now you've intimidated him. It's all going to stick in his throat.'

Mountain manoeuvred the beef skilfully on to the table and seized the carving-knife.

'I'll tell him what I think about *us* and that will even things up. About our politics, for example, hein, mon ami?'

'I'll say something about that,' said I, and I did.

The joint was excellent, a work of art. I was on the brink of saying so but feared they would ask me straightaway if I could name one single German work of art that deserved to be called a joint of roast beef. Better stick to politics . . .

The art dealer had plenty of nasty things to say, particularly about colonial policy.

Yvette turned to me.

'Did you know Jean was an officer in the colonial army. He must tell you the story about the Kabyles and the cook in the Tangier fortifications – as a punishment.'

'I've been punished already,' I said. 'Even if I get something to eat now. My last meal – but I won't be getting until *after* my execution.'

'As a punishment for *him*,' said Yvette, 'for being a chauvinist.'

Mountain smiled. He broke some white bread, threw the pieces on to his plate and mopped up the fat as he began obediently to tell his story.

'It was in the Riff war. A ghastly business. We attacked a foreign people and then treated them like rebels. As you know, it's all right to treat barbarians barbarically. It's the desire to be barbaric that makes governments call their enemies barbarians. I didn't always see it that way, Yvette is right to insist that I tell the story once again to punish myself, because in the old days I used to tell it differently. I used to tell it to illustrate the chauvinism of our enemies. Well, history since then has taught me better. As you know, I was an officer. I won't talk about the war itself. That's better forgotten. We burnt things down and shot things up, and the newspapers spoke of strategy. Naturally our weapons were the better, so the generals were able to praise our heroism. I had been wounded slightly and was having lunch with our commander in the officers' mess in the fortifications. That's how I came to be present when they investigated the murder of one of the cooks by some Riff Kabyle prisoners. Let me tell you right away that they found out absolutely nothing.

'Very early on it became clear that the cook died of his own good nature. The Kabyles had been brought into the fortress in the afternoon, about seventy of them in all. Of course they weren't in particularly good condition, they'd been on the road for two days and those were some roads. On top of that they were starving. But in the fortress that day's rations had already been issued, so they couldn't be given anything until the next morning. They were crammed into one of the stone caves, and there they lay or stood screaming for food. The stronger ones dragged themselves to the iron grating and pleaded with the guards or cursed them.

'The cook, in civilian life a small fishmonger in Marseilles, took pity on them and wondered how he could get round the regulations. Hats off to him, he alone stood for the France of the Convention.

'In the evening he took along a basket with loaves of bread which he had saved up somehow or other and a handful of cigarettes for bribing the guards with. He bought the cigarettes in the canteen out of his wages. As I said, may the earth lie gently upon him.

'It worked. The guards weren't monsters, they were smokers, and the prisoners got their loaves of bread.

'Later that evening the cook went down to them once again because he had forgotten his basket and didn't want it to be discovered at the morning inspection. You understand, the whole affair was illegal.

'Next morning his body was found in the cave.

'When the guard changed the first thing that happened was another great rumpus. The prisoners complained, yelling that they'd been given stale bread. True enough, only one of them had been able to eat his loaf.

'But the cook lay in the corner with his head bashed in.

'That's all there is to the story really. The inquiry got nowhere. The cook had brought the prisoners bread, they had killed him just the same. Nobody could discover how. The most careful search of the cell produced no weapon. It was a complete mystery. Since the mystery was never solved, the story has no point either. It's really not much good as an example of chauvinism, that would be plain silly. Perhaps these Kabyles were chauvinists but we were worse ones. From childhood on, we had been brainwashed, it's my only excuse for the way I used to misinterpret this affair. All it proves is that you can't be kind-heated in wartime. One can't say: we want to shoot the women and children to smithereens but that's as far as we'll go. We won't go any further. We're going to be beasts, but only up to a point. Nor could the cook have said: I'm neither a Frenchman now nor a soldier, I'm just a cook. The stack of loaves didn't fool the Kabyles.'

Mountain had long since stopped eating and was now playing with the crumbs of white bread.

After a short pause the art dealer said:

'But we can drink to the man from Marseilles. He made a mistake, but some mistakes are terrible.'

We emptied our glasses. Then I couldn't help remarking: 'Yet another race that doesn't appreciate bread properly.'

We laughed.

Yvette passed round the cheese. The little art dealer was just raising his knife when something occurred to him.

'There's a solution to that mystery,' he said slowly. 'I can tell you why the cook was killed.'

Mountain simply asked: 'Why?'

'It wasn't despite his bringing those loaves of bread but because of it. They were too stale, just as you said. Inedible. Hard.'

'With one exception,' muttered Mountain. 'Yes, perhaps that's a way of looking at it too. But that doesn't solve the mystery. It only supplies the motive.'

'There's still the little matter of the weapon,' said the art dealer. 'And we can solve that too. I suggest the weapon was a loaf of bread. An old loaf of bread, too hard for the Kabyles to chew. And too hard for the cook's skull.'

Mountain opened his big blue eyes in astonishment.

'That's really good,' he said admiringly. 'Perhaps you know who the murderer was as well?'

'Of course,' said the art dealer without further ado. 'The murderer was the Kabyle who had eaten his loaf although it was so hard. He had to eat it, otherwise they'd have found blood on it.'

'Oh,' said Yvette.

'Yes,' said the little art dealer seriously. 'They knew a thing or two about bread. They had good taste.'

THE AUGSBURG CHALK CIRCLE

In the days of the Thirty Years War a Swiss Protestant by the name of Zingli owned a large tannery and leather business in the free imperial city of Augsburg on the Lech. He was married to an Augsburg woman and had a child by her. As the Catholics marched on the city his friends strongly advised him to flee, but, whether it was that his small family held him back or that he did not want to abandon his tannery, he simply could not make up his mind to leave while there was yet time.

Thus he was still there when the imperial troops stormed the city and, while they plundered it that evening, he hid in a pit in the courtyard where the dyes were stored. His wife was to have moved with the child to her relatives on the outskirts, but she spent too much time packing her belongings – dresses, jewellery and bedding – and so it came about that suddenly she saw from a window on the first storey a squad of imperial soldiers forcing their way into the courtyard. Beside herself with fear, she dropped everything and fled from the place through a back door.

So the child was left behind in the house. It lay in its cradle in the large hall and played with a wooden ball that hung on a string from the ceiling.

Only a young servant-girl was still in the house. She was busy with the copper pots and pans in the kitchen when she heard a noise from the street. Darting to the window she saw soldiers throwing all kinds of loot into the street from the first storey of the house opposite. She ran to the hall and was just about to take the child out of the cradle when she heard the sound of heavy blows on the oaken front door. She was seized with panic and flew up the stairs.

The hall was filled with drunken soldiers, who smashed everything to pieces. They knew they were in a Protestant's house. As though by a miracle Anna, the servant-girl, remained undiscovered throughout the searching and plundering. The soldiers made off and, scrambling out of the cupboard in which she had been standing, Anna found the child in the hall, also unharmed. She snatched it up hastily and stole with it into the courtyard. In the meantime night had fallen, but the red glow from a burning house near by lit up the courtyard, and with horror she saw the battered corpse of her master. The soldiers had dragged him from his pit and butchered him.

Only now did the girl realise the danger she ran should she be caught in the street with the Protestant's child. With a heavy heart she laid it back in the cradle, gave it a little milk to drink, rocked it to sleep and made her way towards that part of the city where her married sister lived. At about 10 o'clock at night, accompanied by her sister's husband, she elbowed her way through the throng of soldiers celebrating their victory to go to the outskirts and find Frau Zingli, the mother of the child. They knocked on the door of an imposing house, which, after quite a long while, did open slightly. A little old man, Frau Zingli's uncle, stuck his head out. Anna announced breathlessly that Herr Zingli was dead but the child unharmed in the house. The old man looked at her coldly with fish-like eyes and said his niece was no longer there and he himself washed his hands of the Protestant bastard. With that he shut the door again. As they left, Anna's brother-in-law noticed a curtain move at one of the windows and was convinced that Frau Zingli was there. Apparently she felt no shame in repudiating her child.

Anna and her brother-in-law walked on side by side in silence for a while. Then she declared that she wanted to go back to the tannery and fetch the child. Her brother-in-law, a quiet respectable man, listened to her aghast and tried to talk her out of this dangerous notion. What were these people to her? She had not even been decently treated.

Anna heard him out and promised to do nothing rash. Nevertheless, she must just look in quickly at the tannery to see whether the child needed anything. And she wanted to go alone.

And go she did. In the midst of the devastated hall the child lay peacefully in its cradle and slept. Wearily Anna sat down by its side and gazed at it. She had not dared to kindle a light, but the nearby house was still burning and by its light she could see the child quite well. It had a tiny mole on its little neck.

When the girl had watched the child breathing and sucking its small fist for some time, maybe an hour, she realized that she had now stayed too long and seen too much to be able to leave without the child. She got to her feet heavily and with slow movements wrapped it in its linen coverlet, picked it up in her arms and left the courtyard with it, looking round furtively like someone with a bad conscience, a thief.

After long consultations with sister and brother-in-law, she took the child to the country two weeks later, to the village of Grossaitingen, where her elder brother was a peasant. The farm belonged to his wife: he had merely married into it. It had been agreed that perhaps it would be best to tell no one but her brother who the child was, for they had never set eyes on the young wife and did not know how she would receive so dangerous a little guest.

Anna reached the village at about midday. Her brother, his wife and the farm-servants were at table. She was not ill received, but one glance at her new sister-in-law decided her to introduce the child then and there as her own. It was not until she had explained that her husband had a job at a mill in a distant village and expected her there with the child in a few weeks that the peasant woman thawed and the child was duly admired.

That afternoon she accompanied her brother to the copse to gather wood. They sat down on tree-stumps and Anna made a clean breast of it. She could see that he felt uncomfortable. His position on the farm was still insecure and he commended Anna warmly for having held her tongue in front of his wife. It was plain that he did not credit his young wife with a particularly broadminded attitude towards the Protestant child. He wished the deception to be kept up.

However, that was not so easy as time went on.

Anna joined in the harvesting and tended 'her' child between whiles, constantly running back from the fields to the house when the others rested. The little boy thrived and even grew fat, chuckled whenever he saw Anna and made manful efforts to raise his head. But then came winter and the sister-in-law started to make enquiries about Anna's husband.

There was nothing against Anna staying on at the farm; she could make herself useful. The trouble was that the neighbours were growing curious about the father of Anna's boy, since he never came to see how he was getting on. If she could not produce a father for her child, the farm would get itself talked about before long.

One Sunday morning the peasant harnessed the horse and

called Anna loudly to come with him to fetch a calf from a neighbouring village. As they clattered along the road he told her that he had sought and found a husband for her. It was a dying cottager who, when the two of them stood in his mean hovel, could barely lift his wasted head from the soiled sheet.

He was willing to marry Anna. A yellow-skinned old woman, his mother, stood at the bedside. She was to have a reward for the service rendered to Anna.

The bargain was concluded in ten minutes and Anna and her brother were able to drive on and buy their calf. The wedding took place at the end of that same week. Whilst the priest mumbled the marriage ritual, the lifeless glance of the sick man did not once stray towards Anna. Her brother was in no doubt that she would have the death certificate within a few days. Then Anna's husband, the father of her child, would have died somewhere in a village near Augsburg on his way to her and no one would give the matter another thought if the widow stayed on in her brother's house.

Anna returned joyfully from her strange wedding, at which there had been neither church bells nor a brass band, neither bridesmaids nor guests. By way of a wedding-breakfast she ate a piece of bread with a slice of bacon in the larder and then, with her brother, went towards the wooden chest in which lay the child who now had a name. She tucked in the covers more tightly and smiled at her brother.

The death certificate certainly took its time.

Indeed, no word came from the old woman the next nor yet the following week. Anna had given out on the farm that her husband was at present on his way to her. When she was asked what was delaying him now she said that the deep snow must be making the journey difficult. But after another three weeks had gone by, her brother, seriously perturbed, drove to the village near Augsburg.

He came back late at night. Anna was still up and ran to the door as she heard the wheels crunch in the yard. She noticed how slowly the farmer unharnessed and a spasm went through her heart.

He brought bad tidings. On entering the hut he had found the doomed man sitting at the table in shirt-sleeves having supper, chewing away with his mouth full. He was completely restored.

The peasant did not look Anna in the face as he went on telling her. The cottager – his name, by the way, was Otterer – and his mother appeared equally astonished by the turn of events and had probably not yet decided what was to be done. Otterer had not made an unpleasant impression. He had said little, but at one point, when his mother had started lamenting that he was now saddled with an unwanted wife and a stranger's child, he had commanded her to be silent. He went on eating his cheese with deliberation throughout the interview and was still eating when the farmer took his leave.

During the following days Anna was naturally very troubled. In between her housework she taught the boy to walk. When he let go of the distaff and came tottering towards her with little outstretched arms, she suppressed a dry sob and clasped him tightly to her as she picked him up.

Once she asked her brother: 'What sort of a man is he?' She had seen him only on his deathbed and then only in the evening by poor candlelight. Now she learnt that her husband was a man in his fifties worn out by toil: was, in fact, what a cottager would be.

Shortly after, she saw him. With a great show of secrecy a pedlar had given her a message that 'a certain acquaintance' wished to meet her on such-and-such a date at such-and-such a time near such-and-such a village, at the spot where the footpath went off to Landsberg. So the married couple met midway between their villages, like the commanders of old between their battle-lines, on open ground, which was covered with snow.

Anna did not take to the man.

He had small grey teeth, looked her up and down – although she was hidden under a thick sheepskin and there was not much to be seen – and then used the words 'the sacrament of marriage'. She told him curtly that she would have to think things over and that he should get some dealer or slaughterer passing through Grossaitingen to tell her in her sister-in-law's hearing that he would soon be coming now and had merely been taken ill on the journey.

Otterer nodded in his deliberate way. He was more than a head taller than she and kept on glancing at the left side of her neck as they talked, which exasperated her.

But the message did not come, and Anna toyed with the idea of simply leaving the farm with the child and looking for work further south, perhaps in Kempten or Sonnthofen. Only the perils of the highway, about which there was much talk, and the fact that it was mid-winter held her back.

But now her stay at the farm grew difficult. Her sister-in-law put suspicious questions to her about her husband at the dinner table in front of all the farm-servants. When on one occasion she went so far as to glance at the child and exclaim loudly in false compassion, 'poor mite!', Anna resolved to go despite everything; but at that point the child fell ill.

He lay restlessly in his wooden chest with a flushed face and clouded eyes, and Anna watched over him for nights on end with fear and hope. When he was on the road to recovery again and his smile had come back, there was a knock on the door one morning and in walked Otterer.

There was no one in the room but Anna and the child, so that she had no need to dissemble, which in any case the shock would have prevented. They stood for quite some time without a word; then Otterer announced that for his part he had thought the matter over and had come to fetch her. He referred again to the sacrament of marriage.

Anna grew angry. In a firm, though low voice she told the man she would not think of living with him, she had entered into the marriage only for the sake of the child and wanted nothing of him beyond giving her and the child his name.

As she mentioned the child Otterer glanced fleetingly towards the chest in which it lay gurgling, without, however, going up to it. This set Anna against him even more.

He voiced a few remarks: she should think things over again; there was scant fare in his home; his mother could sleep in the kitchen. Then the sister-in-law came in, greeted him inquisitively and invited him to dinner. He was already seated at table as he greeted the peasant with a careless nod, neither pretending that he did not know him nor betraying that he did. To the wife's questions he replied in monosyllables, not raising his eyes from his plate, that he had found a job in Mering and Anna could join him. But he no longer suggested that this had to be at once.

During the afternoon he avoided the brother's company and

chopped wood behind the house, which no one had asked him to do. After supper, of which he again partook in silence, the sister-in-law herself carried a featherbed into Anna's room so that he could spend the night there; but at that, strange to say, he rose awkwardly to his feet and mumbled that he must get back that night. Before leaving, he gazed with an absentminded expression into the chest where the child lay, but said nothing and did not touch him.

During the night Anna was taken ill and fell into a fever which lasted for weeks. Most of the time she lay apathetically; only now and then towards midday, when the fever abated a little, she crawled to the child's wooden chest and tucked in the covers.

In the fourth week of her illness Otterer drove into the yard in a farm cart and took her and the child away. She let this happen without a word.

Only very slowly did she regain her strength, and small wonder on the cottager's thin soup. But one morning she noticed how dirty and neglected the child looked and resolutely got up.

The little boy received her with his friendly smile in which, her brother had always declared, he took after her. He had grown and now crawled all over the room with lightning speed, slapping his hands on the floor and emitting little screams when he fell on his face. She washed him in a wooden tub and recovered her confidence.

A few days later, however, she could stand life in the hovel no longer. She wrapped the little boy in a few blankets, stuck a piece of bread and some cheese in her pocket and ran away.

She intended to reach Sonnthofen, but did not get far. She was still very weak in the knees, the highway was covered in slush and, as a result of the war, people in the villages had grown very suspicious and stingy. On the third day of her wayfaring she sprained her foot in a ditch and after many hours, during which she feared for the child, she was brought to a farmstead, where she lay in the byre. The little boy crawled about between the cows' legs and only laughed when she cried out anxiously. In the end she had to tell the farm people her husband's name and he fetched her back again to Mering.

From now on she made no further attempt to escape and accepted her lot. She worked hard. It was difficult to extract anything from the small plot and keep the tiny property going. Yet the man was not unkind to her, and the little boy ate his fill. Also her brother occasionally came over bringing a present of this or that, and once she was even able to have a little coat dyed red for the child. That, she thought, would suit a dyer's child well.

As time passed she grew quite contented and experienced many joys in bringing up the child. Thus several years went by.

But one day she went to the village to buy syrup and on her return the child was not in the hut and her husband told her that a grandly dressed lady had driven up in a coach and taken the child away. She reeled against the wall in horror, and that very evening, carrying nothing but a bundle of food, she set out for Augsburg.

Her first call in the imperial city was at the tannery. She was not admitted and could not catch sight of the child.

Her sister and brother-in-law tried in vain to console her. She ran to the authorities and, beside herself, shouted that her child had been stolen. She went so far as to hint that Protestants had stolen her child. Whereupon she learnt that other times now prevailed and that peace had been concluded between Catholics and Protestants.

She would scarcely have accomplished anything had not a singular piece of luck come to her aid. Her case was referred to a judge who was a quite exceptional man.

This was the judge Ignaz Dollinger, famed throughout Swabia for his boorishness and his erudition, known to the Elector of Bavaria, whose legal dispute with the free imperial city he had had to settle, as 'this Latin clodhopper', but celebrated by the people in a long ballad.

Accompanied by her sister and brother-in-law, Anna came before him. The short but immensely corpulent old man sat in a tiny bare room amidst piles of documents and listened to her only very briefly. Then he wrote something down, growled: 'Step over there, and be quick about it!' and indicated with his small plump hand a spot in the room on which the light fell through a narrow window. For some minutes he studied her face closely, then waved her aside with a snort.

The next day he sent a tipstaff to fetch her and while she was still on the threshold shouted at her: 'Why didn't you let on that what you're after is a tannery and the sizable property that goes with it?'

Anna said doggedly that what she was after was the child.

'Don't go thinking that you can grab the tannery,' shouted the judge. 'If the bastard really is yours, the property goes to Zingli's relatives.'

Anna nodded without looking at him. Then she said: 'He doesn't need the tannery.'

'Is he yours?' barked the judge.

'Yes,' she said softly. 'If I could just keep him until he can say all the words. So far he only knows seven.'

The judge coughed and straightened the documents on his table. Then he said more quietly, though still in an irritable tone: 'You want the brat and that bitch with her five silk skirts wants him. But he needs the real mother.'

'Yes,' said Anna, and looked at the judge.

'Be off with you,' he growled. 'The Court sits on Saturday.'

On that Saturday the main road and the square outside the Town Hall by the Perlach Tower were black with people who wanted to attend the proceedings over the Protestant child. This remarkable case had made a great stir from the start, and in dwellings and taverns there were arguments about who was the real and who was the false mother. Moreover, old Dollinger was renowned far and wide for his down-to-earth proceedings, his biting remarks and wise sayings. His trials drew more people than minstrels and fairs.

Thus it was not only many Augsburgers who thronged outside the Town Hall; there were also not a few farmers from the surrounding countryside. Friday was market-day and, in anticipation of the law-suit, they had spent the night in the city.

The hall in which Judge Dollinger heard his cases was the so-called Golden Hall. It was famous as the only hall of its size without pillars in the whole of Germany; the ceiling was suspended from the rafters by chains.

Judge Dollinger sat, a small round mountain of flesh, in front of a closed metal gate along one wall. An ordinary rope cordoned off the public. But the judge sat on the bare floor and had no table before him. He had personally instituted this setting years ago: he strongly believed in staging things properly.

Inside the roped-off enclosure were Frau Zingli with her parents, the newly arrived Swiss relatives of the late Herr Zingli – two well-dressed worthies looking like substantial merchants – and Anna Otterer with her sister. A nurse holding the child could be seen next to Frau Zingli.

Everybody, litigants and witnesses, stood. Judge Dollinger was wont to say that trials tended to be shorter if the participants had to stand. But perhaps, too, he made them stand in order to conceal himself from the public, so that people had to stand on tiptoe and crane their necks to see him.

At the start of the proceedings an incident occurred. When Anna caught sight of the child, she uttered a cry and stepped forward, and the child tried to go to her, struggled violently in the nurse's arms and started to scream. The judge ordered him to be taken out of the hall.

Then he called Frau Zingli.

She came rustling forward and described – now and again raising a little handkerchief to her eyes – how the imperial soldiers had snatched the child from her at the time of the looting. That same night the servant-girl had come to her father's place and had reported that the child was still in the house, probably in the hope of a tip. One of the father's cooks, on being sent to the tannery, had not, however, found the child, and she assumed that this person (she pointed at Anna) had taken him in order to be able to extort money in some way or other. No doubt she would have come out with such demands sooner or later had she not been deprived of the child beforehand.

Judge Dollinger called Herr Zingli's two relatives and asked them whether they had enquired after Herr Zingli at the time and what Frau Zingli had told them.

They testified that Frau Zingli had told them her husband had been killed and that she had entrusted the child to a servant-girl where it would be in good keeping. They spoke of her in a most unfriendly manner which, indeed, was no wonder, since the property would come to them if Frau Zingli lost the case.

Following their evidence the judge turned again to Frau Zingli and wanted to know from her whether she had not simply lost her head at the time of the attack and abandoned the child.

Frau Zingli looked at him with her pallid blue eyes as if in astonishment and said in injured tones that she had not abandoned her child.

Judge Dollinger cleared his throat and asked her with some interest whether she believed that no mother could abandon her child.

Yes, that was what she believed, she said firmly.

Did she then believe, the judge asked further, that a mother who nevertheless did so ought to have her behind thrashed, regardless of how many skirts she wore over it?

Frau Zingli made no answer and the judge called the former servant-girl Anna. She stepped forward quickly and said in a low voice what she had already said at the preliminary enquiry. But she talked as though she were listening at the same time, and every now and again she glanced at the big door through which the child had been taken, as though she were afraid it might still be screaming.

She testified that, although she had called at the house of Frau Zingli's uncle that night, she had not gone back to the tannery, out of fear of the imperial troops and because she was worried about her own illegitimate child which had been placed with good people in the neighbouring village if Lechhausen.

Old Dollinger interrupted her rudely and snapped that at least there had been one person in the city who had felt something like fear. He was glad to be able to establish the fact, since it proved that at least one person had had some sense at the time. It was not, of course, very nice of the witness that she had only been concerned about her own child, but on the other hand, as the popular saying went, blood was thicker than water, and anyone who was a proper mother would go to the lengths of stealing for her child, though this was strictly forbidden by law, for property was property, and those who stole also lied, and lying was similarly forbidden by law. And then he gave one of his wise and pungent lectures on the infamy of people who deceived the Court till they were blue in the face; and, after a short digression on peasants who watered the milk of innocent cows and the City Council which levied too high market-taxes on the peasants – which had absolutely nothing to do with the case – he announced that the examination of witnesses was over and had led nowhere.

Then he made a long pause and showed every sign of being at

a loss, gazing about him as though he expected someone or other to suggest how to arrive at a solution.

People looked at one another dumbfounded and some of them craned their necks to catch a glimpse of the helpless judge. But it remained very quiet in the hall; only the crowd in the street below could be heard.

Then, sighing, the judge began to speak again.

'It has not been established who is the real mother,' he said. 'The child is to be pitied. We have all heard of fathers dodging their duty and not wanting to be fathers – the rogues! – but here are two mothers both laying claim. The Court has listened to them as long as they deserve, namely a full five minutes to each, and the Court is convinced that both are lying like a book. But, as already said, we still have to think of the child who must have a mother. Therefore it has to be established, without paying attention to mere babble, who the real mother of the child is.'

And in a cross voice he called the usher and ordered him to bring a piece of chalk.

The usher went and fetched a piece of chalk.

'Draw a circle with the chalk on the floor big enough for three people to stand in,' the judge directed him.

The usher knelt down and drew the circle with the chalk as requested.

'Now fetch the child,' ordered the judge.

The child was brought in. He started to howl again and tried to go to Anna. Old Dollinger took no notice of the crying and merely delivered his address in a rather louder voice.

'This test which is now about to be applied,' he announced, 'I found in an old book and it is considered extremely good. The simple idea underlying the test with the chalk circle is that the real mother will be recognized by her love for the child. Hence the strength of this love must be tested. Usher, place the child in that chalk circle.'

The usher took the wailing child from the nurse's hand and led him into the circle. The judge went on, turning towards Frau Zingli and Anna:

'You go and stand in the chalk circle too; each of you take one of the child's hands and when I say "go!" try and pull the child out of the circle. Whichever of you has the stronger love will also pull with the greater strength and thus bring the child to her side.'

There was a stir in the hall. The spectators stood on tiptoe and had words with those standing in front of them.

But there was dead silence again as the two women stepped into the circle and each grasped one of the child's hands. The child had also fallen silent, as though he sensed what was at stake. He turned his little tear-stained face up to Anna. Then the judge gave the order 'Go!'.

And with a single violent jerk Frau Zingli tore the child out of the chalk circle. Bewildered and incredulous, Anna's eyes followed him. For fear that he might come to harm if both his little arms were pulled in two directions at once, she had immediately let go.

Old Dollinger stood up.

'And thus we know,' he said loudly, 'who is the right mother. Take the child away from the slut. She would tear him to pieces in cold blood.'

And he nodded to Anna and quickly left the hall to have his breakfast.

And in the following weeks the peasants round about, who were pretty wide-awake, talked of how the judge on awarding the child to the woman from Mering had winked at her.

TWO SONS

In January 1945, as Hitler's war was drawing to a close, a farmer's wife in Thuringia dreamt that her son at the front was calling her and, on going out into the yard dazed with sleep, she fancied she saw him at the pump, drinking. When she spoke to him she realized that it was one of the young Russian prisoners of war who were working as forced labour on the farm. A few days later she had a strange experience. She was bringing the prisoners their food in a nearby copse, where they were uprooting tree-stumps. Looking back over her shoulder as she went away she saw the same young prisoner of war – a sickly creature – turning his face with a disappointed expression towards the mess-tin of soup someone was handing to him, and suddenly his face became that of her son. During the next few days she repeatedly experienced the swift, and as swiftly vanishing, transformations of this particular young man's face into that of her son. Then the prisoner fell sick; he lay untended in the barn. The farmer's wife felt a rising impulse to take him something nourishing, but she was prevented by her brother who, disabled in the war, ran the farm and treated the prisoners brutally, particularly now that everything was beginning to go to pieces and the village was beginning to feel afraid of the prisoners. The farmer's wife herself could not close her ears to his arguments; she did not think it at all right to help these sub-humans, of whom she had heard horrifying things. She lived in dread of what the enemy might do to her son, who was in the East. So her half-formed resolve to help *this* prisoner in his forlorn condition had not yet been carried out when, one evening, she came unexpectedly upon a group of the prisoners in the little snow-covered orchard in eager conversation, held in the cold, no doubt, to keep it secret. The young man was there, too, shivering with fever and, probably because of his exceptionally weak condition, it was he who was most startled by her. In his fright, his face now again underwent the curious transformation, so that she was looking into her son's face, and it was very frightened. She was greatly exercised by this and, although she dutifully reported the conversation in the orchard to her brother, she made up her mind that she would now slip the young man some ham-rind as she had planned. This, like many a good deed under the Third Reich, proved to be exceedingly difficult and dangerous. It was a venture in which her own brother was her enemy, nor could she feel sure of the prisoners either. Nevertheless, she brought it off. True, it led her to the discovery that the prisoners really did intend to make their escape, since each day, with the approaching Red Armies, there was greater danger that they would be moved westwards or simply massacred. The farmer's wife could not refuse certain requests, made clear to her in mime and a smattering of German by the young prisoner, to whom she was bound by her strange experience; and in this way she let herself be involved in the prisoners' escape plans. She provided a jacket and a large pair of hand shears. Curiously enough, from that time on the change no longer occurred: she was now simply helping the young stranger. So it was a shock when, one morning in late February, there was a knock on her window and through the pane she saw in the half-light the face of her son. And this time it was her son. He wore the torn uniform of the *Waffen S.S.*, his unit had been cut to pieces and he said agitatedly that the Russians were now only a few kilometres from the village. His homecoming must be kept a dead secret. At a sort of war council held by the farmer's wife, her brother and her son in a corner of the loft, it was decided first and foremost that they must get rid of the prisoners, since they might have caught sight of the S.S. man and in any case would presumably testify to their treatment. There was a quarry not far off. The S.S. man insisted that during that night he must lure them one by one out of the barn and kill them. The corpses could then be dumped in the quarry. Earlier they should be given some rations of alcohol; this would not strike them as too odd, the brother thought, since lately he, as well as the farm-hands, had been downright friendly to the Russians, to put them in a favourable frame of mind at the eleventh hour. Whilst the young S.S. man expounded his plan, he suddenly saw his mother shudder. The menfolk decided not to let her go near the barn again in any circumstances. Thus, filled with horror, she awaited nightfall. The Russians accepted the brandy with apparent gratitude and the farmer's wife heard them drunkenly singing their melancholy songs. But when, towards eleven o'clock, her son went into the barn, the prisoners were gone. They had feigned drunkenness. It was precisely the new, unnatural friendliness of the farm people that had convinced them that the Red Army must be very close. The Russians arrived during the latter part of the night. The son was lying drunk in the loft, while the farmer's wife, panic stricken, tried to burn his S.S. uniform. Her brother had also got drunk; it was she who had to receive the Russian soldiers and feed them. She did it with a stony face. The Russians left in the morning; the Red Army continued its advance. The son, haggard with sleeplessness, wanted more brandy and announced his firm intention of getting through to the German army units in retreat to go on fighting. The farmer's wife did not try to explain to him that to go on fighting now meant certain destruction. Desperate, she barred his way and tried to restrain him physically. He hurled her back on to the straw. As she got to her feet again she felt a wooden stake in her hand and, with a great heave, she felled the frenzied man to the ground.

That same morning a farmer's wife drove a cart to Russian headquarters in the neighbouring hamlet and surrendered her son, bound with bullock-halters, as a prisoner of war, so that, as she tried to explain to an interpreter, he should stay alive.

Appendix

LIFE STORY OF THE BOXER SAMSON-KÖRNER

When they ask you to write something about your own life it isn't all that easy to get it together. The trouble is that when you come to look closely there are two sides to everything, and one of those sides gets more or less paid for while the other can run you into a lot of expense. This makes it particularly important that everything should be looked at with a view to the second side.

So let me say right away that I was born in Beaver, State of Utah, U.S.A., in the Mormon area close to the Great Salt Lake. I can also suggest why I was born there: it was because Beaver, State of Utah, U.S.A., is not on the railroad. It is a place where you can marry twelve wives, but if you want to look at the house where I was born you can't get there except on foot.

That's one side of it. It's very important, because that's the only reason why I came to be a proper Yankee and didn't need to spend twelve years behind barbed wire playing poker.

To look at the other side: I was born in Zwickau, Saxony, because that's where I first saw daylight. I remained in Zwickau for roughly thirteen years, most of which I spent in the Hotel Deutscher Kaiser. The hotel was named after the Emperor of Germany and belonged to one of my uncles. There I learned a game known as opening doors, carrying bags and cleaning shoes. This came in very handy a bare year later in England, when the wolf was somewhat at the door: it helped me get a job in Cardiff; for it's the same the whole world over, or so I've always maintained. London and Hamburg are not all that different, and anybody who thinks there are things that matter more in this world than having your shoes cleaned, your bags carried and your door opened is kidding himself.

At the outset there were four months when I wanted to be an electrical engineer in Zwickau, and I could have become one as well as the next man if it had not been for my father's remarriage. It was mainly because of this that I left Zwickau and shelved all idea of electrical engineering. Moving on to Aue – without a word to my father, let me say, since I chose not to consult him – I became oddjob man in a restaurant. There I met someone who got me a job as a farmhand on an estate near Altenburg. The estate in question was my main reason for leaving for England shortly afterwards at the age of fourteen. It was there, you see, near Altenburg that I read about Hamburg for the first time.

From then on I set my sights on Hamburg.

In point of fact I started by first going to Eisenach, where I got to know a gentleman who had a beer business. He set me to drive his beer waggon, but in return he wanted me to take evening classes. And that knocked the bung out of the beer barrel, so to speak. Off I went to Hamburg.

Not that I went by train, even though my father had belatedly sent me 200 marks for the Eisenach trip. These, I thought, might come in quite useful, so I preferred 'Shanks's mare'.

By the time I reached Hamburg there were three of us. The roads were packed with fellows my age wanting to go to Hamburg. Once there I was surprised to find there was so much less water than I could have wished but, in lieu of that, a vast number of establishments for losing your money in. For twenty pfennigs a night I stayed in a lodging in St. Pauli, the so-called Dalbude. We kept trying to find a ship that would take us, but they were terribly strict about papers and anyway they'd only let you come as a ship's boy, which would by no means have been a congenial profession. I tried to maintain my funds at a certain level by buying and selling all kinds of things, mostly oldish shoes, things everybody needs and you can earn a few coppers with; but the money melted away like butter in the sun, and very soon in any case the 'heat' was on. Meaning by 'heat' that the police began taking an interest in us. As soon as they saw a young fellow without papers those policemen's eyes popped out as if on cherry-stalks. I moved on to Bremerhaven.

In Bremerhaven I had the advantage of knowing that you have first to have somewhere to sleep if the money is not to disappear so quickly; for you can't tie your coins to a string in a hotel the same way you can in a dosshouse. But in Bremerhaven once again the ships had no use for me, and I was forced to spend most of my time sitting around in beer houses if I was even to hear talk of the sea. And time was something I had only too much of. I was at least as tall and strong as any twenty year-old and my cheek was boundless. But I couldn't get on to any of those damned ships and once again my money melted like butter in the sun, in other words it was nothing more than a grease-mark. I got to know a young fellow from Saxony who was in the same kind of predicament, and we started chumming up mainly with the English sailors. The point being that they preferred going ashore to cleaning up their ship. Instead of that they now had us, and they were glad enough to pay us to hose down the engine room for them. It struck me that I might stay on board after the engines had started, and sail over to London with them whether or not it suited their book.

One evening I told the young Saxon 'we're going to stow away'. That night when the ship sailed we were down in the coal bunkers, and off we went to London. It wasn't too bad to begin with, though it was rather cramped and dark, but then the first major snag appeared. Towards dawn I started being seasick. She kept going up and down, and so did my stomach, to such an extent in fact that I said 'I'm not staying down here, I'm going up top'.

When they saw us they weren't all that bothered. I said 'me go with'. And they understood, even when I said it in German. They gave us something to eat and put us to work in the open air.

About 9 o'clock the first pilot came aboard, and the first thing we heard was that the ship wasn't bound for London after all but for Antwerp. Right, I said, let's go to Antwerp.

Soon after that things started to get very nice. The weather was better too. We sat on deck and peeled potatoes. We saw lots of ships. That lasted for three days. Then came the Scheldt, which was rather less interesting, and on the third afternoon we did indeed arrive at Antwerp. There they promptly chucked us off.

We didn't know a thing about Antwerp, and it was not easy to stick it out for four whole days. Luckily the ship's carpenter had taken a great shine to my little Saxon and before we got chucked off he gave us a few shillings. What's more, we had regular meal tickets, that's to say at mealtimes we went to one ship or another, queued up and held out our plates. We had begun to learn from experience.

On the fourth day the carpenter told us 'we sail tonight, I don't suppose I'll be seeing you again'.

That evening we stowed away in the coal bunker once more. It's a mistake to keep dealing with a different lot of people. Soon after that we were sailing down the Channel and once again I got seasick. I went above, and they were glad to see us back peeling potatoes. In Cardiff (England) they chucked us off once more.

Once more the carpenter gave us a few shillings and said 'Auf Wiedersehen'.

But we wanted to get to London. Admittedly London was the other side of the island, but it was a great city with lots of possibilities. We stowed away once more.

This time people were not so nice to us. Once they had dragged us out we had to work like beavers, and even so they shipped us off on the pilot boat with a letter baldly addressed 'Police'. They told us that was where we should apply. However, we thought the police wouldn't be the right people for us, and chose instead to throw the letter in the sea. On the pilot boat I got terribly seasick. The pilot chucked us off at Land's End and we hoofed it sadly back to Cardiff. London couldn't be reached that way. Later we got there via Alexandria.

In Cardiff once again there was nothing doing. It was time for more drastic measures. We went to Bristol to see the German consul. But he at once observed our lack of financial backing and chucked us out with a shilling or two. After that we thought we'd go back to Cardiff.

There were a whole lot of boats lying around on the beach without a soul in them. We got into one. But when we wanted to shove off there wasn't any water. The tide was out. What's more it was extremely cold. My friend. . . . But of course there are two sides to what I am about to say. On the one hand it was extremely cold and we only had very thin things on, while on the other the man who owned the boat together with the jacket and boots that were in it would certainly have offered to lend my friend those warm things supposing he had happened to be there. After all, it wasn't our fault if the fellow chose not to spend all day sitting around in his boat. So we simply annexed the jacket and the boots. After which I remember our tramping across a long bridge, roughly half an hour long. Then night fell. We had sneaked into a barn when suddenly a tall policeman stood there beckoning to us. At the police station they asked to see our papers, but we found it difficult to understand them and as for the jacket we prudently said it had been a gift. They were not all that keen to believe us. They asked in an underhand kind of a way where had we come from, and when they heard we had crossed the bridge they told us that was strictly prohibited and jugged us for four days.

We didn't take it too seriously, because episodes like that are the price one has to pay for showing initiative. We hadn't crossed that bridge because we thought it any special fun, and we hadn't meant anybody exactly to suffer; but of course there were other initiatives of ours which we might easily have been jugged for if only they had thought of it, and the same would apply to anyone. What I say about immorality is this: if only one didn't freeze when it gets cold and didn't stop feeling hungry when one has had a slice of bread, moral standards would be a lot higher. Then there would certainly be far fewer people staying in prison.

Just for walking across a bridge, which wasn't even particularly adapted for walking since it was really only intended for the railway – and to say nothing of the more or less gift jacket – we got five days in Bristol gaol.

That gaol wasn't at all bad. They had to feed us like everyone else, and no matter if we had frittered away our reputations it was pleasant to stick your hands in your pockets and walk round in a small circle whistling, hemmed in by specially thick walls designed to stop dangerous people like us from breaking out and menacing the island.

We could also observe the other prisoners to our hearts' content, since the warder considered us very decent and when he said he was keeping his eye on us it was really a compliment. At times when we played cards with him he used even to say he thought we should be in chains, except that unfortunately he hadn't got any in small enough sizes. Because, you see, he taught us how to play cards. He was very fat and not at all healthy and the doctor had told him he needed a bit of exercise, so he played cards. But we had no money on us and playing cards without money is like a meal without salt, so we scratched our heads till Tubby came up with the suggestion that he should pay us to smoke a pipe. We'd never done that, and the warder thought it would amuse him to see us smoking. We agreed, so he brought in a friend of his from two cells further along who used to be in a bank. The pipe was provided by another prisoner; he was in for murder with violence according to the warder, and to judge by the state of the pipe it had been a multiple offence. We had to smoke damned hard to earn our money, and we lost it only too easily at cards.

But when we finally left Bristol gaol we had made good use of our time and learned something that would last us for life.

What's more, Tubby gave us a bit of money, so when we arrived back in Cardiff we were able to get into the Sailors' Home. There are plenty of places in England – you don't need a map to realise that – but Cardiff was the only place we knew, so it was where we always went back to. And in Cardiff we knew the Sailors' Home. That's how lazy people are.

It was my first love that took me away from Cardiff. One day a man turned up at the Sailors' Home looking for a hard-working bloke to work in a hotel. The landlord said we'd be somewhere on the beach and he shouldn't let our appearance put him off.

Right enough, there we were by the water's edge seeing who could spit the furthest.

The man watched us for some time before making his proposition: he wanted to see what we were like and which of us would suit his purpose better. I spat furthest and I was the one he hired.

To start with I was the oddjob-man and did the shoes, but soon I graduated to baker and made the pancakes for the self-service restaurant.

My friend stayed on at the Sailors' Home; I used to see him in the evenings, he was doing very well, he lived mainly on pancakes. But now he had to spit in the sea all on his own and he didn't care for that. He said nothing, but one evening when I arrived with a few pancakes to smoke a quiet pipe with him he had gone. I never saw him again.

To offset that I used every morning to see a young girl in the hotel corridor. She was about thirteen and a maid-of-all-work. Every time she saw me she smiled like a lady. But I myself was a gentleman, being tall as a spruce tree despite my sixteen years. I couldn't help running into her in the corridor now and again; what's more there was nothing to stop me exchanging a few harmless words with her. I must say there's nothing so inspiring as when there's 'nothing to stop' something. The things there's nothing to stop are the things one does time and again. For instance there was me exchanging a few harmless words with her and it turned out there was a fair on in Cardiff and nothing to stop our going to it. In Cardiff at the fairground I saw my first boxing match.

And not only saw my first boxing match but boxed myself for the first time. It happened like this:

They had a canvas booth there for boxing in. That's to say there were two people there whose fulltime job it was to bash each other's heads in, on top of which anyone in the audience who wished to get socked could volunteer. You had to pay 20 pence to watch. It wasn't an exorbitant sum – in fact I've always thought that boxing was underpaid – but for me in Cardiff at that time it was quite a lot, particularly as I had to pay for two tickets. Anybody who boxed of course was let off paying, so after we had hung around outside the booth for some time and the situation was getting embarrassing for a gentleman I told the proprietor as carelessly as I could that I would 'like to have a few words with his man'. He gave a shifty kind of smile and escorted my lady very politely to a seat in the front row where she would be well placed to watch me 'have a few words with his man'. I'd just as lief have had her sit slightly further back. What call had she got to see it all so clearly? Anyhow there she sat.

They put a couple of gloves on me – to stop me hurting their man too badly, I supposed – after which their man arrived and clambered over the ropes. He hadn't a very welcoming look.

Since then I've seen a lot of fellows clamber over the ropes to fight me, better boxers no doubt, but I'm not lying when I tell you many of them have completely vanished from my memory, that's to say, even when I see their names in my cuttings book I can no longer remember what they looked like. I may read some press cutting where it says I was actually knocked down in round two – which suggests that the man wasn't just doing me a kindness – but his face is more than I can recall. My first opponent however is still before my eyes, as if it was only yesterday that we shook hands. He shook more of me than my hands, come to that.

Even now he strikes me as having been eight feet tall and as solid as an ox.

He seemed to have a totally debased character. He looked as

if he'd be no more reluctant to treat a living creature with no evil designs on him as an unfeeling sack of bran than to eat a Christmas pudding. How stupid of me not to have asked for his photograph beforehand. The bell went, and it was too late for second thoughts. All this took place one night in June. Inside the tent it was very hot, people sat round the ring in their shirtsleeves smoking so sinfully in defiance of the notices that anyone in the ring would have had to take a pneumatic drill and bore through the smoke in order to see anything. I remember how once the bout had started the oil lamps overhead began slowly swinging. There must have been something queer going on, or they'd have knocked against the smoke cloud that hung over the ring. Besides that I could vaguely hear the hoarse roar of the fifty or sixty spectators present, mixed up with the devilish noise of a dozen barrel-organs from the neighbouring roundabouts. Right from the start I had a premonition of what was coming, and a very faint premonition it was. Because what came was not a boxing match but a massacre. Quite simply I was beaten up. I'd got in cheap, it's true, but I'd got in for a purpose: to be smashed. The man made no bones about it. He just reached out for my face and made major alterations to it. His blows came from left, right, above and below, apparently without taking aim, and he always scored. Assaulting peaceful people as if they were murderers, when all they wanted to do was sleep, was something he seemed to have sucked in with his mother's milk. My gloves served me merely to hold in front of my face. Then he smashed through them. Somehow I managed to stay on my feet to the end of the round, apart from one or two interludes where I lay on the floor for a while to have a bit of a rest. I hadn't time to notice anything, or I'd have surely have noticed what I came to realise since: that he didn't by any means want to knock me out as quickly as possible but as slowly. He couldn't just abandon himself to his bloodlust but was bound to consider his audience, who wished to see a fight. That's why he always allowed me long enough to get more or less on my pins again, after which he would give a further demonstration of his art.

He demonstrated his art for two rounds. And as art it was splendid. At the end of those two rounds I was as weary of life as if I'd been 120, lay on my back in a corner and wished I could die.

All the same, and despite the fact that I was in no position to wish a love affair on myself, I could see my lady's face in a kind of blur above me past a number of swellings, and she was saying something. Exactly what, I was in no position to say because my ears were too far back. My idea about the girl had been to wave to her now and again, just when I was passing her seat perhaps. It would have been an excellent idea. Unfortunately the fight got in the way.

I must say, though, that she conducted herself every bit as creditably as I did. My appearance before the fight, while not all *that* charming, was at least a lot better than after, yet beforehand she had largely concealed her feelings from me. She'd never for instance have kissed me if I hadn't had a ghastly black eye and, where most people have their second eye, a swelling the size of a fist. As it was she kissed me.

Women are peculiar. Generally they do the opposite of what one wants. But on that occasion I wanted her to do what she did. We went home far better friends than when we had set out, and from then on when she gave me a smile in the hotel corridor it wasn't always a lady's smile.

All the same this agreeable affair became one of those two-sided things such as I described earlier. One side of my love was that it was agreeable; the other was spelt out for me by my friends.

From what they said it was a damned risky business.

In England, so they told me, nothing involving girls is all that simple.

In England, so my friends in the hotel kitchen told me, when people kiss they are supposed to get married. And right away too. Or else, so my friends told me, the sheriff would take an interest in the affair, and the sheriff is even less able to take a joke than the girl herself.

My friends didn't think my situation was really dangerous, but they said it would be better if I disappeared.

Whatever the reason, I must admit that disappearing is always a good thing.

I asked my friends along to a pancake supper which turned into a game of cards – this being the reverse side of the supper, and with a view to the journey – then went off next morning to Barry Dock with some money for the trip.

Barry Dock is a small port.

When I got there, not a single ship was to be seen – something quite exceptional. Four days later all my friends' money had gone and I went home. Home was Cardiff.

Cardiff however contained my lady.

Naturally I had not told the girl I meant to clear out, but when four days went by without her seeing me she must have realised.

My employer wished to take me on again right away; in fact he wanted to have me trained as a chauffeur, but I realised in time that my girl had begun keeping an eye on me, and I was conscious of the sheriff in the background.

I ate myself reasonably full and played a bit of cards with my Cardiff friends, then went back to Barry Dock to look for adventure.

I never saw my lady again. She was very pleasant.

Then I sat on a railing by the dockside and spat into the Atlantic and a desire came over me to have a look at London. If I had had better eyes I might have seen across the ocean to America, but never London because my back was turned to it. To get to London I was forced to make a detour via Alexandria in Egypt: I managed to get a job as messroom steward on a little steamship that was going there, and since my money ran out again I had a look round Alexandria too.

Anyhow the ship itself was a lot more interesting than Alexandria. Alexandria looks much like it does on postcards, only cleaner. (In fact anyone who cannot get hold of a postcard of Alexandria can make do just as well with one of Constantinople, the postcards being very much alike.) Add the fact that the women there go around with their heads tied up, and you'll get some idea of it. I admit I'm prejudiced against Alexandria because I got no shore leave there and couldn't look round the place.

All the same that trip and the one or two that followed taught me a hell of a lot about life. All I had to do was make the officers' beds, clean the shoes, do the washing. That was easy enough, but I also had to get along with the people themselves, and that was a great deal more interesting. They weren't by any means the worst bunch I've come across, but nearly all of them felt a lot better if they could give a tall and rather slow-moving young fellow a good boot up the backside, and they thought it a great thing to trip him up as he went by and pummel his kidneys in a friendly way.

I must say I was dead against that from the outset. It's absolutely senseless. I told them so right away and when they didn't mend their ways I hurled a man against the galley wall to emphasise my point. This is how I did it: it's very important in a fight to be as angry as possible.

Sometimes of course you're naturally angry, but at others it just has to be organised. For instance if I had to hurl my man against the galley wall I would set out by doing my best to get worked up against him. I'd tell myself all the nasty things that could be said about his nose, let's say, and if he merely glanced in my direction I'd instantly mutter something about his insolent habit of staring. I would also put up with all I could from him and keep on telling myself 'don't do anything till you can't bear him any longer'. Because nothing gets you more furious than that, and it's best to keep your fury as tightly bottled up as you can – which vastly adds to it. Finally your man only has to stir a finger and you hurl him against the galley wall. This is a far better method than launching an assault in cold blood. Most of the brutalities I've seen have come from being too cold-blooded rather than too hot.

If I had set about it blindly I would never have known if I wasn't merely getting angry when nobody else was around, which would have meant that it was all for nothing. This way however I could fix things so that enough people were around, then choose the right moment and just let fly. Pretty soon they began to take note of my dislikes.

From that point on my existence improved vastly. It was the very man I had hurled, so I noticed, who invited me into a card game, and not because he was worried – for I was only able to beat him because he didn't get furious too, and he hadn't an evil thought in his mind – but because he had taken a shine to me and I was now somebody to be reckoned with.

That's the most important thing in life: needing to be reckoned with. But good as it was to find out how satisfactory it is to be strong and not to care who knows it, it was even better to have learnt, as I did around the same time, that strength by itself is not enough. I learnt this from the episode with the ship's cook.

The ship's cook was a nigger. He was called Jeremiah Brown

and added up to nothing more than the black contents of a white uniform. He was the most self-satisfied man I've ever met. Whenever he was talking to one of us he would keep looking at his watch or something, to show that almost anything mattered more to him than our conversation. His galley was papered all over with photographs showing him in a variety of roles – from general to householder sitting in a rocking chair in front of a two-storeyed villa – amounting to every kind of glamour a nigger's imagination could conceive.

This man taught me a painful lesson.

The story starts with Brown taking me on to haul coal and bake bread because I was strong – and against Brown I was powerless because he was well in with the officers, who treated him as a kind of a private joke. When I found my kitchen jobs beginning to stretch late into the evening I became quite inventive, for while on the one hand hauling coal naturally calls for strong people, on the other hand it is just those strong people who are best placed to resist such calls. I started by shaking Jeremiah's black hand as often and as heartily as I could. I did so for preference when there were other people standing around so that they could see how fond I was of him and he couldn't swear if I gripped him rather hard. Unfortunately I was foolish enough at the outset to put them wise, and so he came to realise that they were all waiting for him to yowl with pain. He was so vain that he would sooner have put up with any amount of discomfort than cry out in front of everybody. So I was forced to go further. I think it was my first conflict with another man, and as I said it taught me a lot.

One afternoon Brown came into his galley and instantly saw there was something missing. There were others in the galley besides me, and Brown knew we were observing him.

All his photographs had gone. Everyone on board knew there was nothing in the world the cook cared about more than his photographs. We watched his face closely. Brown slowly looked round and took in the empty walls. He stood there quite calmly and looked at each in turn. He seemed rather thoughtful, that was all.

Then he glanced indifferently at us and went over to the stove to make tea.

We found it all very disappointing.

Next day the cook stopped sending for me, and from then on one of the ship's boys hauled his coal for him. The officers, so I noticed, started treating me worse. He must have put them up to it.

I thought he must have realised he'd get nowhere with me, and decided it wasn't worth wasting his time with such a fellow. With his connections he could easily arrange for me to be paid off at Constantinople.

Two or three days later, however, as I was hanging over the rail who should come up behind me but Brown, and when I turned round he was smiling. Then he asked if I felt like coming into the galley and having a cup of tea with him. What's more, when I came into the galley he really did make tea for me and drank it with me.

I thought he was going to start talking about the photographs. I might perhaps have given them back to him. But he said nothing about the photographs at all. He spoke of the weather and told me about San Francisco.

I can't think how he managed not to put me on my guard. We came together every day and he told me his stories. After a few days had gone by I started wanting to talk about his photographs, in very general terms of course. I told him I was so sorry, didn't he miss them and wouldn't he like to get them back?

He gave me a friendly look and changed the subject. He no longer seemed to give a damn about those photographs of his.

In Constantinople I was paid off and left behind. It was an embarrassing position for the cook. He had managed to get me chucked out, but in the meantime he had made friends with me and there was nothing he could do about it.

We went ashore together at Constantinople, and Brown advised me not to throw my money away. He spoke most emphatically and appealed to my conscience. He told me he resented every single bottle of wine we were fools enough to pour down our gullets. I should be saving my money till I had enough to do something with.

Next day he came back and told me he too was fed up with this particular ship and had found someone who could get him a berth on another boat which was carrying liquor to Trinidad.

And I could come along as second cook. Of course I straightaway agreed. We settled everything. First of all the ship was going to put into London.

In London I learnt why the cook wanted to have me with him. While still on the ship I didn't realise; I thought it was just that he liked me. He had bought himself a fresh lot of photos in Constantinople, and I thought the main point of his putting them up in his new galley was to convince me that he wasn't missing the old ones. The latter meantime were all present and correct in my sea chest.

In London my idea had been to push off and use what money I'd saved to make a short visit home. It was not to be, for I was involved in a battle, and to make matters worse I didn't know it. My friendship with the cook was merely the second instalment of our battle: it was far and away the more dangerous.

Brown was really charming to me. He organised little exhibition bouts on deck, supposedly to demonstrate my strength which had so impressed him. Actually we wrestled more than we boxed. Brown would sit there on a small stool looking at me with a fascinated grin and continually drawing the spectators' attention to some trick of mine or something of that sort. He liked feeling my muscles, what's more, and praising them like a connoisseur.

He was a dangerous fellow. In London he finished me off. It was our very first day there, a lovely day with a disastrous finish. Over a glass of rum I had confided to my friend Brown that I meant to jump ship in London, and he had strongly recommended me to take my things ashore the very first day. He'd help me; he was as good as his word, and so we parked my chest in a cheap lodging house and went off arm in arm for a bit of a stroll.

We had various drinks together in various establishments, and together we visited various dance halls; between times we ate together and incidentally, as I well remember, went together to a photographer's at the express wish of the cook. There Brown had my picture taken in some kind of boxing pose with my sleeves rolled up. Together we collected the picture a few hours later, and Brown insisted on paying for it. After that we foundered in an absolute Atlantic Ocean of whisky – together, or so I thought.

Next morning however when I woke up in my bunk I realised it was only me that had foundered, for the cook appeared fresh as a daisy and in good order. I couldn't understand why he didn't have a wet cloth round his head like me. It wasn't till that afternoon when I went to my lodging house that I began to get the point.

My chest had gone. I had come in a cab and collected it myself, in a very drunken state, so the landlord said. Presumably I had left it in the cab.

I went straight back on board. The first person I ran into was Brown the cook. He looked remarkably pleased with life, and before I could even open my mouth he told me he had come across his old photos in a crappy old chest which he had promptly thrown away. As he said this he gave me a frank and concerned look. I still recall how there wasn't the slightest semblance of anger in me at that moment; I simply felt lousy.

I walked past him without speaking and lay down in my hammock. I'd had enough of this world.

For a few days I never left the deck, and then the ship sailed on to Trinidad. That whole voyage was one I prefer not to speak about. (At the end of it all Brown made me pay four shillings, supposedly for burning one of his pans.) I had to digest my lesson, which was that this strength business has got two sides to it. It's the weaker that get the knocks, true enough, but it's the smarter that get the cash.

That nigger now had all his precious pictures back in chest, plus an extra one, a new picture of a fresh-faced, exceptionally stupid young fellow with very strong muscles.

The next time we made London I had had quite enough of the sea. Having again managed to save about twenty pounds I decided I would go home.

I bought myself a suit of good thick material, a big cap and some smart shoes, and went off to Hamburg.

I went first class.

In Hamburg I checked the train connections, found my train didn't go till that evening and decided to go up to St. Pauli as I 'might as well have a look and see what was going on'.

There I remained for four days.

A lot of people were more or less to blame for that.

The 'Cathedral' was in full swing just then, and I drove along the Achterbahn with lots of other people, went with a whole gang to the underground hippodrome and was one of a group of at least ten who saw all the world's accidents depicted in the Panorama.

A whole army of nice friendly people who had the highest regard for me gobbled up my twenty pounds.

At the end of those four days they began to be less nice and less friendly and to hold me in somewhat lower regard. Till finally they just didn't know me and had never seen me. Even that wasn't quite so unpleasant as the fact that I could no longer see my money.

There was one particular lot of swing-boats I and my kind friends had singled out to honour with our custom. After the first three days the owner insisted on serving me in person. He couldn't let just any old swing-boat attendant serve so distinguished a guest as me.

I now turned to him, and he was decent enough to take me on as a swing-boat attendant. I got one mark per day and I worked there eight days. My friends found me the very first day, and of course it was a special treat for them to have me swing them. They brought along any number of fellows who were as able to pay as I had once been and were particularly anxious to have me serve them.

It was pleasant for them to order me about peremptorily; they tried to brake the swing-boats as I was getting them in motion, and bawled me out for only getting them up to a decent height once the music was half over; what's more they never tipped me. 'The man's as rich as sin,' they said, 'he could pay for the whole lot of us if he wanted to.' So once again the owner made a small fortune out of me.

Really there are two reasons why I am telling this story. In the first place I imagine many of you would have been upset to find yourselves serving the very same people you had just been standing rides to. But I didn't care. I served them as willingly as I would anyone else, they were no skin off my nose, it wasn't a bad thing that I should attract custom. It was stupid of them not to realise that at times you're lucky and at times less so.

The second reason is that of course I still had some money

left when I began working. I didn't let myself run right out. I was stupid, but not so stupid that it would no longer have helped if I started to have some sense. Money is like driving a car, as I found when I had a taxi in New York. You and your cab can get into a situation where you'd give a lot to be able to stop it. But you can't let the engine conk out. Once you do this your car is useless.

By the time eight days had passed I'd got enough for a ticket (fourth class) to Bremen. And in Bremen I got a berth as a coal trimmer on the *Kaiser Wilhelm der Grosse* bound for New York. Things weren't so good in Bremen, but I'd never have signed on on the *Kaiser* if it hadn't been a way of getting to New York. In those days anything that took one a step further was like a free ticket.

Admittedly the first time we put into New York I didn't manage to get away. You always had to sign on for the return trip. The second time, though, I managed to get my foot a bit jammed between the cutter and the ship's side, so they had to send me to the Hoboken hospital. I wasn't too badly hurt. One day after the *Kaiser Wilhelm der Grosse* had left dock I was fit to be discharged.

But I wasn't yet able to settle in America. I still had to make a number of voyages. I was successively with the Atlas Line, which carries bananas from the West Indies, the Morgan Line, which carries cotton from New Orleans, and the Clike Line which used to run to Charleston. These last two are American lines, and from then on I only went on American ships. On American ships the money's better, the food's better, there's more work and more sport than on any others even including the German.

Around that time – it must have been about 1907 – I happened to find myself sailing to Africa on a big four-master. She belonged to Standard Oil and was supposed to be carrying paraffin for South Africa.

We took two whole months to get there. There were about thirty crew all told and the work was extremely hard. As coal trimmers we used to do four-hour shifts, but now we spent all our time 'in the fresh air'. What's more a sailing ship is by no means stable. It's a bloody queer business if you ask me. I'm against them.

Once we'd made Cape Town I had no desire whatever to travel back on that old bucket, and a lot of others shared my views. They and I spent a week in the small harbour there working as fishermen. But it was a job with few prospects, and when there turned out to be no other ship that might have been going, say, to India and could have taken the lot of us we went back on her after all. We just carried ballast, mainly stones and muck.

We had one further item of ballast on board, a negro called Congo. This black man was a real boxer, probably the first I got to know at all well. He was actually a pretty good man; he had had a lot of fights in Africa but ran through all his money and so he was working his passage back to America.

From time to time he would do nothing but drink for four weeks on end. If you said anything about it to him he'd tell you that drinking made him a much improved man, one not to be compared with the ordinary sober workaday Congo.

He organised his whole life around these drinking spells. Though he forgot everything else, his periods of drunkenness were registered on his memory. He could never remember what had occurred in any particular year – where he'd worked, where he'd boxed, where he'd lived – but he knew that in such and such a month he'd been drinking in New Orleans or Cape Town or Montreal.

And I don't think he lied about his drinking, though he was a fearful liar in every other respect. He was the kind might tell you with a completely straight face how a shark had bitten off his left arm and when his listeners pointed to the perfectly sound arm in question would just say 'Yes, strange things happen, don't they?'.

But there was something splendid about him: the way he did all kinds of jobs on that sailing ship for instance, without knowing anything about it, and worked so hard that he kept on coughing and looking forward to a new spell of drinking in America. It was he that first showed me how to box.

Fragment

Editorial Notes

THE PRINCIPAL COLLECTIONS OF BRECHT'S SHORT STORIES

1. *General*

Brecht grouped his short stories in three main collections, of which the first two never reached the stage of publication. They were

Die Gesichte (*The Visions*).

9 Kurzgeschichten (*Nine short stories*).

Kalendergeschichten (*Tales from the Calendar*), 1949.

After his death three further collections appeared containing previously unpublished material:

Geschichten (*Stories*), 1962.

Prosa 1 and 2, 1965.

Gesammelte Werke 11, Prosa 1, edited by Herta Ramthun, 1967. The notes that follow give a short account of all these. For details of first publication in newspapers or magazines, see the notes on individual stories in the next section.

2. *The Visions* (1919–1945)

'From the *Visions*' (or 'Aus den *Gesichten*') was one of Brecht's loose labellings to categorise a particular kind of poetic prose writing. Standing as it did for a purely mental grouping, it embraced most notably the prose poems written around 1940 (and included in *Poems 1913–1956* on pp. 323–327) along with the contemporaneous 'Appeal by the Virtues and Vices' from the *Conversations between Exiles*, but also covered both earlier and later pieces. Among the former are the very early 'Das Tanzfest' and 'Absalom reitet durch den Wald' (GW 11, pp. 15–17) and possibly the 'Three fragments' of about 1920 (*Poems 1913–1956*, p. 58); among the latter 'The city-builder' (to come in *Songs and Poems from Plays*) which was first published in 1945 and is thought to have been written in the United States. Though Brecht's diary for June 1920 mentions the possibility of writing 'a book of *visions*' there is no sign of these ever having been physically put together.

3. *Nine short stories* (c. 1930)

For *The Threepenny Opera* and *Happy End* Brecht went to a new theatrical publisher-cum-agent, the Berlin firm of Felix Bloch then headed by Fritz Wrede. In view of the success of the former work (and perhaps of its impending film version) he wanted some of his stories to be circulated to theatres and editors wishing to publish examples of his writing. Accordingly he and Elisabeth Hauptmann persuaded the firm to compile and distribute a set of nine duplicated stories to potential customers in Germany and abroad.

The nine stories were, in order,

1. Letter about a mastiff (p. 63).
2. The monster (p. 107).
3. The death of Cesare Malatesta (p. 49).
4. The blind man (p. 21).
5. North Sea shrimps (p. 77).
6. Conversation about the South Seas (p. 61).
7. Too much luck is no luck (i.e. Four men and a poker game, p. 94).
8. Müller's natural attitude (p. 72).
9. The Lance-Sergeant (p. 38).

Of these only numbers 4, 8, 9 and possibly 5 had not already been published in some form. The selection may possibly reflect Brecht's own preferences among his work, but it is also quite conceivable that it was determined by the availability of typescripts.

4. *Tales from the Calendar* (1949)

The *Kalendergeschichten*, published in 1949 by Gebrüder Weiss Verlag in West Berlin and, under licence, by Verlag Neues Leben in East Berlin, was the only collection to appear during Brecht's lifetime. It comprised eight stories in the following order:

1. The Augsburg chalk circle (p. 188).
2. Two sons (p. 200).
3. The experiment (p. 153).
4. The heretic's coat (p. 162).
5. Caesar and his legionary ('Cäsars letzte Tage' in *Texte für Film II*, Suhrkamp, Frankfurt 1969, p. 372).
6. The soldier of La Ciotat (p. 129).
7. Socrates wounded (p. 139).
8. The unseemly old lady (p. 178).

Each story was followed by a poem: respectively 'Ballad of Marie Sanders' (*Poems 1913–1956*, p. 251), 'Parable of Buddha of the burning house' (ditto, p. 290), 'The tailor of Ulm' (ditto, p. 243), 'Children's Crusade' (ditto, p. 368), 'The carpet-weavers of Kujan-Bulak' (ditto, p. 174), 'Questions from a worker's reading' (ditto, p. 252), 'Mein Bruder war ein Flieger' (GW 9, p. 647) and 'Legend of the origin of the book Tao-Tê-Ching' (*Poems 1913–1956*, p. 314). After the concluding poem came 24 pages of Keuner anecdotes.

Though the Brecht-Archive holds no correspondence about the publication of this volume, there is a preliminary scheme which shows a slightly different arrangement. This left out 'The unseemly old lady' and reshuffled the other stories in the order 4, 1, 6, 7, 3, 2 and 5. 'Lucullus's trophies' (p. 170) then followed 'The experiment', while the penultimate story was to have been 'The strange illness of Mr. Henri Dunant' ('Die seltsame Krankheit des Herrn Henri Dunant' in *Texte für Filme II*, p. 406), which was then crossed out. In place of the 'Ballad of Marie Sanders', 'Children's crusade' and 'Mein Bruder war ein Flieger' the poems nominated were 'Ruuskanen's horse' (*Poems 1913–1956*, p. 353), 'Song of the flocks of starlings' (ditto, p. 204), 'To the German soldiers on the Eastern Front' (ditto, p. 373), which again was crossed out, and 'Von den Osseger Witwen' (GW 9, p. 643). There was no mention of any Keuner anecdotes.

Tales from the Calendar, with translations of the stories and anecdotes by Yvonne Kapp and of the poems by Michael Hamburger, was published by Methuen, London in 1961.

5. *Geschichten* and after (1962–1967)

In 1962, six years after Brecht's death, Suhrkamp-Verlag in Frankfurt put out an anonymously edited selection containing (a) previously uncollected stories, (b) five stories from *Tales from the Calendar*, (c) 'The dispute' (*Poems 1913–1956*, p. 324) from the *Visions* and (d) two further groups of Keuner anecdotes. Under (a) it included 'Bargan gives up', 'The death of Cesare Malatesta', 'Before the Flood', 'Four men and a poker game', 'Letter about a mastiff', 'The monster', 'The job', 'A mistake', 'Gaumer and Irk' and 'A question of taste'.

Prosa 1 was published three years later under Herta Ramthun's editorship as part of Suhrkamp's hardback collected edition which had begun with the early plays in 1953. It contained the remainder of the uncollected stories, including eighteen of those in our edition, and also the unfinished 'Life story of the Boxer Samson-Körner'. The *Tales from the Calendar* were in *Prosa 2*.

In the Gesammelte Werke (GW) of 1967 this material was rearranged by the same editor under the general editorship of Elisabeth Hauptmann in a single volume (GW 11, also confusingly called *Prosa 1*) in roughly chronological order. The German texts as printed there are the basis of our translations.

NOTES ON INDIVIDUAL STORIES

The following notes give the German title to each story, with page references to the first prose volume of the German Collected Works (GW 11) and the earlier *Prosa* volumes (Pr. 1 and Pr. 2). They specify volume and page, and refer to the Suhrkamp (West German) edition. Dates in brackets are those given for each story by Herta Ramthun in GW, except where more precise evidence is available. 'BBA' signifies the Bertolt-Brecht-Archiv in East Berlin.

Authorities referred to or otherwise made use of include:

Arbeitsjournal. Bertolt Brecht: *Arbeitsjournal 1938–1956*, ed. Hecht, Suhrkamp, Frankfurt 1972. Referred to also as Brecht's 'working journal'.

Benjamin. Walter Benjamin: *Understanding Brecht*, New Left Books, London 1972.

Bestandsverzeichnis. *B. des literarischen Nachlasses* volume 3, ed. Ramthun, Aufbrau-Verlag, East Berlin and Weimar 1972.

Diaries. Bertolt Brecht: *Diaries 1920–1922*, ed. and trs. Willett, Eyre Methuen, London and St. Martin's Press, New York 1979.

Letters. Bertolt Brecht: *Briefe*, ed. Günter Glaeser, Suhrkamp, Frankfurt 1981.

Nubel. Walter Nubel: Bertolt-Brecht-Bibliographie in *Sinn und*

Form, Potsdam, Zweites Sonderheft BB, 9 Jahr, 1957, nos. 1–3.

Poems 1913–1956. Ed. Willett and Manheim, Eyre Methuen, London 1976 and Methuen Inc., New York 1979.

Völker. Klaus Völker: *Brecht-Chronik*. Hanser, Munich 1971.

page

3. *Bargan gives up. A pirate story.* Bargan lässt es sein. Eine Flibustiergeschichte. GW 11, 20, Pr. 1, 25.

Published in *Der neue Merkur*, Munich, vol. v no. 6, September 1921, pp. 394–407. A fragment in *Diaries* for 30 May 1921. Brecht seems to have planned a series of Bargan stories, of which two fragments – 'Bargans Jugend' and 'Geschichten von St. Patricks Weihnachtskrippe' – are included in both German collected editions, while another story called 'Jarrys Mama' is thought to have been lost after submission to (and acceptance by) the *Vossische Zeitung*. A retrospective letter of Brecht's to Professor Ernst Schumacher (12 April 1955) suggests that the present story is not just escapist but somehow anticipates the play *Mr. Puntila and his Man Matti* (1941).

16. *Story on a ship.* Geschichte auf einem Schiff. GW 11, 44, Pr. 1, 52.

(1921.) Published in *Vossische Zeitung*, Berlin, 12 April 1925. The name of the sailor 'Manky' is also that of a character in Brecht's third play *In the Jungle of Cities*, which he started writing in autumn 1921.

18. *The revelation.* Die Erleuchtung. GW 11, 47, Pr. 1, 55.

Josef Apfelböck, the subject of Brecht's poem 'Apfelböck, or the lily of the field', was a Munich youth who murdered his parents on 29 July 1919 (see the note in *Poems 1913–1956*). The paragraph beginning 'Then he got into bed' echoes 'The first psalm' (c. 1920) which can be found on p. 43 of the same volume. Note the term 'psalmodising' (translated as 'intoning') at the end, which echoes the term used of Garga in the 1922 version of *In the Jungle of Cities* and there means the chanting of Rimbaud-like prose poems.

19. *The foolish wife.* Die dumme Frau. GW 11, 49, Pr. 1, 58.

Undated MS in BBA.

21. *The blind man*. Der Blinde. GW 11, 52, Pr. 1, 61.

Was no. 4 in the duplicated *Nine stories* circulated by Bloch-Erben.

25. *A helping hand*. Die Hilfe. GW 11, 57, Pr. 1, 67.

On the typescript Lorge was originally Sorge throughout, the name being subsequently amended in Brecht's hand. Compare the embryonic story in the *Diaries* for 27 August 1920 about the man who 'escapes to South America in his forties' and also goes blind.

29. *Java Meier*. Der Javameier. GW 11, 62, Pr. 1, 73.

(1921.) The *Diaries* entry for July 1921 refers to this as a 'detective story'. Brecht at that time was trying to write such stories for a Munich film company making serials about a detective called Stuart Webbs: for instance 'The mystery of the Jamaica Bar' in *Texte für Filme I*.

38. *The Lance-Sergeant*. Der Vizewachtmeister. GW 11, 73, Pr. 1, 85.

Also known as 'Der feige Vize', 'The cowardly lance-sergeant'. Was no. 9 in *Nine stories*. The typescript bears corrections in Brecht's hand, notably to the last paragraph which originally read:

That and no other way is how the Jew Bernauer saw it, who used to sing 'Deutschland über Alles' in the latrine, which was no mean achievement on his part and put him above many great clerics who speak disrespectfully of alcohol and actually know nothing. But Lance-Sergeant Borg . . .

and so to the end as before.

42. *Message in a bottle*. Die Flaschenpost. GW 11, 78, Pr. 1, 91.

Undated typescript in BBA.

43. *A mean bastard*. Ein gemeiner Kerl. GW 11, 81, Pr. 1, 94.

Published in *Der Feuerreiter*, Berlin, Jg. 1, Heft 4/5, April 1922, under the editorship of Heinrich Eduard Jacob (see biographical note at the end of the *Diaries*). Thought to have been conceived in the first place as a one-act play under the title *Der Schweinigel* ('The Whole Hog'). This has not survived.

49. *The death of Cesare Malatesta*. Der Tod des Cesare Malatesta. GW 11, 91, Pr. 1, 105.

Published in *Berliner Börsen-Courier*, 29 June 1924, some two months before Brecht's arrival to work as a dramaturg in Berlin. Was no. 3 in *Nine stories*.

57. *The answer*. Die Antwort. GW 11, 96, Pr. 1, 111.

(c. 1924.) Published in *Magdeburgische Zeitung*, 17 August 1929.

59. *Before the Flood* ('Considerations in the rain' and 'Fat Ham'). Vor der Sintflut ('Betrachtungen bei Regen' and 'Der dicke Ham'). GW 11, 101, Pr. 1, 116.

Published in *Frankfurter Zeitung*, 27 July 1925. The first of these short pieces occurs in slightly different form as a monologue at the end of scene 1 of the 1926 version of *Baal* (where there is more Flood imagery in scene 3). The typescript shows a number of changes and additions in Brecht's hand. The *Frankfurter Zeitung* gave the title as 'Von' der Sintflut – 'About' the Flood – and this misprint was copied in *Prosa 1*.

61. *Conversation about the South Seas*. Gespräch über die Südsee. GW 11, 104, Pr. 1, 119.

Dated 1924 by Elisabeth Hauptmann and published in *Die Dame*, Berlin, no. 18, May 1926. Was no. 6 in *Nine stories*.

63. *Letter about a mastiff*. Brief über eine Dogge. GW 11, 108, Pr. 1, 121.

Also known as 'Erlebnis mit einer Dogge' ('Experience with a mastiff'). Published in *Berliner Börsen-Courier*, 13 August 1925. Was no. 1 in *Nine stories*. The typescript leaves blank the date of the San Francisco earthquake (p. 67) and omits the two sentences following, from 'on that day' to 'not to be', which were added on a new page.

68. *Hook to the chin*. Der Kinnhaken. GW 11, 116, Pr. 1, 130.

Published in *Scherls Magazin*, Berlin, no. 1, January 1926. Brecht's 'Life story of the boxer Samson-Körner' (p. 207) and his essay 'Emphasis on Sport' ('Mehr guten Sport') were also published that year.

72. *Müller's natural attitude*. Müller's natürliche Haltung. GW 11, 145, Pr. 1, 161.

(1926.) Elisabeth Hauptmann recalled its publication in the later 1920s, but could not give details. This was no. 8 in *Nine stories*. The story misplaces the Taunus mountains, which in fact are north of Frankfurt.

77. *North Sea shrimps*. Nordseekrabben. GW 11, 153. Pr. 1, 169.

(c. 1926.) Subtitled 'oder die moderne Bauhauswohnung' ('or the modern Bauhaus apartment'). Said to have been published in the *Münchner Neueste Nachrichten* in early January 1927, though Elisabeth Hauptmann dated it three years later. Was no. 5 in *Nine stories*.

85. *Bad water*. Schlechtes Wasser. GW 11, 163, Pr. 1, 180.

Published in *Simplicissimus*, Berlin, nr. 19, 9 August 1926.

90. *A little tale of insurance*. Eine kleine Versicherungsgeschichte. GW 11, 170, Pr. 1, 187.

Published in *Uhu*, Berlin, 12 September 1926 under the title 'Eine Pleite-Idee' ('A bankrupt notion').

94. *Four men and a poker game, or Too much luck is bad luck*. Vier Männer und ein Pokerspiel, oder Zuviel Glück ist kein Glück. GW 11, 175, Pr. 1, 193.

Published in *Simplicissimus*, Stuttgart, no. 5, 3 May 1926. This issue had a cover drawing by Th. Th. Heine showing 'Caesar Mussolini' giving the Fascist salute and acknowledging God on condition that he became an Italian. The story seems to carry anticipations of Brecht's libretto for *Mahagonny*, notably the names 'Johnny' (name of the *Ur*-hero of that work) and 'Jenny Smith', as well, of course, as the American mythology and the Caribbean location.

100. *Barbara*. Barbara. GW 11, 184, Pr. 1, 203.

Published in *Dortmunder General-Anzeiger*, 27 August 1927. The description of Eddy as a 'ball of fat' recalls Mjurk's words to Baal in the nightclub scene of *Baal*, also the picture of Galgai (or Galy Gay) given in the *Diaries*.

104. *The Good Lord's package*. Das Paket des lieben Gottes. GW 11, 189, Pr. 1, 208.

Published in *Magdeburgische Zeitung*, 25 December 1926.

107. *The monster*. Die Bestie. GW 11, 197, Pr. 1, 217.

Published in *Berliner Illustrierte Zeitung*, Berlin, no. 50, 9 December 1928 after winning first prize in that magazine's short story competition. Was no. 2 in *Nine stories*. In 1934 when Brecht was in London working on a film project (*Semmelweis*) with Leo Lania the latter submitted an English translation to Lovat Dickson, who rejected it for magazine publication as having been written 'without a perfect knowledge of English'.

One of the surviving typescripts sets the story in the Paramount Studios and gives the actor's name as Murphy, while another mis-spells the studio's name as 'Moszropom'. It is supposed to have been based on a true incident at the Mezhrabpom studios in Moscow in 1928 when Jacov Protazanov was directing the actors Giarov, Sistiakov and Anna Sten in *The White Eagle*, a film based on Andreiev's story 'The Governor'. These studios, responsible ultimately to Willi Muenzenberg's IAH or International Workers' Aid, employed a number of German directors and actors in the 1930s.

112. *The job, or In the sweat of thy brow shalt thou fail to earn thy bread.* Der Arbeitsplatz, oder Im Schweisse deines Angesichts sollst du kein Brot essen. GW 11, 224, Pr. 1, 245.

(c. 1933.) This story is based on a real-life episode reported from Mainz in 1933 (allegedly in the first issue of *Ein Buch für Alle* that year). How and when it reached Brecht is uncertain. Anna Seghers wrote two fictionalised versions of the episode under the title 'Der Vertrauensposten' ('The Responsible Job') which she sent to Brecht's collaborator Margarete Steffin that summer and which finished up among Brecht's papers; but it also seems that Elisabeth Hauptmann must have written it up independently before leaving Germany at the beginning of 1934, since on 1 September she wrote to Brecht from St. Louis, Missouri, asking 'Have you ever used *your* Mrs. Einsmann story? If not I'd like to try and rework my version for here. I've got . . . notes on the real case and about the transitory nature of sex distinctions.'

It was filmed for East German TV in 1977 by Christa Mühl with a script by herself and Werner Hecht, under the title *Tod und Auferstehung des Wilhelm Hausmann* (Death and Resurrection of W.H.).

119. *Safety First.* Safety First. GW 11, 210, Pr. 1, 230.

Dated about 1933 by BBA. Also called 'Der Feigling' (The Coward). Herta Ramthun thinks that Brecht or one of his friends came across a report of some such incident in a shipping magazine and thought that it might make a film story. He evidently showed the finished story to Lania, since the latter in 1935 wrote suggesting various additions to it. The names and the setting recall the world of the *Three-penny Novel*, on which Brecht was working during much of 1934, while the insurance swindle is akin to that in Traven's novel *The Death Ship*.

129. *The soldier of La Ciotat*. Der Soldat von La Ciotat. GW 11, 237, Pr. 2, 73. In *Tales from the Calendar*.

(1935.) Published as 'L'homme statue' in *Internationale Literatur*, Moscow, 1937 no. 2. Originally called '27 September', the date in 1935 when Brecht read in a Danish paper of Mussolini's impending invasion of Ethiopia. The first version of the story started:

Today's *Politiken* says that the Italian troops in Eritrea are enthusiastic for the war and plagued by epidemics. Once again there loomed up before my eyes that strange sight which I first encountered years ago and have often seen of late: the *poilu* of La Ciotat.

La Ciotat is between Marseilles and Toulon, not far from Sanary-sur-Mer, where Brecht visited Lion Feuchtwanger in September 1933.

131. *A mistake*. Ein Irrtum. GW 11, 241, Pr. 1, 263.

Typescript dated 17.6.38 by Margarete Steffin.

135. *Gaumer and Irk*. Gaumer und Irk. GW 11, 247, Pr. 1, 270.

Date uncertain. Walter Benjamin's conversations with Brecht about Kafka took place in September 1934.

139. *Socrates wounded*. Der verwundete Sokrates. GW 11, 286, Pr. 2, 76. In *Tales from the Calendar*.

Typescript dated December 1938 by Margarete Steffin. Mentioned as a finished *Novelle* in Brecht's working journal for 12 February 1939. In 1955 Liselot Huchthausen, an East German teacher, wrote to ask why Brecht had turned the battle of Delium (where Socrates did indeed distinguish himself) from a defeat by the Spartans into a victory over the Persians. This, she said, 'must surely detract somewhat from the internal credibility of the story, or mustn't it?'. Brecht replied (letter no. 817) that he must have been writing from memory, without reference books, but would see if it was feasible to make an amendment in the next edition. The amendment was not made.

153. *The experiment*. Das Experiment. GW 11, 264. Pr. 2, 28. In *Tales from the Calendar*.

(1939.) Also called 'Der Stalljunge' (The stable-boy). It may have been Brecht's concern with the ideas of Aristotle, particularly in connection with the writing of *Galileo*, that drew him to Bacon, whose anti-Aristotelian *Novum organum* was later a model for the 'Short organum for the theatre', Brecht's own major theoretical work.

A film project of about 1942 also bears the title 'The Experiment' but appears to have no other link with this story.

162. *The heretic's coat*. Der Mantel des Ketzers. GW 11, 276, Pr. 2, 41. In *Tales from the Calendar*.

(1939.) Likewise mentioned as a finished *Novelle* in the journal for 12 February 1939. Published in *Internationale Literatur*, Moscow, 1939 no. 8 under title 'Der Mantel des Nolaners' (Nolaner means a man from Nola). Giordano Bruno is referred to in *Galileo*, whose first version Brecht was revising at the start of that year. Story and play reflect similar thinking.

170. *Lucullus's trophies*. Die Trophäen des Lukullus. GW 11, 304.

(1939.) Third of the finished *Novellen* mentioned in journal for 12 February 1939. Brecht's radio play *The Trial of Lucullus* followed after the German invasion of Poland that autumn; it took two weeks to write and was completed by 7 November. Its picture of Lucullus is much less tolerant. Lucretius's *De rerum natura* was the model for the vast unfinished 'Didactic poem on the nature of man' which occupied Brecht in America around 1945 and was to have included his version of the *Communist Manifesto* in hexameters. The second, 'deleted' passage quoted by Lucretius in the story forms part of this. The first is from *De rerum natura* 3, lines 830 and 870–887.

178. *The unseemly old lady*. Die unwürdige Greisin. GW 11, 315. Pr. 2, 96. In *Tales from the Calendar*.

(1939.) The character is evidently based on Karoline Wurzler (1839–1920) of Achern in the Black Forest, who married Brecht's grandfather Stephan Brecht, a lithographic printer, and had five children. Karl, the book printer who features in the story and continued living in the family house at Achern till his death in 1965, reportedly dismissed his nephew's account as 'a fabrication from start to finish' (see W. Frisch and K. W. Obermaier: *Brecht in Augsburg*, Aufbau Verlag, East Berlin and Weimar 1975, p. 26). It was the basis of René Allio's film *La vieille dame indigne*, SPAC Cinéma, Paris 1964.

183. *A question of taste*. Esskultur. GW 11, 337, Pr. 1, 310.

Published in Swedish in *Göteborgs-Posten*, Göteborg, 18 December 1943. Brecht's journal for 26 January 1940 records his writing of this 'little detective story' based on an evening spent with Jean Renoir and the Berlin film director Carl Koch, an old friend, presumably during one of his Paris visits in the 1930s. Meeting Renoir again in Santa Monica in October 1943 he watched him eating a sausage and found it 'so amusing as to be almost exciting. Nothing much wrong with *his* senses'.

188. *The Augsburg Chalk Circle*. Der Augsburger Kreidekreis. GW 11, 321, Pr. 2, 7. In *Tales from the Calendar*.

(1940.) Dated by Brecht 'Lidingö January 1940' and sent by him on 20 November that year to Mikhail Apletin of the Soviet Writers' Union for transmission to *Internationale Literatur*, who published it in their issue of June 1941. An earlier, fragmentary version was called 'The Odense Chalk Circle' and was set in Denmark. Augsburg was Brecht's home town in south Germany. The BBA contains a scheme by Paul Dessau for the composition of a 'dramatic ballad for music' in three parts based on the story. This appears to date from about 1944, just when Brecht was turning his Dollinger figure into the Azdak of *The Caucasian Chalk Circle*, whose music Dessau eventually wrote.

200. *Two sons*. Zwei Söhne. GW 11, 363, Pr. 2, 24. In *Tales from the Calendar*.

(c. 1946.) A note in Brecht's journal for 12 May 1945 gives the outline of a film 'which one might make for g[ermany]'.

> . . . a peasant woman who spends 2 days struggling with herself and her family (including her son who is on leave) to decide whether to slip half a loaf of bread to a starving prisoner. she does so, and brings her soldier son to the allies in a cart, bound with cattle-ropes – to make him safe.

A later entry (24 March 1947) shows that he sent the story to Slatan Dudow, the Bulgarian film director, in East Berlin. It was not however filmed till 1969, when Helmut Nitzschke directed it for DEFA as the first part of the film *Aus unserer Zeit*, with Felicitas Ritsch and Ekkehard Schall as mother and son, and a commentary by Brecht's widow Helene Weigel.

207. *Life story of the boxer Samson-Körner*. Lebenslauf des Boxers Samson-Körner. GW 11, 121.

Published in *Scherls Magazin*, Berlin, January and February 1926 and in *Die Arena*, Berlin, in four monthly issues from October 1926–January 1927 inclusive. Paul Samson-Körner, the German middleweight champion, was a friend of Brecht, whose collaborator Emil Hesse Burri was one of his sparring partners. A scheme in BBA headed 'approximate résumé' suggests that Brecht intended to write a short book of some 70–80 pages, of which only about one third was completed. The rest was to have covered the following themes:

> Training at sea – boilermaker in Hoboken – cold Chicago: the bed of newspapers, the freight car and the free lunch – hitchhiking across America – making a living as porter, dishwasher, short-order cook, banana stevedore, card-shuffler, dumb-bell artist, snow-shoveller, boilermaker, boxer – half an hour driving an excavator in the Mormon quarter – the fight with the 'Prussian Lion' – among the cardsharpers – back to Hoboken as a cattle man – first bouts – to Panama as a steel construction worker – 1916, champion of Panama – taxi owner in New York – foreman

in the Chilean copper mines – champion of Chile and Peru –
outstanding fights with Dan McClure, Tom Gibbons et
al. in New York – story of Jack Johnson the black world
champion – behind the scenes of the Dempsey-Carpentier
fight – return to Germany – championship bouts in
Germany.

However the February–March 1927 issue of *Arena* merely
carried the well-known photograph of the champion about
to deliver an uppercut to Brecht's jaw, together with an
apologetic note reading:

> The next instalment of our serial 'Life story of the boxer
> Samson-Körner' is missing from this issue. Samson and
> Brecht wish to take a break from their story. Brecht felt
> a little run down after all that writing, and asked Samson
> to take him into training. Our picture shows the two men
> before things got serious. They are now boxing every day.
> They will resume their story with renewed energy in the
> next issue of *Arena*.

Not so. There the matter rested. According to Herta
Ramthun's note in GW, Brecht's theatre projects had begun
to take up too much of his time.

Index